I0714192

All Rights Reserved. No part of this publication may be reproduced, distributed, or transmitted in any form or by any means, including photocopying, recording, or other electronic or mechanical methods, without the prior written permission of the publisher, except in the case of brief quotations embodied in critical reviews and specific other noncommercial uses permitted by copyright law. For permission requests, write to the publisher, addressed "Attention: Permissions Coordinator," at the address below.

Cover art by Clement Eastwood

Novel Eden Publishing

Ordering Information:

Quantity sales. Special discounts are available on quantity purchases by corporations, associations, and others. For details, contact the publisher at the address above.

Orders by U.S. trade bookstores and wholesalers. Please contact The Author @ 856-417-1827, offredfc@gmail.com.

Printed in the United States of America

The band Somber Nights had been working on pulling themselves together, but their Bassist Flatfoot had sprained his fingers. Their openers had the time of their life, finally having a captive audience for their album.

One man down struggling to reorganize themselves, the crowd grew restless, beginning chants for the Nights in the middle of a song forcing the entire performance to a halt. How could they perform without a bassist? They needed a solution quicker than a jiff.

Jared Mitchell Wright was pacing wildly in the campus' premiere auditorium corridor where the Presidents of Kismet and Lord Commissioners of The Regulator Regime had spoken. He welcomed the pressure months in advance. Not even the experience of a hundred lifetimes can prepare you for the inevitable or uncontrollable. Though, it played a significant impact on how one reacts to a crisis. Jared rattled his mind with names he knew of local artists and influencers who may know of someone. His mind kept slamming against his roommate.

"Excuse me, excuse me. Hey, move out the way. I'm with the band! Yo Jay! " A man standing at 6'2ft wearing a pair of True

favorite cartoons, a birthday gift from his Uncle.

Jared's eyes shot to the face connected to the name running to have him let into the hallway they've converted into a dressing room, connected directly to the stage and AV department.

"Yoza! Mate, sneaking into the backstage, that's bold, my guy!" Jared wrapped an arm up and around the man who had him by 5-8 inches.

"Dude, this opener is trash people starting to leave." Terrance let out a sigh, "What's good with y'all, man?"

"I need a bassist. Hey, you know a guy, don't you? That guy who hangs out with Mya, yeah? God sent you, I know he did, I see it in your eyes!" Jared claps his hands, knowing victory was afoot.

"You mean Tor'jun? Ugh, yeah, maybe he'll do it, but he's always with his girl. Honestly, it isn't even his scene anymore." Terrance groans.

"Sounds like a miserable lad already. Give him a call. I'll speak to him." Jared holds out his hand.

"I'm serious, bro. He's probably not going to come. He's a hermit." Terrance crosses his arms.

"You know what's wrong with the world, mate? People are constantly manifesting the worst-case scenario before even trying. If your mate is depressed, you should want him here, not

eyes began to turn a deep white as his voice deepened.

Terrance uncrossed his arms, raising them in the sky, "Remember the roommate agreement. You use your weird powers on me, and it's a month's rent, boy."

"I am money, and it flows abundantly unless your friend gets here! Give me the phone, mate! Let's do this the easy way." Jared warns.

"Come on, use a little bit. I could save up the money!" Terrance nudges him.

"You think- Fine, mate. Whatever, let cloth control your life. I'll pay the full month's rent. Save your water. Now, please, mate. HELP ME!" Jared squeezes his hands shut, shaking Terrance from across the room. "Call him!"

"Alright, alright, bro, chill the hell out. You didn't need to do all that." Terrance struggled, unable to lift his hands. "You lucky, you're my boy."

"You're lucky. I took my medicine today." Jared's eyes turn back to their golden color, and he grinned, "No hard feelings mate?"

"Nah, bro, never that, but you got to use that for some good. If you can get Chris out here, drinks are on me tonight. I happened to have come into a few extra hundred dollars." Terrance relinquished his cellphone, moving on to greet the band.

the entire inner circle knew. He held down the home button to get the voice command.

"Cassie, Call Chris Tor'jun!" Jared said as clearly as possible.

"Calling Chris Song Joy." the robotic female voice stated.

"Chris Tor'jun! TOR'JUN!" Jared stressed.

"I heard you. It's a translation, you idiot." The phone said sharply, shutting Jared up before going to the ringing screen.

"Your phone has a fresh mouth, mate," Jared muttered, walking toward the stage listening to the mix of cheers and shouts for The Nights.

"Whoa, it sounds live, bro. How's the concert party?" a surprisingly cheery voice greeted, "I'm working on some new sketches!"

"It's not a party. It's a bloody concert, mate. And- Are you- are you listening to my music in the background!? I'm less than a mile away, you know? Jah'Rakil, I hope you're not a lost cause. I need a bassist mate, get over here! The people are crying for us!" Jared holds out the phone to the cheers and screams for The Nights.

"Holy crap, you're Jared Mitchell... you're here? I thought Terrance was at some party!" he sounded flabbergasted.

"It's Jared Wright right now, mate. I'm working. You need to be here like yesterday. You play bass, right?"

"Wow, that was bad. Don't try to sound cool, mate. Be relaxed and let cool run through you. I can send a ride for you. You need to get here now!" Jared stresses his urgency.

"I'm sort of in the middle of doing some sketches and cleaning before my girlfriend gets here. We're supposed to watch a few movies tonight." Chris sighed.

"And now you can be doing something important. Is your name Tor'jun right? Song-Joy, your family was of the Warsingers of Ancient Ecru, correct? My Mother was a Tor'wu, Song-Wise, we are nearly related. I have $10k invested out of my pocket, not to mention what the school is spending and what the fans have spent to be here. They are about to rush the stage and beat this poor opening act to death if we don't get on. My favors are worth more than gold, and I freaking need you, bro!" Jared explains as quickly as he can, "I will bless you eternally if you come. I swear your life will improve if you get down here!"

"She's knocking on the door right now... you put me in a tough spot, bro. It's completely out the blue."

"I know I know it's unfair to ask you to give up a night of Netflix and chill to become the spectacle rather than the voyeur." Jared sighed, nearly giving up to Terrance's words.

"Hold on, fine, bro, I'm on my way, but I need a bass. Call the ride." Chris felt defeated, unable to refuse the man's pleas.

You must come!" Jared cheers up.

Chris hung up the phone tossing it on his bed. He took a moment to breathe between the insistent knocking and urgency. Chris buried his face into his hands, letting out a contained scream before taking a deeper breath and going to the door. He opens it to find an anxious and skeptical auburn-haired girl. She shoved herself inside the single bedroom, looking around rampantly—Margot checks under the bed, in the private bathroom, and the closet.

"What's up, Margot? Good to see you too." Chris rubs his neck.

"You think I'm daft? To whom were you speaking with, Sir?" Margot crossed her arms over her chest.

Margot perked up when her investigation came up short. She threw her arms around his neck tightly, pulling herself up to kiss him all over the face. He carried her into the room by proxy, closing the door with his foot as he worked toward the bed. She was in her pajamas and one of his hoodies. She wrapped her petite frame around his torso, beginning to whine in his ear as her stomach growled.

"Did you cook?" Margot pulled away, looking him in the eyes.

luck. I have leftovers from my study session earlier." Chris shook her off on the bed.

"You love giving me sloppy seconds...." Margot mutters under her breath, rolling her eyes.

"It's an Asiago and Feta steak quesadilla, but since you're sleeping on the leftovers, I guess you're not trying to doctor it back to life, huh?" he asked, reaching into the mini-fridge and popping it into the microwave.

Margot tightened her eyes, "You got that from Antigua's Cafe in Asset Hall?"

"I don't know. Mya bought it when we were smoking earlier. We were studying after the presentation bombed. Then Opal went to talk to the teacher. Mya sparked me up because I was feeling blue." he explained.

"How do you expect us to keep a relationship if you're always hanging out with other girls? Are you kidding me? You told me you were studying. You're over at her place smoking weed like some pothead?" Margot screamed, hitting the bed, finding one of Mya's hoodies, then throws it across the room.

"Fair point... We didn't do anything if it makes you feel better." Chris noted.

"Sharon and Maple said you two were sitting by the lake together like you were on a date. You didn't even answer your

tell me anything."

"Probably because they didn't think it was a big deal. Mya and I are farther than two poles." Chris attempted to banter.

"I can't trust any of you. You're not supposed to touch a Nakan woman. I would burst into flames if you weren't the glimmering hope in this world." Margot crossed her arms over her chest.

"You lost me there. You feel okay?" Chris asked, taking her temperature.

Margot smiled up at him, gripping his collar with a wild grin touching his face. Margot's playing possum got Chris close enough to kiss him on the lips, then his ear, his neck, and his shoulder. She rubbed his crotch, kissing the bulge in his pants but never reaching inside. God forbid they remove their hypocrisies and inhibitions to commit to something.

"Another night of blue balls, right?" he groaned.

"I don't want to have sex, so what? You're supposed to be a nice guy, and nice guys don't ask for sex," Margot says for the hundredth time.

"Whatever, Margot, yo, we need to get ready. They need me at this concert on campus. The lead singer called a cabby." Chris said, slipping on a pair of shoes over his fuzzy socks and throwing on a jacket.

and my friends were all going. Tickets were like $50 a piece. I wasn't spending that to see Somber Nights." Margot groans.

"I'm pretty sure you'll be getting in for free. Jared of Somber Nights asked me to play tonight!" Chris cheers.

"What...? You don't even play an instrument. Why are you joking with me?" she rolls her eyes.

"I used to be in a band back home in Ecru. We split up for college, I wanted them to come with me, but it was a no-go. My Bass broke, and I spend too much money on you to buy a new one. I play a few instruments." Chris corrects her.

"I don't care. Let's stay in!" Margot begins to whine, stretching out, crying, and crawling into the bed.

Chris stared at her with the universal look for 'If you ruin this for me, I will burn down your crops and reign discord on your family for generations.'

Margot replied with a look of, 'Fine, but you owe me so much for this.' before letting out a sigh and hopping off the bed to grab her purple bag stashing some clothes in the bottom drawer of his dresser.

There were particular body language and gestures that eased their cultural barriers.

"What, you kept that here? When did you put that here?" Chris scratched his head.

know it's here. I see Mya has been trying to mark her territory here." Margot gritted her teeth.

"You're on some hardcore Nakan ranting right now." Chris shakes his head.

Margot stared at him dead in the eyes as she squats down to grab Mya's hoodie. She holds a pair of shears from her purple bag and begins cutting the sleeves off.

"What the hell, that's not either of ours. You can't do that."

"You want to see hardcore Nakan, right? You think I'm crazy with the two of you and whatever the hell you are? She should thank me. Now it's fashionable. It's more her style, urban chic." Margot cut off the other sleeve, ripping it off as it tugged to the body.

"You should try telling her that to her face. You're going to explain why that hoodie cut up like that, Margot. That's crossing a line." Chris holds her wrist before she can cut the other sleeve.

"You'll defend that rock-eater against me? Oh hell no! We're staying home! If you think you're treating me like that, you can go by yourself!" Margot crosses her arms and sits on the bed.

"Why do you two hate each other so much?"

complex," she says as if he's stupid.

"My mom, who you never met before-

"We spoke on the phone once, when you hit me remember?"

"When you were screaming and cursing me out?" I raise an eyebrow.

She glares at me, "Excuses."

"I said I was sorry." I remind her, "And anyway, my mother is of Ecrun and Nakan ancestry. She's much more like you, so maybe you're right. You're the oedipal complex. Besides Doctor Dalio, you are my girlfriend, and that means everything to me. I wouldn't try to ruin what we have. Can we please get ready to go? I need to call him back and let him know what's up!"

"If you want to prove you love me, give all this up and stay home with me. You don't play guitar or bass anymore. Stay here, and let's watch, Haunted Houses of Wetmore. I'll even let you play with my breasts if you're good. And if you're outstanding, you can have some sex." Margot pushes her chest together.

"Are you kidding me, Margot? I expected you to support me, not stand directly in the way." he slaps his forehead.

"Support you? I'm trying to save you from yourself! I don't want you embarrassing yourself in front of everyone." Margot rolled her eyes.

Margot looked away from him, poking out her mouth. She grabbed a pair of black tights from the purple bag, sliding out of her usual pajamas. She strolled to the mirror, shaking her rearview, trying to get his attention.

"You don't mind a little fire, do you?" she purrs, poking out her butt, "Stay home, and I'll let you into heaven."

Chris's phone rings before he can look. Margot calls for him, but he was already picking up the phone.

"Mate, you were supposed to call me back!" Jared groans.

"I'm sorry, I'm sorry. I'm on my way out the door, trying to get my girl along with the program."

"That's supposed to be the easy part, mate. Like, the solidified bit before you start wanking, right?"

"You don't know my relationship. Just- where's the ride?" Chris rubs the bridge of his nose.

"Sheesh, mate, at least get me drunk before you try to punch me in the face. Or at least get to the concert and do it after the bloody performance! It's the opportunity of a lifetime mate and-

"Where are my shoes?" Margot shouts, pulling shoes out of the cubbies beneath his bed.

"ARE YOU COMING?" Jared shouts loud enough to be heard through the whole auditorium, nearly causing Terrance's

with growing fervor rather than dissipating.

Margot cleaned out her ears, nearly feeling knocked unconscious by the soundwave aimed at her. Her ears were ringing as she heard the subliminal, "Don't mess this up for him." refusing to escape from her ears until it rattled into her subconscious. No one else in the world could have heard it. It was the power of a man who mastered his sound chakra hundreds of years ago.

"I'm dating a rock star." Margot wrapped her arms around his neck, slipping into her Chuck Taylors fresh out the box, a pair she bought to keep in his room for special occasions. She had almost given up on them ever going out on dates.

"You need to get here to be a rock star, mate. Rakil, honestly, it's only showing up and the results that count. Now, get downstairs. Your chariot awaits!" Jared hangs up.

"Boy, if I knew I was dating a freaking stud, maybe I would act right. An impromptu date and you're the entertainment for the evening? That's so you, baby." Margot giggles, pinching his cheek.

"Uh, haha… it's amazing how quickly your mood changes." Chris chuckles nervously.

Margot ignored the comment fantasizing about the man he should be and will be with her careful crafting. Her first plan was to get him to think of more than sex finally. Though, her desired to settle down before graduation but for various reasons. She held her dreams around his arms as they walked down to the first floor, where a modest car sat out front in the night air.

The driver was a young Eshan man who spoke little of a common tongue, using the Cabby App to learn the language and meet people. He drove them away from a night of binging on television, lousy food, fighting, and sex, back to the memories of playing shows in abandoned buildings, parents' basements, warehouses, and The Underground fighting circuits, or dive-in bars. Music always came naturally to him, stopping less than a year ago, still playing time and again if someone else had an instrument. He tried like hell to get his other three bandmates to come to New Haven University in Erdu. They had never left Ecru and had no intentions of leaving Ecru. They would never believe what could have happened had they followed him.

Chris looked over to see his girlfriend going through various emotions as they approached the auditorium to see a line still forming for people with tickets to enter. Another group was leaving or corralling outside, waiting for the main show to start. A few stayed close enough in case they got their money's worth, eyeing the Ticketmaster for a refund. They got out, and Margot watched in aggravation as they approached the line. Her eyes grew as she saw Chris passing right by, walking to the

mind people's opinions of him.

"Yo, I'm the bassist. JMW called for me." Chris nodded.

The security guard eyed Chris wondering where he got the audacity to cut the entire line then lie about such a thing. To a point where he feared questioning the young man's guile.

The Security guard chirped it in, "There's some guy here, says he's the bassist."

"Let him in, let him in. This Jared guy is about to flip his freakin' lid if this guy doesn't get on stage soon. What are you waiting for!?"

The voice from the walkie flooded out the stagehands with anxiety. The disembodied voice tugs their rope and directs them on their way.

Margot looked back in amazement as Chris kept trucking along, looking for the dressing room.

"Yowza!" Terrance shouts from across the room.

"Yo, bro!" Chris calls back as he's waved toward a giant curtain separating the media and fans from the talent.

Terrance dabs Chris up as they meet by the curtain. Terrance looks to Margot in shock and looks away, trying to find words.

"Hey, Terry." Margot teases.

"I hate that name...." Terrance mutters.

for us, bucko." Margot shoots at him with her fingers.

"I'm more worried about you fu-

Chris stops Terrance before he can continue pushing him along behind the curtain. Margot follows tenaciously, wanting Terrance to finish his sentence before she popped him. Chris stood between the two until Terrance leaves to inform Jared.

"I think Terrance is jealous of you…." Margot chides.

"Jealousy isn't a Terrance-like trait. Tee is too austere to want what someone else has. He's a good guy and a better friend."

"The one you're always talking about me with, right?" she rolls her eyes, "Or is that one, Monique?"

"You know her name. It's Mya. I don't talk about you to anyone. Jah'Ada, Margot, can you cut it out? Please?" Chris pleads.

Margot rolls her eyes, "You asked me to come here."

"I asked you both to come here. Should I regret that also? You just arrived." Jared greets, walking up to them.

Chris smiled ear to ear, "Dude, I've heard all your music. Even in your weird hip-hop phase, you had a few good songs."

"You ras clot, my rap album won awards!" Jared challenged.

"It was generic." Chris looked him in the eye.

bass, you're some kind of virtuoso? What's my best song then, mate? Let's hear it. Quickly, let me see if I just have to play two instruments tonight." Jared snaps his finger.

"The only time you did that was a harmonica and a piano, not the most challenging feat, my friend. Your best song was "Eshan Cymatic Tempura" you were doing more mixing and producing then. You made this amazing ambient, chopped, and screwed song no one heard of before."

"That's because it was a bloody DJ session, bro. I didn't think anyone ever heard of the song before outside of the listeners. I was trying to make my next leap and had to pay rent. I started making beats. That was like five years ago mate, who the hell are you?" Jared says in complete awe.

"Chris Tor'jun from Little Penah, Ecru. I study History here at NHU." I say modestly.

"Right on, mate. I appreciate you coming out. I'm not playing that song, but everything else will be simple for you if you know it. And how about you, my lady, what's your name? Where are you from?"

"I've never been a huge fan of yours. Your music is way too sad. I'm Margot Dalio Hoska from Hubertus, Naka. My great-great-great-grandfather knew your grandfather. He studied under him. I have no idea how old you're pretending to be, but you need to cut it out and get a real job." Margot commented.

ways—anguish incarnate in this one. Speaking of gramps, your family happens to have a few of our things, little lady. I want them back." Jared chides in his usual banter.

"You're a disrespectful twit! Hit him, Chris!" Margot shouts, sucking her teeth at Jared.

"Both of you, chill out, please!" Chris demands, exasperated.

"You want me to chill out?" Margot shoots a glare at Chris.

The men gulped. Jared took a step back, and Chris went to calm Margot.

"Mate… I'm not trying to be in your business. I just want to get on with the show." Jared leans back on his heels.

"I got this. Give me a minute. You didn't help the situation any!" Chris shouts back at Jared.

Jared holds up his hands, backing away, "Five minutes to show time, my friend. Your bass is ready by the stage. I just need you to decide whether you'll spend your life in heaven or hell. I'll be waiting."

"Screw you. You are so pompous!" Margot says to herself under her breath.

"He's a freaking celebrity. I usually don't care at all about celebrities or any crap like that, but you're seriously treating him like he's some bum on the street. You really can't imagine

tries to explain.

"Someone has to check his privilege and ego." Margot stretches out, "You two need to toughen up. You should have fought him over me."

"You need to find a good spot to watch the show. I'm about to practice a few chords. Can you support me?" Chris asks.

"Yeah, whatever..." Margot mutters.

"Margot, I sat through a five-hour dinner theatre with your little friends. You can't enjoy a concert?" Chris looked befuddled.

"I said yes! Don't yell at me!" she retorts.

Chris takes a deep breath, "Baby, I know had an exam today, and you have another in a couple of days. You're stressed out. You're a major introvert. You want to be curled up watching your show. Give me a few hours. I'll be all yours tonight, and we can spend more time together tomorrow."

"I want this jerk off to pay you so we can go on a real date. Make that happen, and I'll be good. You're a great musician. You told him off, so you must be good. Rock it tonight, baby. You have a huge crowd out there, and I know you'll do well. Now, kiss me and go save this dude's career." Margot kisses him on the lips then pats his cheek.

"Thank you, baby." He kisses her again even deeper then rushes off to find Jared and the bass.

parts and people operating the show. There was an entire crew functioning what seemed more like a science experiment than a simple rock concert. Then again, he thought, who wanted simple anymore? Suddenly, two hands grabbed Chris tearing him between the curtain and the hallway. He spun around, shoving away the crabs in the bucket, freeing him from the delusion on the other side of the curtain.

"Who do you think you are walking back here, buddy! This is a restricted area, prohibited to plain pedestrians playing themselves with popularity complexes. Get out of here before I have- you're eyeballing me pretty hard." The stage director stepped back, raising his hands.

"Not a fan of your tone. I'm about two seconds from punching you in your throat and finding my bass." Chris's anti-disestablishment agitation began kicking in.

The director began to check his tone and tilted his head to the side, seeing if this was a fight he wanted. He was used to throwing his weight and words around. With a stranger, he didn't like his odds and reconsidered his strategy.

"I'm the bassist, you idiot," Chris replies, rubbing his neck.

This is the bassist!" The stage director fetches his reinforcements.

Chris slaps his face, "You're lucky I don't kick you in your teeth bro, don't ever run up on someone like that again unless you're ready to taste clouds."

"Clouds?"

"Means rest in peace partnah, adios to life. I used to be a Mask, my guy. You don't ever talk to me like that again." Chris points the man in his throat and pushes him aside.

A group of stagehands immediately surrounds him. He crouched down, ready to pounce, but their hands were all over him with headsets, wires, mic testing, and cleaning his face. He raised his hands in surrender to the process of being groomed for the stage. The swarm of stagehands dispersed and went off to their next assignment of tasks. Chris still couldn't find the bass. Without sight of Jared, he was brought to the harsh aimless reality of the other end of the curtain. It seemed without someone demanding, directing, or indoctrinating. Nothing got done. Suppose he wanted to be a free spirit. He had to move his soul. People want your soul for anything but heaven.

Chris noticed the onlookers far more intently now. No one paid any mind, no one cared, and no one interacted outside of necessity. Everyone was set upon their tasks. It was the ones seemingly doing nothing which had the real power and

leading upstairs, poking open an eye if someone stepped close. The Stage Manager was still as stone, leading with head shakes and nods to critical decisions. You could see emotion wretched on his face, yet all the same, he keeps his head for the sake of the stagehands.

It mattered here.

They were people again released from the monotony into the fire seeing the eternal light of the stars. These people did all they were told and couldn't think for themselves. However, they seemed to love it. This was their purpose, their occupation, their placement, or their decision. They took orders and fulfilled them with a smile or a satisfaction Chris never knew. He couldn't smile getting someone's coffee. He couldn't go home at night adjusting someone's headset.

He moved quietly, observing the adjustment as The Stage Manager moved closer to the stage.

"Are you following me?" The Stage Manager turns on the dime, "How did you get back here?"

"I'm Chris Kirin Tor'Jun, the Bassist for the evening." I bow.

"Oh god… we're getting desperate." The Stage manager fawns his mouth, japing to himself before responding, "Oh, little bunny lost in the world, where is your carrot? If you're a bassist, your head will spin."

"Do it." Chris looked him dead in the eyes without so much as breathing or palpitating in total stillness and silence like a panther about to pounce.

The Stage Manager wore sunglasses, hiding his gaze, trying to break eye contact, but as a trained professional, his head cocked straight. As a mortal, his lips were shut.

Chris looked behind him to the stagehands realizing nothing separates the two other than a few more years and a few more connections. He felt a strange feeling looking back at the Stage Manager, realizing the same laid true for him. He's the same Gatekeeper from earlier. I guess it was the same for Jared. Nothing separated him but his faith and grit.

Chris gave the Stage Manager a curt nod and pushed forward to the stage. He noticed Jared still wasn't around, but the rest of the band had assembled, apart from the drummer still sleeping. The rest tuned their instruments and practiced their chords scoffing at Jared for tardy and mocking the drummer for sleeping on the job. Yet, their anxieties loomed as their prepared for something they do every day and night.

"Hey, are you the bassist?" A Mayan woman with a blue mohawk eyeballed me, "Who let you back here?"

"I've been exploring...." I shrug.

She cracks a smile and waves me forward.

"Chris Kirin Tor'Jun." I greet with a fist bump.

"Tor'Jun... Tor'Jun, I know that name from history class in the fifth grade. We were studying Ecru Mythology. There was some hero back in the 2nd Age, The War Singer. Led to some revolution, right?" Miranda asked.

"I have no idea about mythology... I'm pretty sure you're right." I chuckle.

"Pretty sure isn't sure." she rolls her eyes.

"Chill, I think you're right, alright? The actuality is that The Warsingers were a clan underneath Jibril Tor'vidya, the Grand Sameera and ancestor. He created the four clans with proverbs in the songs of Joy, Knowledge, Inhibition, and Wisdom from the four sons born to Rakil. It was the world's oldest religion, not a myth, but I guess they wouldn't know much about Ecru to other regions. Let's get the hype. We a got a show, right?" I try to boost her up.

"You're a smart guy, but a weird one. I guess that's what happens when we're running on short supply. Are you any good?" she asks.

"Ha, I used to be pretty great." I shrug.

"Ugh... have some confidence, pretty great? Are you pretty sure? Do you have balls? Tell me one thing you're certain about now!" she claps her hands.

"What?" I ask.

else you're not going on that stage, you'll mess up everything, and then I'll choke you out with my guitar strings. I don't need that type of violence tonight, but I know myself. So answer my question and show me you know yourself." Miranda persisted.

"I am a bloody good bassist, and I know every single one of your songs, every note, key, octave, word, intention, and melody. I am perhaps your biggest fan." I gulped, hoping my answer was satisfying.

"Do you have Jared's face tattooed on your stomach too?" Miranda chuckled.

"I don't have any tattoos." I grin.

"That's strange. Mostly everyone I know has tattoos, brands, something. Why don't you have a little ink?" She asked.

"Crazy thing about life, sometimes you have completely different experiences. You see, I'm only 22, so like everyone I know has been under 18 for like all my life. So, it was kind of illegal to have tattoos. I guess I got so used to my skin I decided to keep it, don't cha know?" I smirk.

She smiles, shaking her head, "You're right. However, you forgot to mention after 19, and everyone gets their first tat, or peer pressure surrounds them."

"I don't deal with peer pressure. I either start fighting harder when people gang up on me, or I dip out before they can respond.

"You must be great at parties." Miranda giggles covering her mouth politely.

"I guess you'll see in a bit. I'm my own man. As long as someone can respect that, then we're fantastic. The second they try to put me in their ego-driven perspective, I shatter their perspective." I didn't laugh, feeling her schema's box beginning to suffocate me.

We were only feet away from the stage. Japes and snide comments weren't going to steal my focus or shake me up. I had left the effects of all that in my dorm room. I'm here to excel in what I love most. If I wanted fear to drive my life, I could have stayed in my bedroom half the world away in Nadia. Fear had never controlled my life before. It might have made me miss a few opportunities, but ultimately insecurity or laziness had been my prime limitations. Laziness would have been resting and sleeping back in my dorm room watching reruns, avoiding fights with Margot. Insecurity would have been letting Miranda shut me down. Here I stood.

"Ay, mate, where is your bass?" Jared asked, patting my shoulders, "I see you met my love and devotion, thee Miranda Maroni."

"Today, I'm your devotion. Tomorrow it's the bottle." Miranda rolls her eyes, tired of hearing it.

had the same talks Jack has with me or my buddy Jim Beam. We have deep pulsating conversations about life, love, and recovery."

"So, you're like an alcoholic…?" I asked, scratching my scalp.

"Ha, if he weren't famous, he would be an alcoholic. He's functional enough." Miranda chides as she leaves us.

"I am an avid drinker, yes. I prefer a drink with my breakfast, lunch, dinner, snacks, or because it's 16 o hundred. Sometimes, I prefer a drink with a cloud of smoke to soothe my mind. Some people like yoga, counselors, and long talks. I prefer wine, whiskey, and blunts. Do you have an issue with that, mate?" Jared asks as if my opinion mattered.

"I'm a smoker, not a drinker. I prefer wine because it doesn't get me too drunk. I guess if I had more tolerance, I would drink. I could never manage to be drunk for more than a few minutes even then I wonder when it all ends."

"You stop drinking then…." Jared smirks.

"About two or three drinks in, then I get a headache." I chuckle.

"So, that's what a normal guy is like… 2 or 3 drinks, brother? I think half a handle to feel buzzed. Two drinks seem social to me. So, we'll have a couple of drinks. A couple of blunts,

show, kick back and talk?" Jared asks.

"If there's an after-show, let's hope this crowd doesn't rip me apart for not being Flat-foot. I thought you knew where my bass was. Without it, I can't go on." I sigh.

"Well, you could go on, but I don't think you'll serve any purpose. You can dance for moral support." Jared jokes before walking ahead of me. "Hmm... give me a second."

Jared holds out his hands then closes his eyes. He starts humming a prayer under his breath then claps his hands twice. As he turns around, a stagehand approaches us, carrying a black case with my name imprinted on its side. Jared smiles innocently as the stagehand delivers the black case then runs off without many words.

"Your instrument, mate." Jared winks.

"You just did that with your head?" I ask.

"God already has a design. A prayer here or there can swing it in your timing. That's all. Place your faith in him. All I did was pray." Jared shoves the case in my hands, "Come on then, open her up!"

"Alright, alright, you're more excited than I am." I accept the case and crack it open to a cherry red four four-string electric acoustic bass guitar staring at me.

"Your face has WOW written all over it." Jared chuckles.

right. My mind has WOW written all through it. I've never had a bass this nice, especially not on short notice. I couldn't imagine how much he already invested, then go and find a piece of art like this bass.

"Am I putting her in the right hands?" Jared asks me.

I cradled my new baby girl in my arms, gently easing the strap around my shoulder before strumming her lightly. I began fiddling a low melodic classical tune I had first learned when I began, one of the few pieces I mastered. I leaned into a beautiful folky beat as my fingers began to speed up. I even managed to catch Miranda's attention as she passed by, nodding her head. Jared watched curiously unimpressed until I began playing YYZ by Rush, having the time of my life with a bass in my hands. I played without breaking a sweat for five whole minutes to the point I hadn't even realized the show had started. My microphone was live, and Miranda had joined me by stage side as a live camera feed showed us jamming backstage.

Jared pointed to the camera with a wild grin as the crowd joined him in, laughing everyone part of the little joke. I grinned it off, following my new bandmates on stage as Jared led us into the first song. The show was about 20 minutes late, but it seemed like the perfect time as we began jamming. Jared and Miranda both played guitar but had such different sounds and styles. Miranda had an electric acoustic guitar. Her sound was

resonator guitar seemed to reinvent the wheel, experimenting with new sounds and chords on the same songs he's been playing for years. The drummer Jax had perfect rhythm, never missing a beat, managing to match Jared's freestyle as if rehearsed hours before the show in natural harmony. Something that would come from years on the road but more reminiscent of twins who shared a single mind.

Somber Nights had several ballads from their early days in smoky jazz clubs. Ever since hitting the main stage, something clicked. None of his hip-hop days reached the stage, but most indie-rock hits were loved and requested.

Chris played as if it was back in the garage. The raging of the crowd was deafening. It's all he heard above the music at first. He rocked with the beat dancing around his bandmates to their surprise and delight. He lost himself entirely to the music as if becoming a new creation altogether with that bass in his hands. Any microphone he could chime into during his favorite parts would lean onside Miranda or Timber. God forbid he and Jared got close enough together. They paraded about as two drinking buddies nearly falling off the stage to the crowd, wrapping an arm over the other and belting out the word in a lovely competition between Chris' tenor and Jared's dabbling between falsetto and natural smoky bass singing voice.

the crowd. Jared had to wrap an arm around Chris to get him to stand still.

"Hello all, we didn't see you there!" Jared chuckles into the stage microphone, "Are you all having a good time?"

Chris saw the crowd cheering, and finally, embarrassment had hit him. He spent so much time building up his reputation as an aloof, standoffish, and impersonal soul, the majority of the campus now knew him as a dancing fool. No one seemed to mind but him.

"Tor'jun! Tor'jun! Tor'jun!" The crowd screamed, recognizing the shy man despite his wishes.

Chris blushed, waving his hand, hiding behind Jared as best he could.

"They're screaming for you, mate, not me." Jared laughs, stepping out his way.

Chris accepted the other side of the musician's life as people screamed and cried for him to keep playing. Most people tried to silence his rants of Nakan creationist history, but he couldn't get enough with the bass in his hand. Had he prepared a ballad of human rights violations committed against his people, maybe they would listen? They said luck is when preparation met timing as much as he wanted to use the stage to preach on the myriad of causes in his mind. He simply frowned and took a few steps back, leaving Jared to his natural gift.

The largely Erdun crowd replied, "SCREW NAKA!" even louder than either could imagine chanting it and repeating it wildly.

Chris could only imagine Margot's face. He could see Mya and her girls in the front row, none too far from Sh'rn and Maple, joining in with the chant. All were screaming as loud as they could, hopping up and down with the rest of the crowd screaming out the simple sentiment on everyone's mind. Chris looked back at the band with a grin on his face. The simplicity had astounded him.

"BRING BACK ECRU!" Chris rose his fist up.

The small amount of Ecru, Western Erdun, and Eastern Nakan students erupted with the chant.

Jared laughed, patting Chris on the back as he joined in the chant. He wrapped an arm around his new friend as they recited with the entire campus.

"BRING BACK ECRU! BRING BACK ECRU!" the students began shoving and screaming, sending security into the crowd.

Jared sighed, "You want to fight over creation but cheer for destruction, ain't that just the way?"

The crowd began to subdue itself from the disappointment of the living legend.

"Why is it generation after generation it's easier to rally a crowd into the killing, pillaging, or warfare but never to fix me?" Jared asks before he sits on the edge of the stage.

The crowd began to quiet down. They watched on in curiosity as the mood changed and gave itself the way to a brand new experience.

"I am over 310 years old. My birthday is in a few months, so 311. Can you imagine in three centuries how bloody depressing it is when humanity has yet to get it together? Instead, there is more of the same hatred, systematic oppression, denial of basic resources while new groups step into power while the same old families sit above it all? Then you young lot either fall into the furnace apart of the vicious cycle or can't wait to rule over your colleagues. I wasn't born to be a musician. Most of you have no idea who my family is or was, for that matter. I am a figment and monolith, yeah? Music is something I picked up to voice my anger, sadness, frustration, and perspective. Then I hate chicks saying it's depressing, you're not listening. You dance, you sing, you scream, but you're not listening." Jared monologues.

The crowd was crossed between cheering, confusion, and booing. The truth he spoke shattered the chains of hundreds in the crowd bubbling up with his truth to scream out in support. The multitude hadn't known, cared, or understood. Chris was stumped when the man who looked no older than 30 confessed to being ten times older. The last segment was outraged from singer trying to preach wanting to scream. The crowd was seconds away from an explosion into a mosh pit. What to do, what to do?

Jared stares off as memories of riots, wars, and bloodshed ran across his mind watching the frenzied crowd. He began to doubt whether or not he was meant to perform at all. Perhaps he needed to see how little the world had changed.

"It's the mystery of the world today.

People speak, but what do they say?

It's the way of the world today.

Things spin until they fade away.

Can I prophesy, can I speak?

Can I cry without being weak?

Is it a time, or is it space?

Have mercy keep me out of my place!"

Chris begins to sing, trying to get the band to join in.

Jax begins tapping his cymbals before the bass drop, feeling the vibe in the air as well. Miranda let out a sigh, strumming lightly to one of their oldest songs, wondering how this kid could have even heard something written 15 years ago when the band first formed. Jared couldn't believe his ears, stunned as he looked behind himself to Chris, trying to rally them all together.

standing to his feet.

"Don't tempt me with a bad time,

Show me the truth of your mind.

Show me the truth, the way, and the life.

Don't lie to me with twisted truth,

Show me the uncouth.

Show me you, not the lies.

I don't need the appearances,

I don't need the fear,

I need love over distance,

I need grace so dear.

Don't baptize me in blood,

Give me water, alive,

Just pray I survive,

Release the traps of my mind!

Don't tempt with a bad time, No!

Show me the truth,

The truest of your mind.

Show me the truth, the way, and the life.

Free me from lies, free me from lies!

Yes, please free me from lies!

I don't need the appearances,

I'm already in fear,

I need love over distances,

Jared joined Chris in a duet together as they played, staring straight at the other.

"Help me, help me, God, and raise me from the dead like Lazarus. Help me, help, God. Free my spirit from this trap of mind!" Jared began improvising as his body rattled with the spirit.

Chris took a step back, letting Jared take center stage their classic song.

"Save Ecru, Save Erdu, and me!

I never did it for money,

I did most of this for free.

Let me show them the way,

The way, the way

If you show me a brighter day.

I'm so lost in appearances,

So lost in these lies.

I turn on the TV and end up crying.

There's more than corruption,

There's more than just crime.

There's more than just hatred.

We're dead, not alive.

Can you please lift our spirits?

Save us from ourselves.

Save us from these liars, thieves, and spells.

They all want consumers,

Can someone create the way, the truth, and the life?

Please! Please! Please! Save me,

Save from appearances,

Save me from lies!

Please! Please! Please show me,

Show your grace, your mercy, and light!

Even just for a day,

Even just for a moment.

Show me your grace, your mercy, and light!

Even just a day,

Even just for a moment.

Please, someone, save a life."

Jared fades out, bowing his head and lifting his hands as he sang straight from his spirit.

The crowd erupted in tearful cheers after the singer finishes pouring out his soul to end an hour-long performance. Jared was the first to flee the stage. The rest took their bows and waved their way off the stage. Jax kept a heavy drumline taking the time to indulge in a wondrous solo that kept the crowd on its feet. He rocked out as the stagehands began striking the stage, and the crowd filtered out.

Chris went off in search of Jared, who had nearly vanished before Chris caught him nearing the parking lot.

the heavy gym doors.

"Come with me." Jared offers, extending his hand.

"Where are you even going?" Chris asks.

"To think out loud… To figure it out finally, why are you here?" Jared sounded exasperated.

"Let's go…." Chris sighs, following Jared to his tour bus.

Jared shook the rusty handle until the door creaked open on the old moonbeam van. He drove across the world more times than he could count. Only he and Jax still rode in the van. Miranda preferred to fly in. Timber and his husband, Flat-foot, drove their trailer everywhere. Jared clung to his memories within the van.

"311 years, mate…." Jared said as he took a seat on the shaggy couch, cracking open a swisher and emptying its guts into a plastic baggie.

"You have to be a multimillionaire. Why not get a better ride?" Chris asks.

"You think it's about the money, mate? What the hell does a man do with a million dollars? We're the same humans who lived off apples, squirrels, and grapes for 10,000 years. Where does humanity possibly delude itself to believing he can use a million dollars?" Jared shakes his head.

"Ha, you could probably buy a jet." Chris joked.

me as a joker. I'm serious, mate. When did we give up the simple life for the complexities and intricacies? When did we all choose to give up freedom for this life of slavery?"

"The same time when the shiny stones became more valuable than our own lives." Chris offered, taking a bag of bud out of his pocket.

"I got it to mate. This kush is straight from the Garden of Eden." Jared raised his hand then took a metal box from underneath the couch.

"If you want to hear my theory, I'll share it." Chris put the bud away.

"That's why you're here, right?" Jared said in a callous deadpan tone.

Chris looked away from his hero for a second and then saw the exhausted spirit before him. He thought his life had strung him dry but seeing what 300 years on the planet could do. He realized he had a lot of life left.

"We are living exactly as we have always lived. Bear with me a second here. First, we believe we have evolved, changed, and somehow reached some higher status of life. In truth, there are billions still living in the Stone Age, survival of the fittest mentality. Second, we believe in the shiny stone theory. I believe in the ownership theory. If we stare at life from a pure survival root chakra standpoint, the strongest survive, so we huddle them. When there are only twenty in a clan doing this, it's almost harmless, but it replays itself to a village of 200 underneath a King, Duke, or Tax Collector. Then it scales itself greater with 2 million under the exemplar of their cultural beliefs. It's the same root chakra standpoint. A dependency upon an avatar emulating some perceived strength or needing its protection. Third, the only ones who uncover this truth either exploit it, living above the perceived strong controlling and manipulating what is perceived as strength based on who they can control. Or-

"So, you saw your first secret society videos late at night on YouTube?" Jared shakes his head.

Chris rubbed his neck, unable to respond.

"I'm not only talking about secret societies. I am talking about the strong, the ones who mold and shape society."

"It's not strong. Do you know the strongest man alive?" Jared asked.

"The Lord Commissioner, Ray Bradley Warren of the Regulator Regime," Chris responds without hesitation.

"Wrong," Jared says as he grinds up the buds in a platinum grinder.

"Patriarch Colin Gregor?" Chris asks, unsure.

"Wrong," Jared says as he dumps the greens into the wrap.

"You?" Chris throws up his hands.

bloody fighter, mate. I know a few tricks, but no, I met the man. I stared him in his eyes. Those eyes, The King's Crimson Red Eyes, the ones the Warsingers protected. Strongest force living or dead, he's a recluse and doesn't want to be bothered by anyone. Most of the strong are like that. That's the only hole in your theory. No one is sitting above the strong, no one at all, no lord, and no patriarch because only strength defeats or controls strength. What you have, your theory is correct, is a group of cowards attempting to control what is perceived as valuable so they may assume such a role. Sadly, the strong are in hiding, refusing to display their strength. It's the emperors and god-kings sending their fledgling armies to conquer the defenseless. Whenever there is a slight resistance, those armies lose. Did you notice that? The only time these armies seem to win is when the opposition doesn't fight back. That's it. Then, you have the forces stronger than armies. You have the Guardians. You have God Almighty. It seems like you need to reject both The Guardians and God to join these armies or to become one of these Emperors because only a fool or a blasphemer believes they can play either role. I agree with you, mate. Sharpen your theory if you add a hint of mysticism to it, it might become more believable." Jared explained while lighting the blunt seal.

"Uh, thank you..." Chris gulped, never having thought of such a thing so boldly before.

you can call us friends or anyone around him as such, he's a Guardian as well. He's far gone. I wouldn't be surprised if he popped his head up one of these days to claim his place on the food chain truly, but it seems out of his character. If he could die in hiding, he would. A sad reality is that true power haunts the powerful. Once you know what you are, it's bloody hell to be it." Jared continued.

"What do you mean? I thought once you knew your purpose, life got easier." Chris scratched his scalp.

"Ha, if your purpose is being a dad or a nurse, yeah, I'm sure it's freaking easy. Can you imagine when your purpose is replacing George Henry Wright, Obatta Sameera, Anka or Ada, to lead a planet? It's a bit more difficult accepting the lives of billions under your control and influence. Billions of people looking toward you for guidance, for protection, for grace, for truth becoming a Guardian, a leader, or a prophet is not as easy as you think."

"But if it's your purpose, why is it so hard?" Chris asked.

"You see, there are men who lust for power. They typically have never had any. They lust for it and know nothing of it, like a chronic masturbating virgin. They lust for authority because they are vacant, yeah? Then you have men who have the talent, the power, the charisma, and the purpose. How does a man compete for what he already has within? To constantly

there eating its tail and you need to train for your purpose. You spend years of your life in isolation, distant from those people, and you spend even more years studying, training, and practicing to lead. You spend even more years lecturing, being lectured. All the while, the world keeps falling apart. You're bloody smarter, bloody stronger, and bloody whatever it was you sought after, and the worst was worse than when you began your training. There's no answer yet. That's why they needed you to go through the process."

"That sounds very personal," Chris notes.

"As personal as it gets when it's your shoes, mate. I became a musician to feel closer to the people I was supposed to save. I'm not sure I saved any yet." Jared looks away, trying to gather himself as not to cry.

"And the strongest man alive?"

"He's shed a lot of blood to keep people safe. The oxymoron of war for peace paralyzes him." Jared presses the blunt to his lips and lights it as he takes a shallow inhale.

"Is there a meaning to life?" Chris asked.

"Save as many as you can before you die... then die again once the last one remembers you. Hopefully, you never die because you did such a good job. Hopefully, you never die twice because you're never forgotten." Jared closes his eyes, answering without hesitation.

mind didn't rattle with questions or float away with thoughts. He was solidified upon the singular idea of two deaths. It was the first he had ever heard the idea before, especially from someone so prominent.

Jared passed him the blunt, and the two sat in near silence aside from the light music in the background.

Jared looked at Chris with a smile and then chuckled.

"What?" Chris asked.

"You were my fan before this, right mate? Now, what are you?" Jared grinned.

"I guess your friend." Chris shrugged.

"Ha, you were already Terrance's mate. We could have been friends. My point is that the veil is lifted now. There's no longer any mystique, no distance, no curious ideas of who I am or what I am. Now, you see no difference between the two of us."

"I see a lot of differences between us, but I get your point. I feel like I could hold my own with you."

"Hopefully, soon you'll feel like you can replace me. 311years is pretty old to be running around like a 30-year-old. For my species, though, 311 is like 31. I have a long time before I die in spirit or start to slow, but I'm tired of this plane. I need to return to my real duties soon."

"What species is that?" Chris made sure the weed wasn't speaking to him.

life. I should have been on a shiny throne lording over everyone, but it's not my style. I prefer being among the people but- it's not what I thought it would be. I sing, they dance, but nothing changes, mate." Jared took long drags, already preparing to roll up another.

"Do you believe you changed?" Chris asked.

"Now, you're asking the right questions." Jared grins.

"Well... have you?" Chris persists.

"I've changed as much as the wind and as little as a breeze. It's been dramatic shifts at times. When I was truly young, I spent a lot of time in Kismet. Then on my traveling around the world, I studied under the Grand Masters of their region. Then, when I returned to Kismet, they tried to put me back in their indoctrination to forget everything I learned. I left to travel with my band traveling, doing more insulated travel around Erdu, Maya, never returning to Esha. Not allowed in Naka, ha. I've been changed, I have grown, but in 300 years, you'll be unsurprised to know there's still further to go." Jared stopped all he was doing and stared at the ceiling, passing the remnants of the blunt to Chris, "Imagine a mortal man, living to 100... to 120... there's still so much to see. The goal isn't always to change. Sometimes you must be."

"You think you'll be happier had you changed?" Chris asks.

desire. There is only Rakil above the clouds, and no one can take it away. Looking at the world makes me sad. These simple moments make me ecstatic. It's not about happiness. I learned that in my 20s. It's about service to the world, not slavery but service. You have to give to others ever to feel as if you have meaning. If you don't, then nothing truly remains here. It's a shame most think only about and for themselves then pretend they don't know why they're miserable. If you spend all of your life-giving your gift to others, you'll never miss out on anything. You'll always know where you stand. You'll always know you did the right thing. I feel melancholy at how much is left to be done, but I have hope because of how much has been done. You cannot save the world. If you save yourself from the world, then the good you do becomes immeasurable. Remember that, my friend. Save yourself from the world first." Jared refuses the blunt as it's passed back to him, pointing to the half-rolled blunt before him.

"How do I save myself from the world?"I ask, chiefing on the cigar-sized blunt as a larger one is rolled before him.

The door clattered as Jax fiddled with the handle outside.

"It's down then up," Jared shouts.

After a few more seconds, Jax got the door open with a large sigh of relief. The drummer jumped up and steps and spun kick the door behind him.

"Greatest twenty-minute drum solo this school has ever seen."

"It's already been twenty minutes?" I asked, thinking on Margot.

"Yeah, bruddah, the auditorium is clear, and everyone is home. Miranda is in a cab to the airport. Timber and Flat are heading back to their hotel in Penu, and then they're off to look at a vineyard. Where's our next adventure, captain?" Jax had spoken more than I heard all day.

"Here for a while. I have to head back to my apartment for this little after-party in an hour. I told my roommate I would go."

"A party?" Jax raspberries.

"Ha, that's the major first step. You need to give up the parties, clubs, and spending hours getting ready. The social appearances have to die to you to some degree. Sometimes you can't avoid it, but that need for validation will cripple you. Learn to keep to yourself, study more, take yourself out on dates, and figure out what you think. Then the rest comes easy." Jared finished rolling.

"How to be kept?" Jax asked.

"Yes, sir, to be kept in the holiness." Chris answers.

"My advice, learn how to take naps instead of making bad decisions. Instead of dealing with negative energy, over-indulging, or doing something you'll regret, sleep on it first, and better you'll be when you wake up. A good dream is better than drugs, sex, or anything else out there. If you can master that, then you'll be kept for sure." Jax grinned, beginning to close his eyes.

"I have classes... and a girlfriend," Chris comments, rubbing his chin contemplating the party.

"I have a full tour schedule. Naps save my life." Jax yawns.

"Touche..." Chris chuckles as Jared hands him the unlit blunt.

"You do the honors, mate. Jax will probably take a few hits then pass out. We have a party to get to after I take a shower." Jared stretches out.

"You're not a smoker?" Chris asks Jax as he sparks up.

"I was a huge druggist when we started. If it was a drug, I tried it. My favorites were coke, weed, alcohol, and upper pills. Then, this guy over here started going overboard, and being his mentor, I had to give it all up. Now, he's down to weed and alcohol. We did it, but life's better without all that crap. We have much more money now, too, not trying to get an entire city as high as possible. We buy premium in bulk and ration it out." Jax explained.

"His mentor... you'll older than him?" Chris began coughing, holding out the blunt for someone to take it.

taking the blunt.

"Is he?" Chris asks again between wheezing.

Jared rolls his eyes, "He's what the Mayans call a Tortuga-perezoso. They don't age, they don't move, and it's a wonder he plays drums."

"Neither of you are human?" Chris took a closer look at the buds sitting on the table.

"Humanoid." Jax shrugs, breathing the weed-like air then blowing it out his nose.

"Is that laced?" Chris asks.

"Nah, it's weed. Angel Kiss Kush from Anka but weed." Jared winks.

"Do people know you're not human?" Chris asks.

"Do you realize how many non-humans live on this planet? Open your eye, kid." Jax points to his forehead.

"I need some water and air." Chris chuckles.

Jax and Jared look at each other before breaking out laughing. Jax passes along the blunt shaking his head.

"You're my favorite so far, Chris. You can tour with us as long as you like." Jax offers.

"This wasn't a one-time deal?" Chris asks.

"Flat sprained a finger, bruddah. He's down for four weeks. We could use you, and you're wavy with the bass. All the

explains their situation.

"Hell yeah…" Chris says without hesitation.

Both break out laughing again.

"You didn't even think about it. Why don't you maul it over first?" Jared asks.

"Why?" Jared asks.

"It's the type of lifestyle that once you get a taste of it, you forget what you're eating, and you're not aware it's all you'll be eating for a while. Imagine today, every day until the tour stops. "You'll have the best moments and the arguing with your girlfriend every day for the next 4-5 weeks. Then imagine giving it all up once his finger heals." Jared explains.

"Do you have any regrets?" Chris asks with a straight face.

"Absolutely…" Jared looked away.

"Nope." Jax offers.

"Jax!" Jared exclaims.

"What? I love tour life." Jax smiles.

"You're not married and never had a girlfriend. You just go wherever the van goes! This kid has to live a life." Jared shoots.

"It's his life, isn't it, Jared?" Jax asks honestly.

Jared looks away again and shrugs, "Yeah, I guess that's the beauty of it all. It's your life, kid. Welcome aboard."

Chris frowned, "Is it that bad?"

behind his head, "You won't be in long enough to deal with that. I at least have control over that much as your bandleader. Once Flat is recovered, you're a full-time student again. You got it?"

"Got it!" Chris salutes.

"Great, now hit the blunt and pass it. This is giving me a headache." Jared rubs the bridge of his nose.

"I can't wait to tell everyone I'll be on tour with The Somber Nights!" Chris cheers.

"You'll realize who your real friends are... I'll tell you that for sure." Jax sighs.

Chris began to second guess the situation looking at both the veterans with new eyes. He had a lot to learn from them and intended to squeeze a lifetime of learning into the next month on the road with the two. He looked around for where he would sleep. There were the cockpit and beanbag chairs. He wondered how they managed for so long, then remembered they weren't even human.

They finished up smoking then parted in three separate directions. Jax crashed in the van after dropping off Jared and Chris. Jared ran to his apartment to take a shower. Chris meandered about heading back to his room in Horus Hall, texting his friends about the new opportunity to go on tour. A few demanded he come to the after-party to celebrate, knowing

Margot was radio silent with the message left on unread.

Chris left out a sigh wishing Margot could have been more supportive.

What is a man at his core? Is he his word, his wealth, his girls, or his dedication to one woman? Chris was born into the most confusing time to be a man. A time where it seemed every girl seemed to think it's a competition, and so many men were opting out of the urinal club. Chris felt like the last of a dying breed as what it means to be a man is redefined.

A man's glory, what is glory to a man? What was glory to God? Chris had wondered, studied but couldn't seem ever fully to know. He rose at 5 am every morning to put a day's worth of work at the local foundry for $12 an hour before attending classes. He felt alone, buried in work, and barely functioning. Most nights, he smoked two blunts without a wink of sleep. The days blurred together. Sleep was the cousin of death, so he couldn't let life pass him.

Chris thought he needed the job to get money. Money got him what he needed. Handling his needs got him, girls. Chasing girls brought him to college. He's in college to get a better job to repeat the cycle until he had more money than he could spend. His girl would find a way to spend up all his life's earnings. Until one day, he was wrinkled girls wouldn't bother loving him

lady wanted a night on the town.

He felt conquered by exhaustion and emotional depletion toiling for love, working so hard to feel appreciated when his value felt so conditional. He had passed out on the two-hour ride home in the temp agency's van, waking up at the transport depot to catch an hour-long bus ride back to campus for his evening classes. Every day he attempted this dance. Enduring and pushed because this is all men did, right?

He was raised off late meals, lonely sporting events, and walking to school. Both parents worked with great degrees. He never knew a real gender role, but he took great joy in being a man. Long in the tooth, stoic, and self-soothing, he cared for others and protected those he loved fiercely. He craved discipline and sacrificed for his family. He refused to be controlled in his life or control others. He controlled only himself.

He wished someone taught him to break stoic psychosis to know the depth of his emotions. Along came Margot Hoska Dalio, a beautiful young lady with fire in her heart and green in her brown eyes. They wanted each other the moment their eyes locked. She moved hell and earth to meet him. Heaven and hell pardoned their judgment at the chance of love.

bloomed into two years of bipolar love. He thought he was the only one who could understand. As if she either didn't see it or didn't mind. He needed rest, and she wanted to talk about her anger, sadness, and frustrations. As he was either walking in the door or preparing to take a nap.

Another day fading away, the line went dead after thirty minutes of arguing and explaining himself. Chris Tor'jun was dripping wet from the shower and fighting tears. Combatting this manic and emotional dysmorphia that he once thought was love. It was obvious to anyone he and his girlfriend never saw things eye-to-eye. Fighting had become the only way to know for Margot to know he still cared. He was tired of fighting.

Chris was in the middle of getting ready for a date they planned a week before. He needed sleep, but she reserved things for right after his shift so he wouldn't go off. She thought it was the perfect time to laundry list all the problems she rediscovered an hour beforehand. It must have been perfect timing for her. Chris had grown tired of the pattern before they were supposed to do something important.

It's been a couple of years of the modern experiment of dating, the new age term for flirting, sex, arguing, and acting out every negative quality inherited from their parents before growing tired of the other. He managed the strength to look

relationship. If it didn't work out, there was nothing left inside him. He never wanted to try this again.

Margot Dalio was home, crossed between anger and worry, wondering why he hadn't called her back after hanging up. He used to be so noble. He had no issue fighting for her love before. She remembered the thrill of it all a year ago. He would go so far out of his way to remind her he loved her. They would go out on expensive dates, buy her outfits to show off in, and the sex was mind-blowing.

He always wanted to defend himself, explain himself, or needed space because his feelings were hurt. The pit of her stomach told her he must have been cheating on her so she would fight harder. It's as if he completely withdrew to his world, and she wasn't allowed. It felt like everyone and everything made him happy but her. She wanted the joy he used to fill her with, the life and energy used to keep her stuck on him for days on end before she needed a reminder. Now, it felt barren, and there was nothing to replace him.

Why wouldn't he just break up with her if he wanted to so bad? It's like all he wanted to do was change her or be her father, trying to teach her some life lesson. She barely listened to her father. All she wanted was someone to enjoy these few years of college with and explore herself fully. Why did he make that so

handle her attitude. She had no real idea what he wanted from her. The fighting no longer made her feel loved.

Chris stared himself in the mirror. He was known as a handsome guy. His mahogany skin, a deep earthy and chocolate color, a strong jaw with a dazzling smile quickly fading from his face. However, it no longer meant anything to him. His smile had lost its way back to his face a year ago, and his look always seemed burdened. He no longer recognized the exhausted, broken man staring back at him. His body shook and constricted as the phone rang, knowing it was a problem he couldn't fix. A fight he couldn't win. His view of himself had shattered, left with nothing but the dread of love.

Yet, his phone rang regardless—Margot's number flashing on the bathroom sink. The phone stopped ringing only a few seconds before it picked back up. He sighed, knowing it wouldn't end. He reluctantly picked up after just being cursed out.

Margot greeted, "Haha, sorry about all that before, baby. Your girl is hangry. Do you still want to go out?"

Chris was perturbed. He hadn't wanted to go out when the plans had formed. He didn't have money for her every whim and desire. Nor did he have the will or the energy to keep working to

were the only thing he still seemed able to identify.

"How do you ignore everything you just said to me?" he took his time sorting out his thoughts.

"Ugh, I just said sorry, didn't I? That wasn't easy to do. Can't you just get over it? It's not like you let me have my way anyway. So, you can deal. I'm hungry, so if you want me in a good mood, you better take me out. Let's go!" Margot continues.

Chris felt sick to his stomach. How much could she be so chronically self-centered and insensitive, then boldly accuses him of the same. It's like she saw no issue with her behavior. For so long, he blamed himself, usually too nonchalant or indifferent to register. The pain he felt made it blatant he had no idea how to respond. He didn't want to respond. He didn't want to speak to her at all. He wanted silence and a blunt.

"I don't feel well." He responds distant.

"Man up, Chris. God, we had a little fight. Can't you get over it? This used to turn you on. What about all this now?" Margot sucked her teeth.

"Can I have some time to myself?" Chris rubbed his temples.

handle me? Be honest." Margot snickered on the other end of the phone.

"I am a man!" Chris gritted his teeth.

"Act like it then, man up and take me out to eat. Suppose you can't deal with my attitude that's on you, not me. I always get what I want. So hurry up and cry, then let's go!" Margot hung up again.

Chris stared at his phone with murderous intent. He snatched it up and smacked it down on the window seal. He opened the wooden and vinyl blended window pane, slamming it on his phone repeatedly until the battery fell out the back. He considered tossing the pieces out the window, glad he wouldn't have to hear from anyone again until he decided to cash in on his warranty.

He loathed his love life, the pain and hardship it brought. Who the hell tells someone to have a cry and give me what I want with a smile on their face? Chris sat on the edge of his bed with his head in his hands. He vowed to never speak to her again. Chris was hunched over naked, in tears, ashamed, and dripping wet with snot dripping from his nose. Chris sobbed himself out of his frenzy, wondering how he even allowed love at all.

Handsome used to mean something. Now it meant nothing. Intelligence used to mean something, but knowledge unapplied was the enemy to mastery. It meant now meant nothing. The charm used to mean something. Everything women seemed to love about him felt like lies out of desire and delusion. As if with Margot all these things disappeared, fight after fight, week after week. She saw him as nothing more than an arrogant, know-it-all. Eventually, in her mind, one of them would cheat or walk away. Eventually, it was just a matter of who did it first. Nothing remained in his life but anguish and misery, the dread of believing this would be the rest of his life.

She wanted a subdued and weak man to fit her whims. Yet, asking her to be nicer, reasonable, and more patient was a human right violation. She needs to combat, fight, argue, and scream whenever confronted with the reality of her shadow. He never felt the same need, reflecting and reviewing her complaints with hopes of growing from it. Deep down, he began to believe he deserved it. Relationship after relationship, it became normal. He began to hate himself because his nature wouldn't let him hate Margot.

brushed it off, but it was unceasing without reason and unstoppable.

Chris felt it must have been mutual. Every reason he once thought they'd be inseparable was the very reason he wanted to leave. He couldn't take the endless fighting, anger, or frustration anymore. There was always something wrong she would never acknowledge, forget about fixing it. It was killing him inside. He never saw his friends or family anymore being so far from home. This life was killing him, depleting him, leaving nothing left but a husk and slave to the societal image. All he felt was aloneness, either by God's design or mishap of the dark one. He didn't know who else he had left but Margot as she filled him with her image.

There was a light knock and scratching outside the bathroom at the front door. It went on for a few minutes before he knew who it was on the other side. Does he just forgive her so easily and go out to dinner, another day pretending it just didn't happen. Or choose his solitude and peace of mind. What was a man's true glory? The endurance of surviving war or the joy of a life lived in the face of hardship?

Despite knowing the woman on the other side of the door was his woman, his girlfriend, who he once loved so dearly, and the woman who he sacrificed so much of his identity and life for to keep happy. Though none of his efforts lasted, hours of talks, all came and went with the wind, wondering what was next all the time instead of savoring the experience or week prior. Her needs were a bottomless pit, and her wants soared to the sky. He was neglected and completely depleted.

He was fighting a losing battle only God could turn around or save him. He no longer knew what was desirable. His devotion told him to make things work and endure into marriage, but she didn't see things the same. Her desires seemed unquenchable. She worshipped materials and money. Chris couldn't risk losing his soul to sate a woman guided only by avarice and egoism. He sat quietly as the light knocks turn into banging.

"Come on! I said I was sorry! I'm hungry!" Margot scratched, trying to coax him out.

Chris felt like a prisoner of war in his room. He hung his head in shame as she banged and screamed on the other side of his door.

"Open the door! Pick up your phone! I know you're in there! How dare you try to ignore me?" Margot banged even harder.

He didn't see any way to make things work. He chooses his silence, solitude, sitting by his bed in a full-lotus, continuing

helped to his extent but made him realize, you can calm the storm within, but there was nothing to stop the storm outside. He did not know what God's glory could show him, but he knew at the moment he had himself. His mantra was a tearful apology forever entering the relationship for losing himself within it.

If lateness were close to godliness, Chris Tor'jun would be Ada himself. I came fifteen minutes late and not so much as a text message for my troubles. If we weren't partnered for this presentation, I needn't be bothered with him. I've avoided it all year. Why the hell, for my biggest final exam, am I being bounded to Jared? He's notorious for being uncommunicative, tardy, and far more lax than any human being deserved to be, but he was freaking smart.

"Hey Mya, Sorry, I lost track of time and then had to catch the bus to get here. Hope you weren't waiting too long!" His bright smile was comforting on such a dreary day. He came dressed in his pea coat, a pair of jeans, and a basic T-shirt. Only Chris could make such a plain outfit look fashionable.

"No worries, you're only what...?" I glance at my wristwatch "half an hour late after I came fifteen minutes, so forty-five minutes. Nearly an hour of my life, that's worth a frappe and scone at least." I let out a sigh.

I chose the quint café sitting along the waterfront. He said he'd never been along with a million other excuses to avoid coming. I thought it would help to build some rapport by killing a few birds with one stone. It was a beautiful view of the Tigris River running through New Haven. I loved the location but

my time.

"This place is swank." he looks around as he hangs his coat on the back of his chair, "do I need an arm or a leg to get some coffee?"

"Coffee is a kidney. Tea is a limb of your choosing. Don't worry. I know the owner and a few waitresses. They give me a major discount. It's only a foot or a finger for an iced frappe and a scone, left or right?" I grab the butter knife as he sits.

"So just a couple fingers then?" His smile was contagious, all pearly whites.

He had a softness that didn't belong on his modelesque ebony face, boyish and handsome with the sternness of an older man.

"So, did you have any ideas for this presentation? I thought we could steer away from Nakan and Ecrun politics. Do something a bit more scientific and documented. I really can't afford to get esoteric or historical this time around." Chris begins sorting through his backpack, fishing out books and tomes with sticky notes along with the pages. He grabbed a beat-up notebook, the spirals crushed from the overpriced textbooks.

A waitress had been staring at me since Chris sat down. She was otherwise uninterested in me the entire time I sat here. She began speaking to the server who got me my water, pointing at our table. I gave a wave hoping to get some service. Both of

Rebecca was so nice too. I wonder what I did?

"Hey Chris, can I get you tea with honey and a bit of milk?" Our waitress's eyes lingered on Chris, who let out a sigh.

His smile faded.

"Hello, Margot. I'm not that thirsty, but you can help my friend here if you kindly." He says flatly, tapping his fingers on his notebook.

Do I want to know how these two know each other?

"Are you going to introduce me to your friend? Hi, Chris's friend. I'm Margot." Her smile was nightmare fuel as she glared at me.

"She's my assigned partner for our final project. Nothing is happening here, Margot." He rubs his temples.

"If you could excuse us, I think we still need a moment." I pipe up politely, shrinking in my seat.

She looks me over, sizing me up before nodding, leaving with a smug smile. I felt embarrassed how easily he wrote me off as a lab partner. I mean, I thought we were at least friends or something! Margot was cackling with her friend waiting for us to leave. Reassured she still had a grip of her beau as if he was some poppet.

"You're welcome." I finally take a deep breath and then exhale.

flames and past romances" Chris rubs his temples.

"Who was she? Dude, she's terrifying holy crap." I whisper out of fear she would turn around and start even more drama, but I was going to stand my ground.

He stands, "come on, let's get out of here."

"Nope... I want more details then we can leave. Besides, I need a coffee before, and after dealing with all this drama, you bring. And you are paying for me." I say firmly, crossing my arms over my chest.

He weighs his options and sits reluctantly but sits regardless.

"Okay, the abridged version is-

"Oh, no-no. I haven't even gotten my coffee yet! And we have plenty of time. I want the whole story."

"Don't push your luck, Mya. You get the gist, and you get coffee, then we leave." He stands up and crosses the room to Margot.

She beams as he approaches. They share a cold embrace but enough to sate her at work. Her coworker seemed equally enthralled to see him. Jared was an infamous campus gigolo his freshman year. I can see why and would be a liar if I wasn't hoping this evening didn't end with him and me, especially now. Margot remains surprisingly cordial throughout their exchange.

meeting was as brief as he hoped. I got a bit of pleasure from it.

"Happy?" He groans as he sits, "your coffee will be here in a minute."

"I never told you what I wanted," I muttered.

"You said frappe like fifty times. Oh, we care about what the other wants now? Thanks for the trip down memory lane. An excursion I could have gone without but whatever. Now, she'll be calling me far too much." He says matter-of-factly, the stress had already left his voice. I have to remember this is the norm for him.

He sits, trying to collect his thoughts, "alright, I had a class with Margot. We hooked up on a train going home. We spoke for a bit. She wanted more than I was willing to give. We drifted away, and then we ended up shacking."

"Wait... What the-? Are you going to pretend you didn't say you had sex on a train?" I can't hide my laughter.

Chris shrugs, "eh, it happens."

"No, no, it doesn't. It doesn't happen to anyone ever!" I continue, "How was it?"

"It was rushed and uncomfortable." He says curtly, shifting uneasily in his seat.

"Was she not good at it?" I asked.

"Look, I'm not a fan of kissing and telling." His smile fades altogether as he taps his hand on the table.

He looks mortified, "You're enjoying this way too much, Mya. Can we focus on our project? I don't want to hear you complaining again. I put a lot of work into our last project. I did days, literal days in the library of research. Margot is great. I need to focus right now! If we're going to stay, can we at least work so this doesn't mess up my rotation?"

"You're a chauvinist," I said, offended.

"I don't even want to talk about this with you. Damned if I do, damned if I don't, call me whatever name you want. Can we get this project done?" he said unmoved.

I relented with a sigh. A day with a gigolo who's disinterested in talking about his escapades seems lackluster. It makes me curious how many he's been with 10? 100? 70? 3? I've heard many things but nothing more than whispers of schoolgirls. Rumors could corrupt everything. Negative energy was contagious. I never really knew how many women he's slept with or dated. It seemed like sleeping with Chris was like a notch on your belt. I could relate. My culture is less embarrassed about such things. Sex was natural. It was normal for brothers or sisters to share a spouse to help manage a farm. I didn't understand why they were trying to hide their relationship.

"I can't get past this, bro. I feel assaulted by your drama and want to know what I got myself into, Chris." I looked in the

Chris' tea.

"I am not dating anyone right now. I did. We have. It's this off again, on-again relationship. I don't understand it, but I'm in it."

"Tsk, tsk, you got yourself a situationship. No title and no good. You didn't even update your relationship status but keep posting about that stupid mob wars game."

"The game posts automatically! I play it on my phone! Okay, sometimes I play it on the PC. Maybe, I want to play social media games without using social media." Chris gets lost in his rationalizations.

"Okay, whatever you're saying, sure. My point is that you're in the wrong. If she's your girlfriend, then you should be proud of that fact. Why would someone want to date you if you're not even going to acknowledge that you're together?"

"I've been with more women than none and far less than the rumors imply. Why, don't you guess?" he leans back in his chair, wrapping his hands behind his head with a smirk. "I'm curious of what you think of me."

I bite my lip, stirring around in my mind to find a number that's practical but not insulting. I take a deep breath and shrug "20?"

He raises a brow, "Hmm... not bad, not right, but not bad. Want to guess again?"

insulted you or whatever, but-

"Please, I'm genuinely curious about what you think. No offense to you, but I rather not be working with a woman who thinks I'm a raving sex addict. There are many beautiful women in the world. Sometimes beauty isn't everything." He looks away in reflection, falling quiet.

I blush, looking away. "I mean… I don't think that. I just think you get around more than most. I mean, for good reasons, I hear. You're a good guy. People are going to want to be around you. Some people are women. You don't need to be inside every woman you see to enjoy the human experience." I suddenly find myself in dire need of another interruption from Margot as I began preaching at him.

I want to know, but do I risk insulting him? He's late and a bit unreliable, but the man's far from stupid. He has one of the highest averages in the class, competing for the number one position. If he walks out on this, I lose an easy A.

"I don't disagree with you and manage pretty well. You're a woman. You know what girls are like when they want someone." He shrugs.

"What does that even mean? Women are different. Not every girl is going to push up on you or try to seduce you. A woman will only come at you like that if you show that's all it takes. It's easy to spend $50 on a sundress and a thong for a

women want more." I insisted.

"Show me one." He looks over his shoulder to see Margot approaching with two cups.

"Okay then. How long have you two been together?" I ask, not even knowing they had ever met.

He pauses, tapping his finger to his lip. "I've had the opportunity to get 100% on this project. It's the easiest project since I've gotten to college, but I rarely find someone worth my effort. Mya, can you please get out of my relationship life? I'm a bit of a serial monogamous, or at least like familiarity. I've had sex with about 30 women. I'm generally speaking to about three women at a given moment but for attention, not sex. I don't even really live that life anymore. So, if you had to know, that's everything. Can we please move forward?" Chris whisper shouts as she gets closer.

"I'll let you live." I back off, not wanting to get banned from this place.

I need him to get her schedule so I know which days she doesn't work. I had a few guys in my DMs who would die to take me here. I could try a few items on the menu on their tab then ghost on them.

"Here you go!" Margot says with a disarming delightfulness making me forget she had tried to skin me with her eyes.

his tea.

"Of course, baby. It's on the house for you, sweetie." For someone who seemed disinterested, he sure was milking this whole thing. Margot turns to me with her plastic smile and pleasantries, setting down my coffee with a dour scowl.

"Sorry, our ice machine is broken, so I got you a hot coffee. It looks like you like your coffee, Black." Margot could have poured it in my lap, and I would have been less offended. I saw my drink sitting on the ice tray, and she walked right past it to pour a mean cup of coffee.

"Um… can I get some cream and sugar?" I ask.

"You definitely can. Ask for some from the barista or bartender at the coffee bar." Margot instructs me, turning her focus to Chris.

"It's on the table," Chris notes, pointing to the small dish of sugar and micro creamers.

She strained at him, helping me, tapping her fingers on Chris' shoulder, "Can I get either of you anything else?" she doesn't bother turning to me.

"Uh… no, I think I'm fine," he scratches his goatee, "How about you, Mya?"

"No!" I answer far too quickly.

as if she was imagining stabbing my coffee stirrer through my eyes.

"I'm sorry, um. No, I'm fine." Chris chuckles at my missteps as Margot nods.

He doesn't bother pretending not to look at her walking to other tables. Her body was far shapelier from the back, slender legs leading up to a taut butt.

"She's a dancer," he informs me. I turn back to his wide grin, "You look bothered."

"She's a bit two-faced, you know that?"

"I don't hate her. It was just inopportune seeing her. We spoke a bit back there, and she said she understands. She's a nice person when you get to know her. The whole thing can just be a bit draining, you know? So, I don't want to talk about it."

"What?"

He takes a moment to sip his tea, "I'm sorry. What exactly are you waiting for?"

"What did you two speak about?"

He raises a brow, "I fail to see why it's any of your concern," he's barely able to keep a straight face, "Last time she and I spoke, she dropped the love bomb. It wasn't a good time. She was speaking about marriage and kids. We're only in our twenties. I'm interested in her, and I'm not sure what the future holds."

He nearly spits out his tea, "Ha, I'll drink to that" he raises his mug.

I remember I haven't had added my sugar or cream, drinking a bitter cold coffee like her hatred for me.

"I want to enjoy myself while I'm in college, you know? Not get bogged down or cuffed."

"Why didn't your girlfriend make my coffee like your tea?" Hopefully, he was aware I wasn't ignoring him. I honestly didn't have much to respond to.

"I suppose I agree." I quiver as I look at the artificial sugar on the table while brown sugar floated in his coffee.

"Why do you think?" he pushes the sugar toward me

"She's doesn't value continued service?" I push my coffee away, "Give me your tea."

He shakes his head. His smile was already contagious but seemed to grow warmer with each sip he took.

"Dude, take that cup of hatred your girlfriend gave me. Give me your friggin' tea! I need this to deal with your crap!" I felt like ripping out my hair.

"You're competition." I sigh, "In her eyes anyway. Neither of you is my type if I'm honest. You have major chips on your shoulders. I'm just living and growing, learning from everybody. I don't understand how women keep ending up in my life. I'm honestly not even trying to run game."

"Oh whoa, hold on there. I never said you didn't catch my eye. I said you weren't my type. Completely different. It's more like a capability thing."

"You mean compatibility?" I suck my teeth rolling my eyes.

"No, you smart aleck. I'm talking about capability, longevity, and practicality, like could I spend five weeks in a room with you without blowing my brains out? Type of deal, am I capable of surviving your drama and my drama together. My intuition says Nah."

"You wouldn't date me?"

"I need someone who follows my lead, not stepping on my toes. I need someone who listens without putting words in my mouth. It's not about you. It's about me wanting to be happy more than I want to someone women lust over." He crosses his legs and arms turning away.

"You're not going anywhere...." I groan.

"Ha, last time I checked, we're at the same place in life. All you're doing is projecting your trauma at me. I'll keep my personality over here. You keep your personality over there. And we fill the distance with something more meaningful?" he returns my dread.

"Wow, you're a heartbreaker." I sigh, "I dodged that bullet."

sweet smile and laughter was a hunger. A hunger I'm not sure I can sate. I tried to hide my lip biting as I stirred enough crème to call my coffee milk justifiably. But I kept peeking up to notice his meandering gaze passing by as he pretended to look around.

"You're quite handsome, Chris Tor'jun," I say, stirring my coffee. He nods, unmoved by the sentiment he must hear far more often than it appears he likes. "I would have been glad to partner with you if you ever showed up to class...."

He chuckles, "I usually stop by her office."

"Don't tell me that," I groan, breaking into laughter, "Are you and Miss-

"No, she's married!" he laughs, "I did try, though...."

"Really?"

"No! I'm not that depraved. I'm just messing with you, Christ!"

"How am I supposed to know? You're charming enough to sway her. I feel she would have been lucky." He blushes as if he was capable of a genuine look of shock. He quieted down and looked over his shoulder. "You look antsy."

"Well, Margot is glaring at us. I hear women aren't fond of seeing a man. They're interested in having fun without them." He whispered.

"Was the sex good?"

He hesitated, reading my face before continuing.

idea what she's doing, though. I just enjoyed seeing her naked. Her body is perfect. I wish she did more with her flexibility..." he stops speaking. His eyes drift off to space.

I glance over at Margot. Does she truly love him, or was the sex just that good? Or both.

"So, what do you want to do for this project?" he asks, redirecting us to the reason we came here. He pushes his tea aside, "I'm thinking about researching seasonal depression, finding some homeopathic cures, and maybe we can turn it to a paper if it's reviewed well by Profe?"

I nod, "Why seasonal depression?"

"Eh, sometimes I get a bit blue when it's cold. I want to get some information under my belt before I'm left facing the black dog without a leash."

"Killing a few birds with one stone, I see."

"Ha ... So, are you down?"

"Yeah, so I guess we'll be seeing much more of each other, huh?" I sip my coffee. It was getting frosty. I should have spent less time yapping. "I look forward to it as well as the likelihood of running into another one of your trysts."

"I was under the impression you wanted me to yourself?" his smile faded, and his hunger was more than aware. He leaned in, lacing his fingers with mine. "Are you trying to get out of here?"

you'll refuse to share. When we have sex, it'll mean something."

"Ha, when? You're sure of it, are you?"

"Do you think I'm passing up on this opportunity? Not on your life, buddy." I stand up, tossing my purse over my shoulder, "However, on that note, I think I'll dip out of here before we move too quickly, ya know?" His eyes watched me far more intently than he paid mind to Tiffany. The way he bit his thumb let me know the view was more than satisfying. I filled out my leggings far better than she did. A few years of dancing can't compete with a lifetime of track running and education from the military

"You're quite beautiful, Mya. I didn't mean to offend you. I'm not looking for anything physical right now.."

"About time you apologized," I give him a wink, leaving him all for Margot to pluck up. I felt his eyes following me as I sashayed toward the trolley, letting them tend the bill.

In anger, in spite. Is she lost in lust and hate? Every day leaving seems like the only option. Nothing goes right, she's a constant adversary, and her mind only focused upon herself.

Though, my mind is within the abstract and unseen. Can I be angry for her not understanding me? No, but I can certainly leave knowing she never tried. Anger though?

That's her frequent accusation. It's my anger or my frustration. How does someone see the world we live in and not feel somewhat compelled to have emotion? As if what I feel is unjustified or beyond understanding. However, that's because she doesn't see the same issues. She loves this culture. She loves capitalism, Naka, and materialism.

I need more than some food and trinkets to have real love. To be happy let a long joyous. Of course, I'm the malcontent because I see the glaring issues while she lives in lalaland. I want to fix them, find solutions, and stand against this crap.

My mother once sat me down and spoke to me about love. Sadly, my parents are only friends now. Their marriage ended. Their values, beliefs, and finances were so estranged. Best of both worlds, I suppose. I guess I'm supposed to be the

holds a prominent place of understanding or sense to me. How did millions of poor people accept this crap? A life with no meaning but money, not even a concern for humanity.

From my perspective, humanity sold itself away for sex and money a long time ago. Far before Nakan principles swept the world. Nah, I love history. The poor allow themselves to be lesser than constantly because those metals and cloth grant life! I suppose free enterprise versus a bourgeois class is the solution. Maybe I would prefer an agricultural society, but even then, I fear using food for money would leave many starving. I wish I had a solution, regardless of my capabilities. It didn't take long for Naka to degrade into the same oligarchy, plutarchy, of the few commanding all.

All for One.

My girlfriend doesn't care. Conversation and mental growth aren't her waves. She prefers opinions, baseless and unproven. What's before her is all she can perceive. To her, God is only in church, and a simple apology solves everything even if you return to the same behavior. She used niceties. I preferred good.

It's been years, unhappy happy years for me. She was astounded. I can't even talk to her about my thoughts or our relationship. I can remain blind and hopeful, but the reality of my situation presents nothing to be desired nor wanted.

understand them?

The second I'm "out of line," the whole world needs to stop for her. She wants to flip out and demand changes. We either argue, or I walk out. When I have issues, she can't imagine why I can't just be happy in the world. It's been two years, and not a single one has even been entertained. It's not supposed to be like this, and I know this isn't being loved.

I will rather be single at this point. No woman, no cry. There is no stress within solitude.

Solitude to finally understand me and my thoughts since most just look at me as if I'm crazy for using what God gave me. Years of this life being ostracized or misunderstood. I could hope things improve, but I don't want to die waiting. Maybe things will improve? Hope is nice. Faith is better. She's shown no signs of changing. She'll probably sleep around seeking validation and telling the worst of me. It's the least of my worries now.

I have no interest in being validated or liked by a society I reject. Good, it's better. More women will avoid me. I can be to myself as long as I need. I am done.

"Mr. Tor'jun, you're looking glum." The Office Director, Bradley Smalls, knocked on my desk. "What's good? You're usually the positivity here! Being the new guy already wore off?" He chuckled, sitting on my desk.

leasing office.

His surname didn't compliment him being six-foot-five. He said he had been a linebacker since he could hold a ball. He switched gears. Bradley was dressed in a pinstripe suit and a bowtie.

"I'm in my thoughts. I can be pretty neurotic at times." I yawn, having no idea how long I had been brooding, "What's up, boss?"

"Nothing, I'm worried about you. Opal said she tried speaking to you, and you acted as if she wasn't there. She thinks you might be sick. I was going to send you home."

I rubbed my chin, trying to recall even seeing Opal today. I shook my head, shrugging my shoulders, glad I could head home.

"How did you miss all that booty? She was just out here five minutes. I didn't see anything. But, haha, I've been standing in the doorway for about three minutes, and you were still spaced out."

"I wasn't interested in her, I guess." I sigh.

"Whoa, whoa, hold on, brotha bear!" Bradley stood up off the desk, holding out his hands, "I didn't know you were the ump and not a batter! I'm not with it, bro, not even a little bit. I mean, I respect your preference and whatever but-

but I'm just... I'm going through a lot right now."

"Sup?" he shrugs.

Brad was my boss, but I doubt we've ever had a real conversation before. He's a sportsman and finance guru. He's been a manager here for the past three years. Three years ago, I was getting out of high school. He drove a mustang, paid his apartment of in full, in advance. We didn't live the same life at all. He isn't the man I'm prepared to discuss this with, considering most it isn't even my relationship.

"It's nothing, Brad. I'll be fine. No need to send me off. I didn't even realize I was so lost in my thoughts." I yawn once more, lowering my hands, "Just chill, dude."

"I'm ice cube cool, brother man. You're a 180 from where you're usually vibing. The Baddest girl in the office came straight to you. Opal doesn't even speak to me! You're not even on Gaia right now, man." he breaks out laughing.

"I know... I know, weird, right. It's a cool Brad. I'll be fine. We don't have to talk."

"Why not?"

"We have nothing in common."

"We're both from Ecru. We both piss standing up. That's two things right there. So, what's up?"

"I-I want to leave my girlfriend, but I have nowhere to go. I'll have to quit my job. Probably be homeless and derail my relationship. Now, it feels like it's over, and I'm losing everything! I'm not even married. Not to mention, all my thoughts are on crap I can't control. I'm driving myself insane, and my girlfriend is just finishing the job."

"Huh... " Brad rubbed his chin, "I get it, bro. I went through the same thing with my girl. I think many men do. It's hard to settle down so young. My girl and I worked it out. We're engaged now. Living together is hard, man."

I smiled, a weight lifted off my shoulders with the commonality.

"How about this... I give you a paid vacation. Take a few days off. Find a new pad or work things out with your girl. If you can't find a place since the school year already started and most places are booked. I'll lease you one of the two bedrooms we have left, half off."

"Deal," I said declaratively.

"Alright, I know I pay you enough to make rent every month. I get it if it's late, but I don't want you running any balance when I'm signing your checks. You're making bonuses, no excuses, man."

"Gee... thanks, Brad." I rub my neck, unable to think.

"Come to me next time, bro." he daps me up, "I'm your boss and your brother."

"Thanks so much, man."

big dog!" he pats my shoulders. "Keep me in the loop. The offer stays open as long as the room is available. If I get an offer, I can only give you a day after."

"Why are you doing this, Brad? Why even bother giving me a day if you can make the full price?"

"Ha, you're a good worker! I can't lose because your girlfriend doesn't know how to act!" Bradley breaks out laughing.

I smirk, leaving my desk, stretching out long as I move to dap up Bradley. He hugs me, patting my head before letting me go.

"Why didn't you want to talk to me, bro?" he asks as he releases me.

"I... uh... I didn't think you would understand me. Money isn't my motivation. I didn't think a guy like you would understand."

"Boy, you never talk to anybody. How do you expect someone to understand you? I feel the hype, but it isn't about money if you have ever been starving or in debt. It's about you. Money is everywhere, man—energy over Time, boy. You work, you eat. If not, you go hungry. This ain't about riches. It's about financial liberation, little brother. Being free from the system altogether, then you don't have to spend your time worrying about politics because it doesn't affect you unless they got guns disgruntled and broke. I've been there, but nobody listens to you when they don't want to be like you." Bradley usually spoke as his $5,000 suit looked, but he dropped it, revealing a country twang. "You can make good money and help others. Or struggle, barely able to help yourself at all, let alone anybody else. I can't make that decision for you."

I wiped a tear from my eye, holding back my sobs, "That means so much to me, Brad. It lifted a weight off my shoulder."

"The revolution won't be televised. You must build your dynasty, baby brother. Now, head out. We'll end up spitting for hours. I can tell already we'll get along. Let's get a beer and catch up on one of your days off."

"I don't go to bars, dude."

Brad got stern, "I gave you a paid vacation, and you won't have a beer with me?"

"I-I-I'm sorry. Can we go to a restaurant or something? I'm down to hang but, I'm not a club or bar type of guy." I shrug my shoulders.

"You smoke, bro?" Brad asks, "Come by my place. My girl is a great cook. I'll roll a couple of swishers, and we'll talk about the nine. I needed an old head to tell me. Only right I pay forward."

hospitality. "Sounds great. Probably a better setting as well. I'll be there for sure, thanks."

I said my goodbyes to Bradley. Taking my time lingering around before coming back to my apartment. Luckily, I was home alone. For a while, I stood in the shower, letting the hot water rain over me. My body finally felt the ease I hadn't had in a few years.

I dried myself, walking around my apartment nude to the kitchen, throwing some leftover pizza and wings into the oven to warm up. I grabbed a couple of beers, turned on South Park, and began rolling a blunt.

I am the King of my castle. Maybe if I can just relax, then the relationship won't seem as bad. I'll just relax.

I was half-awake, half on the couch, slumped. My torso laid on a throw pillow and my legs across the arm of the couch. I know how comfortable either could be, but I needed to know how both felt after two swishers and a beer. I made a glorious decision. My body feels incredible. My mind is my greatest tool. Everyone acts like it's some curse.

I stretched out, slipping off the couch as my body fell over and my mind flew. I was suddenly on an entirely different level than usual than visual. I felt as though my soul was swimming as my body watching. I lost my mind to my soul. I lost my body to joy. I came up to a conclusion of my existence. I am not a body.

significance. I am a soul having a human experience. I recognize every other soul in my field of aura.

I am liberated, boundless. This idea, this is life. I am the soul in a body, not a body, not a husk. My body does not control me. My body is controlled by my mind, my soul, my feelings. I am focused on my true thoughts and purpose. What is it? Why am I here?

I smile at the endless possibilities God opened to me at that moment. My whole life opened before me my life. No door ever closed or passed by. I see them. I see all of them. My ego lifted the veil. My perspective was clouded, my mind was drained. I left myself in this new world. It was far too soon to leave.

"Chris!" I hear my name too soon for my body to be present, "Where the hell are you, Chris? I left my project!"

Margot came into my dorm, huffing and screaming.

I watched with all four of my eyes, my mortal and celestial cloud of smoky eyes. She ran to me, speaking some foreign language from a different frequency. It sounded little less than gibberish. My mind was absent any interest in her mortal experience. I felt like watching a rerun on the television, watching her so desperately seek my attention then storming off cursing as I don't respond. Screaming how much of a jerk I am. I felt no real need to respond.

jacket self. Looking around blankly as if I had no recognition of the apartment I've lived at for nearly a year. My body even felt different. It fit better and felt more natural to be in my skin after returning to it.

I used the raggedy Salvation Army couch to stand. My feet shuffled through the coarse blue rug and white sanitation walls as if living in a mental asylum how I felt living here so long trapped in this short-term relationship millennial madness. I woke up to two years of my life fleeting away before me.

Though, I felt natural and better than ever. The apartment was completely foreign to me. I felt the walls, holding myself up to my bedroom. Leaving Margot in the living room as she shouted and screamed after me. I heard nothing but felt the vibrations as I packed a knapsack instinctively. Muscle-Memory to the emotionality. I grabbed my grinder, my stash, and my wallet, moving to the door on autopilot. I finally saw through the illusion. I can't hear my thoughts or beliefs over her lower frequency explosion. None of it mattered more than my core muscle memory and very soul telling me to leave, not another night romancing these demons.

I had never noticed how often this happened. This girl held my heart, pierced with her manicured nails. She couldn't care. She couldn't even understand. She was convinced I hated her.

me, tapping her foot. I left her without a word, having learned from 730 nights never to turn around. Keep walking, Chris, keep going, or else you'll be dragged down with her.

I reach the elevator with her right beside me. Now she wishes to stand by my side.

"I was leaving anyway! Do you not hear me talking to you!?" she asks as the doors closed.

I cleaned my ear, "Those were the first real words I heard since you got back. The rest was hell's wrath on audio. I'm not with it, girl."

"Well, you never listen to me!" she continued.

"I don't think I recall that relationship experience... I'm tired, Margot." I raise my hands, "I don't have any energy left."

"You can sleep in bed, upstairs in our dorm room. Are you going to some other bird's house?" she screeched, "Go to bed if you're so tired! What is leaving going to do!?"

The blow was deep in my gut. Once again, I was reduced to nothing but a coward in her eyes. Her emotional attacks never quelled. My sacral essence cramped, the pain surging through my entire soul system, alerting my whole aura of the danger at hand. I have no witnesses, no friends out here anymore. I am alone, being yelled at like a dog and treated like garbage. If leaving is wrong, so be it.

the elevator descended. The elevator finally stopped, the door slowly opened. I let myself go through the threshold, leaving out my old life with my exhale, entering into the newest life and most natural feeling like my lungs filled with the lobby air. My love, my old flame, I need to let this go. It's turning me into a monster. It's making me lose myself. Making me know even more, I need to leave and never return.

I lift my tolerance and my head, embarking on the new journey. I lift out of the cloud of smoke, of the feelings of loneliness in my own home. I left my mind, my spirit, finding myself back at my office downtown Nadine. Not too far from Nadia University.

Brad was the first to greet me, "I give you a vacation, and you come back with baggage."

"Boy, you hit the nail right on the head." I laughed a bit, walking into the office in a pair of black shorts and a tan tank top, "I have a change of clothes in my bag."

"Dude, what are you talking about? Go home, Chris. I'm serious, man. You're looking crazy."

"I can't go home. I don't have a home to go to, and I'll just- I'll work 'til I figure out my next move." I sigh, "I'm sorry to put you in this position, Brad."

Did she kick you out? Want to talk about it?" he rubbed his neck. The discomfort was evident.

Today was the first day we spoke. Now we were faced with this awkward mess. I hated bringing segments of my personal life to the attention of coworkers. Especially my vulnerabilities.

"I do want to talk. However, I have no interest in talking about any of this, you know? I'm going to need a new place ASAP. So, I have a proposition for you." I sit on the front desk, "How about I change my clothes, work the three days for time and a half?"

Brad sighed with relief, "Boy, I'll give you overtime for not bringing your drama in here. My deal on the lease stands as well, of course."

"Do I get a signing bonus for my lease?" I rub my chin.

"Ha, my dude left for three hours and came back trying to finesse King Smooth. Boy, you got it! I like this side of you, Chris." Brad daps me up, patting my back, "We'll make you an office manager yet."

"Thanks, I'll get changed."

"I'll waive the deposit if you can open for the next five Saturdays and two Sundays."

"I'll work three doubles and a Sunday."

my hand with a grin, "See you for dinner tomorrow. I'm about to take my lunch. Had to take over the front for a bit while you were gone."

"Alright, Boss, thanks again!" I wave, heading to the back office.

We had a nice office. A beautiful rose-colored painting. With different Nadian and abstract art pieces. The vibrant colors and rich joy emanated from the pastels and oil-based paints. There were a few couches and bookshelves with a selection of sales, self-help, religious, and fiction books from Brad's library. The bathroom, however, was quite standard. Though, the back office was its slice of heaven—Bean bags and a fluffy carpet to decompress. And a wall-length desk with laptops for our personal and business use. Hot chocolate and coffee stayed in stock.

I was stopped before reaching the bathroom by Opal. Beautiful Erdun woman, most men would have sold a kidney to be with at this point in my life. I could care less.

"Hey, you're back! I thought you were sick or something." Opal smiled at me, "How are you feeling?"

"Uh… tired and pretty blitzed, to be honest. It isn't the best condition to work in, but it would have been ruined if I

leaving you here. How are you?"

"Oh, I'm great! I let it go immediately. I knew something had to be wrong with you ignoring me!" Opal truly was a beautiful woman, deep brown eyes and mahogany skin. Long natural braids cascading down her back, "You wise up?"

"Honestly, I broke up with my girl. I've felt like I need more time alone." I say, honest and uncomfortable, "I just need a year or two to myself."

"For real?" she feigned sadness, "She's missing out, Chris. So, that means you're single right?"

"I think it does, but I'm emotionally unavailable. I'm not ready for a relationship, Opal."

"Well, are you mentally and physically available?" Opal held my hand, "Let me know if you ever need to talk. I'm here for you."

"Uh… Nah, I'll be good. I don't want to talk about it. Thanks, but I gotta change." I wave, locking myself in the bathroom, sitting on the toilet to gather my thoughts.

Sorry, there was no way I was giving up being a bachelor to return to another relationship. I can't imagine dating again after this fiasco.

I struggle with the thought that I even made the right decision to leave Margot.

sense of responsibility or concern for others. Then whenever I address her with it, she acts as if I'm the one blowing things out of proportion. She just goads me on until I finally snap to prove her point. I can't win.

If I confront her with what bothers me, she rolls her eyes and points out my irritation until I'm just consumed. Or if I ignore it, I'm left constantly giving up my position until she's walking all over me. It feels like she doesn't care about compromise or what I want. She just does whatever the hell she wants and expects me to deal with it.

A girlfriend ago. Maybe I could see myself falling for this. Now? I don't have it in me to deal with someone so self-centered. I keep tallying. The fights, the losses, the broken promises. I ask myself why I put myself through it. Why bother?

She doesn't consider me. She doesn't hold concern for me. And when I tell her, she rolls her eyes and waits for it to be over. How do I speak to her when, when I need her, she gives me little more than her butt to kiss? I tell myself it isn't on purpose. It isn't malicious. It's just how she is, but how does that make it any better? Isn't that worst?

If I knew it was malicious or on purpose, I could just leave. Tell her to get bent. Deuces. But no. It's just how she is. A part of me finds it sickening she can act so selfishly, apathetic, and selfish toward someone she claims to love. Another part

he's helping. Who thinks she'll be more. Who thinks things will improve despite how constantly this happens. I try my best to see the good in people, but what if sometimes that's all there is? What if there isn't more? What if it isn't worthwhile to be patient and grow with your partner?

It's like I feel this guilt for this boy I used to be. That was turning my back on her is as if I was turning my back on myself. Then I remember. It wasn't until I realized how alone I truly was that I wanted to grow. It wasn't until backs turned to me that I realized how far away from my higher self I truly stood.

The current love of my life has brown eyes, a petite frame, and a hair-trigger temper. I fell in love with the former two. Once I was hooked by her anger, it was all-consuming. I met Margot Dalio on a cloudy day. Lovestruck us hard. We held each other and lifted on the new ideas. The other exposed us to two completely different lives and worlds. I wish we spent time talking as we did when we first met.

I fell in love with unquenchable fire, believing I could cool her flame. Every time I thought I saw the end of the firestorm, another swirled around. I felt like the hero, Crimson, fighting off crime, day after day, after freaking day. But why, seriously, why live in chaos?

I'm already enduring Stress, work, class, generational curses, upbringing, pride, ego, and the human ego's refusal to witness the shadow of the soul. Most people I grew up with preferred the shadows and the fire. They never truly see the light of the sun.

It was like blowing trick candles from a birthday cake. Every day I endure fights over any and everything. I feel like I can say nothing to her without her feeling challenged or

We'll make it up with resolutions and promises of change for the same thing to happen again the next day. Her idea of conflict resolution is sex and cuddling after simple apologies. It sounds like someone is still drinking breast milk. I believed the only true solution was attempting to solve the problem. Someone grew up with self-righteousness and hard to please.

My parents both had defiant warrior spirits, which I inherited. My mother was the type to stand her ground whenever she was right, and she was rarely wrong. My father had a permissive arrogance, allowing anything to escape his mouth. I felt trapped whenever the two collided, rarely ever seeing them sort things out. The car ride seemed to end simply. That or my parents grew tired.

I promised myself my relationship wouldn't be the same, but repeating the sins of your parents seems inevitable. God must be challenging us to go through the pain or become it. Those were the options most took anyway. I saw something different entirely, fixing the problem entirely so it needn't exist.

I loved empowered women, ones who balance their grace with internal fortitude. Some women look the part rather than be the part and then fault a man for bringing her outside her comfort zone into reality. Many men do the same. I've resisted blaming all women for my problems, having women in my life I adore and respect like men who complain about Nakans or

pathway to hell. You can't spend your life blaming others or pretending to be different. The only change in life occurs when you become different. Change isn't so difficult when we realize it's inevitable.

I've learned to hate love while dating in college, relationship after relationship, of half-baked ideas and rushed soul bonds. Spotting someone you think is cute or thinks you're cute. Next thing you know, it's been three months, and you've had sex nearly every day for two of them. You don't know her favorite color, just her name and major. I was taught to work things out, which most women didn't want to do. Nowadays, it seems we're taught to leave the moment. It doesn't work. Now, I see exactly why the two competing ideologies are at odds. My theory is there are two people, The Stay-together types and The Nevermores, the couples who work it out no matter what, who had one bad relationship and ruined it for everybody. Then there are The Farewells that leave at the first sign of danger. I can see it clearly in the dying days of this relationship.

My best friend tells me my problem is I like empowered women. She believes I use it as a paradox of constant imperfection and unattainability. We get into talks and discussions about what power is: being outspoken, balancing grace with internal fortitude. Traits not necessarily male or female, things I want a person to have. The more we talked, the

husband/wife became. The more my relationships made sense, at least their ending, the less I wanted a girlfriend, and the more I wanted to prepare to be a husband.

She criticizes me, saying an empowered woman takes taekwondo or weight-lifts. The concepts I discussed were the form of a good person. In essence, a good woman is a good person, and being a good person is unattainable for most humans, let alone a woman. She inquired, "Why to learn what I'll never use?"

Mya and I became best friends through a borderline nihilist philosophy class her freshman year, my sophomore year. My gift of gab during class and my love of reading made me stand out. It wasn't long before we were studying together. She knew me through her best friend, Opal. Once Opal and I decided to be friends, she called me "emotionally unavailable." Her other friends weren't afraid to hang out with me. Every girl I dated hated the entourage I had around me. The women claimed we were all archaic dreamers refusing to accept reality or the Nakan Lifestyle.

None of us are Nakan. Our homelands predate all of theirs. And their ways lead their civilizations into ruin and depression. Theirs destroyed our ways of civilization, but they worked longer than all these inventions and theories. We coped with long conversations late into the night. We bonded over the

soothed ourselves with libations and music. We've only gotten Ds this once, and it was my fault. And we keep each other focused. It took us each a long time to understand there's too much hatred, negativity, and jealousy in the world to be involved with the world.

Mya and Opal were both renown from their childhood in The Academy, training before college. Jared was the lead singer of Somber Nights. Every song he records is a hit. We get to hear all the bad ones before the studio. Terrance was his own man, an old soul who bothered to entertain us with his witticism, satire, and spiritual view of the world itself. I never met a man so pained yet at peace. I suppose I was the standout. I had yet to explore my talents or have a moment until recently.

I was known for being handsome, the ideal husband, and having potential. I hated the idea of it all. What the hell is handsome when I wear sweatpants five days out of 10 and don't even bathe? What is an ideal husband when every single girlfriend I dated, love them or not, made me severely doubt I would ever be married? If I were, it wouldn't be for long. And potential, this one bothered me. Who doesn't have potential?

The woman I dated fell in love with a fantasy driven by their delusions of self-entitlement. They thought they deserved a guy like me, and a guy like me was lucky to have them. No, their hormones and the television have misled them, and the young

for love and appreciation.

My girlfriend did Zumba and cycling. She failed to see a need for self-defense despite the mouth on her. I think learning to duck or block might be beneficial. We never talked about anything. She never wanted to speak. We rarely did anything together besides sex or watch television until she fell asleep. It was the greatest insult to my intelligence I had ever witnessed or participated within. Yet, this will of having a good relationship, having a wife I met in college and set off to live forever, living in Graham, Nadia, and running an after school program in Exigo for the kids to learn skills, get tutored, and stay off the streets, kept me going.

I guess all I wanted was to help people and be a husband. I never cared who to and never understood what it took to have a real relationship. I thank my past loves for the experience and paradigm shift. I decided to stop dating indefinitely and long gave up on the idea of marriage. My childhood dreams were lost to the wind.

I met up with Opal and Mya for their scheduled study sessions after my ballad on Nadian Sovereignty over the Western reaches beyond Nadine. My professor was furious. In the end, she stated I was correct in my information, but my manner of presentation and tone was off-putting, and she considered it hate speech. She said I should be lucky she didn't

research to write the paper. Gotta love college.

We were meeting at the library, not the grand library but the public library. We usually held up a spot by the kid's section around the circulation desk while the kids were in class. Opal loved asking questions. She was our researcher usually because she had the library reference plug. Her crush has a master's degree in library studies and reads all day. He had a major crush on Opal from her freshman year a couple of years ago as her Teacher's Assistant. Mya usually scheduled everything. It was the usual time we spent wasting it, hanging out or smoking weed, all with a new venue and actual purpose—the two-degree difference to success.

It was another day at New Haven University. The last testament to a giant stone tunnel monastery running through the Eastern Nadian and Western Erdun border to the middle of Erdu. New Haven had always been a metropolis. The ancient stone monuments still stood and joined every century with greater modern architecture. The City was a living museum with buildings still in use dating back 10,000 years. Some of the older buildings have been restricted as historical monuments.

New Haven was a culture shock for most students traveling from outside of Erdu with their backward ideology. I guess the Archaic Dreamer mentality paid dividends over the centuries.

world. They said no man could be an island, but I never listened to the bewildered herd. Most never tried to live their dreams or live beyond what they knew. We lived and thrived on seeing a world beyond this one. Jared was honestly our leader, but we lived our own lives. As we got older, there was so little time for each other. I feel like I'm prepared for a life in a suburb. The dream can't die in the burbs with two kids and a barely held together marriage. I knew that firsthand. We all did.

The shame was I saw how deeply I connected and felt with others. It's the Nadian in me. I'm sensitive and empathetic. I'm also a warrior. My family name Tor'Jun is from the Ward Singers. Opal was the only person I met who knew anything about it. You can't base a whole relationship around only that. Especially when that's all they know about your culture besides mythology and stereotypes.

My bag was tossed over my shoulder as I sang along to my favorite *Somber Nights* song. I held out my arms, walking along the stone railings with ideal balance. I swung along the light pole as I got close, hopping down the five-foot jump to the railing below, then grabbing a running start on the railing before kong vaulting over the last pillar.

It was a run I practiced my freshman year before the Dean shut down Free-running on-campus and no skateboards, only longboards. Probably for the best anyway, DJ went to

were simpler freshman year. It was simpler anyway. Before the validation and opinions of others became so instinctively woven into survival. We climb, and climb and pull ourselves up until we become joyous and righteous without being self-righteous.

"You see today. It fades away. Another day, words to say. Don't hold it, let it go, sing it, scream it, meant it, and believe it. You see, these days, they blur away. Another mouth, with words to say. When all you need is a friend away, let it go, let it go, scream it, scream it, let it go!" I blared.

A group of girls walked by, pointing and laughing at me. I waved, continuing to sing until entering the library and finding my friends.

I was chilling with Opal and Mya in the library. My textbook concealed my face so I could avoid looking up at the Syren Temptation before me. The summer heat brought Opal out in a halter top and shorts, spilling out of both. Mya wore a sundress with no straps. Her cardigan tossed aside, pulling up her braless breasts every ten minutes. I wore jeans and a T-shirt. My book concealed my face to avoid looking up.

Opal and Mya created a quiz to make sure I knew everything for our next exam with Dr. Hisaka. We were making a full history of the world and needed to investigate the four regions and their foreign policy.

You only need four correct to pass. There are five questions. You'll have an hour in class, but I'll give you about 5 minutes a question." Mya explains the rules.

"I'm guessing they're shorter questions?" I ask.

"Nope." Mya grins, "The first question, what year did Maya create an embargo with Naka? Why did they choose this political move? How did it benefit Naka? How did it benefit Maya?"

"First question about yourself, huh?" I mutter.

"This is coming out of your time. I started the clock." Mya smiles.

"Maya and Naka were enemies for centuries before the first embargo of the 1430s. It lasted five years and completely cut the freshwater from Naka. As Nakans began to die, they initiated peace negotiations. The second embargo was in 1720 due to Naka's refusal to pay water tariffs because no other nation was receiving Mayan water needed to pay. Aside from Erdu, who received packaged water at a large shipping price. Nakans wanted to go to war. Instead, Mayans blocked all waterways entering Naka, restationed all their peacekeepers and military, then built up their border cities. This strengthened the Maya domestic military, sense of culture, and control over water. Did it force Naka to make allies instead of imperialism

Naka."

"We came up with the questions with Hisaka. She wants to know how it benefits Naka as well. It's what they're like, and they don't believe in losing even when they lose." Opal yawns.

"Well, Naka reentered a peace program with Erdu to purchase water through Erdu. However, it wasn't sufficient, so Kismet provided aid under George Marvin Wright in 1721 to recruit a group of Nadian scientists to purify the highly salinated water on the coast of Naka. This saved Naka and ended bloodshed from Nakan hands. Though, rumors are Naka funds The Regulator Regime and continue under-

They both stared at me as military brats who came through The Regime to enter university. I trod carefully with my views of the Military.

"Which gives a more... managed method of war?" I shrug.

"You pass." Mya claps.

"Why are there five regions, and who created the five regions?" Mya asks me.

I stared at them as if the questions were real.

"Answer it! If you pass, we can raise our grade depending on how many you get right." Opal demands.

"Alright, alright... The five regions are Naka, Ecru, Erdu, Esha, and Maya. The first region was Ecru in the center of Gaia. It harnesses the power of the ether within its capital Zilaypenah.

major cities. The second region was Erdu to the east of Ecru. In the early ages, it had the richest agriculture and largest livable landmass. The Third was Maya which controls all the purified waterways. It has the least landmass, mostly islands, which a mainland connected to the landmass. It's said to be paradise on Gaia. The fourth was Naka. The fifth was Esha, with major mountains along its Erdu border and wide-open borders through the Mayan waterways. Esha is mostly great plains, with the freshest air on Gaia. The Almighty God created Gaia-

"Chris, it's for our grade." Opal pleads.

I roll my eyes, "Naka created the regions. Is that what she wants to hear?"

"Basically…" Mya cringed.

"Why are you so anti-Naka?" Opal asks.

"Is that for our grade?" I smirk.

"No, a real question. We're both wondering." Mya confirms.

"Naka is the core of all world issues. It has zero natural resources but attempts to exploit the natural resources of every other nation. It turned a great region like Ecru into Nadia through media destruction and turned the people against themselves. Now it's buying up all the property and sending the men to Erdu and Naka prisons for slave labor. Would you like me to continue?" I gritted my teeth.

Regulator Regime, and why was it formed?" Opal stabs my chest with her pen. The cap was on whether she knew it or not.

"Hmm... The Regime had a beginning 20,000 years ago under a group from Erdu called the Axesons. It was the first Royal Army with a banner of a flaming battle-ax. They had the strongest military power in Erdu until the plains folk, mountains folk, and coastal folk banded together to defeat and remove the Axesons from existence." I answer.

Mya shakes her head, "What the hell are you talking about, Chris? That's not the Regulator Regime at all."

"Did you know that the first General of the modern regime, Igor Axelson said he dedicated The Regime to his strained bloodline at his coronation in 1540? The modern regime began in 1540 but didn't reach prominence until 1717, when The Warrens banded together with the other mountain folk to defend against the massive bloodshed, pillaging, and murder from a radical group. There was a united military agreement to defend the lands in 1540, but there wasn't a true organization and agreement until the early 1700s."

Opal high-fived Mya with glee, then turned to me smugly, "Not bad, not bad. Next questions! So, what year did the Erdu region divide into four parts?"

divide between Old Erdu of the West and New Erdu of the East. 1750 is when the Gregors moved into Erdu."

"Ehh! Wrong!" Opal blares, "1752 is when the Gregors made allegiances with New Erdu of Central Erdu. They designed the plans to divide Erdu in 1750 but didn't begin the war until 1752 because it took two years for Gregor Forces to march around Nadia. Ecru if we're polite to Chris here. It took 30 full years to divide the region and enforce the division set by Gregors. Now, We have Old Erdu before the Nadian and Erdu border nations still under siege nearly 300 years later. New Erdu in the center. And The Coastlands. They've made mother Erdu a reflection of Naka."

"See what I told you about these Nakan textbooks? They're different. It shows Erdu with different divisions than the map. They planned the war and the outcome before they even started the invasion, a devious lot indeed." I turned the book around to her for her to see for herself.

"Published in Naka... and I wondered why we got a D. Sorry for blaming you." Opal blushed.

I had her riding me all week about the grade, not to mention stressing over Margot every other day over the tiniest things. It was starting to drive me out of my skin to transfer home. There weren't too many people I willingly give my time out to, especially with how even the Nadian descendants of

from the ones who did it willingly or as a personality defect. Erduns had great cultural pride, especially their women. Most Erdun men were still stonemasons or laborers. The few who came to a university focused on engineering, construction management, business management, or finance to fight in the new war for their home. I had to pick my circles wisely. Spending most of my time alone, I had to be careful not to get caught up with all the tension and ignorance.

"Rakil, save us all!" She prays to God, "How could they ever teach such lies?"

"If I may enlighten you. The reason they call it Nadian is that Ecru could not be conquered. They started trading with currency, basically IOUs, to buy up the land. The natives didn't know any better. Imagining Naka to have been so far advanced compared to their ways. The Natives had no idea what they had until they lost it all." I shook my head.

I could tell by the looks on their faces that they were mad they called me crazy for calling my home Ecru. The same thing happened to their people. Most people treated me like I was crazy for knowing the history of my home when they knew little to nothing of theirs. Most lacked empathy. They could only sympathize with what they dealt with personally. People liked to conveniently think the downfall of Ecru was of its own doing. Ecru was destroyed by the same colonizing happening within inner workings of Ecru. They could only take the unoccupied and unprotected lands. The conquest of Erdu is to this day one of the most well-orchestrated internal heists of all time. Their leaders and politicians are selling away its people and land to Naka for Nakan dollars. Common sense would point to firing the politicians. Instead, they're driven and consumed by everything but their fate.

We went to university seeking truth, but instead, we got educated perspective and theory graded by the opinions of our peers and professors.

Mya studied broadcast journalism and political science, so she was hip to it all. She kept quiet when she wasn't writing articles. She steered away from direct political issues. However, she was rather masterful in how she got to the points causing those mass political issues: family life, global employment, education shortages, and the global prison complex. We were no longer rehabilitating people on a universal level. Mya believed we had lost the value for life entirely. I was her test subject for such a theory. I hated the idea of living in a Nakan controlled world, and she said it was the life I was given regardless. All my other actions are outright against this structure of power.

Opal was a finance major completely unconcerned with any political, legal, or global issues. Opal focused upon Opal. I study History with minors in Political Science and Art History. I

needed for my major. Then she introduced me to Mya and the rest of her friends. I introduced them to Terrance and Jared. We all became friends soon after with the vibrations and driving around. Mya and I were thick as thieves once our political science schedules started lining up. We picked most of the same classes by pure chance.

Mya has always had some boyfriend, and I was always occupied with a lady or two. I suppose I never considered the idea with either. I couldn't imagine dating another girl who isn't from Nadia. There are thousands of books on Ecru history, tens of thousands after Nadia was instituted globally by The Regulator Regime and Nakan Government. I never knew outside nations could name and write territory in outside nations. I could never imagine them doing such a thing in Maya or Esha. Then I learned it's rare to find an Erdun who had heard of Ada or Rakil, let alone worship them. Most barely knew their sovereigns or history actually to have a connection to God. You can't study history without seeing God's hands shaping humanity. In Naka, they either worship Enshishi as God, or they worship nothing. Enshishi and The Gregor Family threw away any concept of God the average human could consume. Associating such a family with the concept was blasphemous yet natural to most of the world.

out. Speaking a belief or notion different from the accepted rhetoric seemed to throw people in as much confusion as it did fear. People were more likely to criticize you behind your back than confront you with a discussion. More still will only confront you to espouse their beliefs far more extremely than you care to listen. The University lacked clear debate because we lacked enough students who knew what they believed, let alone possessing critical thought or truth. This is mandatory to survive now! Without a degree, you can only ever work entry-level or grind hoping someone notices you. There are but only so many managers.

I see the bigger picture. Big picture thinking seemed lost. They call you a dreamer for seeing beyond tomorrow. I don't think I ever lost women after I had a five-year plan. These girls who I remembered called every year on the dot, checking to see if it came to fruition. It's either out of spite or to ride the bandwagon and get back together. People without a vision or plan rarely changed, though. I let myself become the man I must become two years before getting back into things with Margot. Kicker, we got together after cheating on my ex-girlfriend. This seemed like a slice of hell, being punished for all things I've done before having it all brought upon me.

"Hey! Hey!" Opal claps her hands, "Do you hear me talking to you? You're daydreaming."

chuckling to myself.

"At least then you'll be seeing something real. Did you hear anything we said?" Opal asked.

"I was thinking about Margot... how I met you all. My slice of hell after ruining things."

"All your relationships were train wrecks waiting to happen. None of them loved you for who you are." Mya cut me off.

"What was the one girl... Julia or something?" Opal asked.

"Giulia, such a soft soul. She said I yell too much." I rubbed my chin.

"You said she was annoying as hell, then one day you yelled at her for what was it, Mya?" Opal tried to recollect snapping her fingers.

Mya sighed, "She was nitpicking you about wiping your hands on your jeans, then you told her to chill the hell out. Then she broke down crying, poor girl. Snot and everything."

I rolled my eyes, getting in my feelings, "I knew double dating with you was a bad idea. You and an ole buddy from your math class. How'd y'all work out?"

"He asked a million questions about you and Jared because of the show. It was the most annoying night of my life. No guys talked to me at all. You could have at least let a girl go back to hook up with you and snotty." Mya giggled.

everything to be perfect. She felt like you were trying to take me from her." I confess.

"Thank Margot for that one." Opal rolled her eyes, "You sure know how to pick them, Chris. You have terrible taste in women. What the hell do you even think about when you date them?"

"Usually, which one seems most interested in me?" I shrug.

"Gross." Opal laughs, rolling her eyes, "I didn't stand a chance."

"Nah, your ignorance on Ecru is why we could never be a thing. And you're too insensitive. I have feelings. I fit none of your stereotypes about men." I chuckled.

"None of them? Haha, you think you turned me down? Let's go. He sleeps around, has no sense of morality, talks for literally ever nonstop like a one-person show, has zero emotions whatsoever 75% of the time, then he gets into a fight with bae, and he's depressed. Rants about Ecru and Nadian Pride overcompensate for the other 25% of the time he's dead silent. You picked a dumb major and two repetitive minors instead of applying yourself. Did I miss anything?" Opal asked.

"I'm an amazing bassist... That was an ad hominem attack. My feeling hurts." I drop my pen on the desk, rolling my eyes.

"You should be a freaking finance major. At least major in Philosophy, then it would make sense. What the hell are you going to do with History? Teach? You would make a hell of a lecturer. I'll give you that."

"Margot says I lecture her, and it's abusive. I try to talk to her for hours about issues in our relationship." I rub my neck.

"Well, don't... that's completely abnormal. No one can handle hearing how horrible of a person they are for more than thirty minutes tops. No wonder you two are brawling. You are making your life poetry. That's why they say never date an artist." Opal sneers, "Dodged that bus."

"So it's my fault?" I throw my head back, "That makes a hell of a lotta sense."

"It's never anyone's fault that's the golden rule of toxic relationships. You should never have dated those chicks and applied yourself to get a real woman!" Opal laughs.

"I think it's her fault." I clarify.

"Chris, you have a million problems. I still love you for them, but you can be harsh, bro. Like, unnaturally harsh and very temperamental. Not to mention all the stress you two are under right now. You need to chill if you're going to make that last." Mya fires at me.

"I don't think it's just Margot's fault. It'll last unless I-

At least break up with her like a decent person. Stop forcing it if your heart's not in it." Mya advises. She's been super helpful throughout.

"My heart is in it. It's hard not to when she makes everything about her feelings literally." I smack my forehead.

"She's a girl, you psycho." Opal looks at me as if she couldn't believe what I said.

"Yeah, like that. Everything is so personal and unnecessarily rude. Then when it's down to her, she goes ballistic! I can't stand the double standard women have with men." I protest to no avail.

"What about your issues?" Opal asks.

"My issues are being worked on. I'm aware of it. I'm throwing the garbage away with the stuff and trying to keep the human. Not treat everyone like crap because I haven't worked on myself. I'm sculpting marble. It takes time." I reply.

"Well, it's the same thing!" Opal shouts.

"It's not the same if you're not actively working and focusing on it. It doesn't happen naturally. It's a very unnatural process. The natural thing to do is be emotional, erratic, reactionary like a cornered animal whenever it comes to your inner workings of the mind. I don't do that at all. She irks me and keeps working at me like you are now, for what?" I sigh.

"You're right."

"Sure." I yawn.

Opal glares at me then licks her lips, "I see why she puts up with you. You're a handsome guy. You're smart. Things come easy for you. And you have loads of wisdom and experience. You wouldn't need to change or break up with so many girls if you weren't messed up, to begin with."

"I admit it. None of you do. You blame men for everything, and then when it is the girl's fault, you do nothing. You keep blaming the man. I accept it like a man, and I'll be blamed for everything, but this double standard is ridiculous. I get it. I'm a man I have a bunch of unnecessary responsibilities you don't-

"Like what?" Mya asks.

"Not being emotional." I stare at her, taking a deep breath.

"What? That's not an actual thing." she begins getting frustrated immediately.

"It's one of the main human experiences. Men are neglected. We aren't taught how to deal with our emotions healthily. Fighting wars, working undignified jobs, and dying young all for you girls. None of it is appreciated." I reply.

"It is appreciated for the men who did those things!" Opal replies.

went through them," I reply.

"What? What the hell are you talking about, Chris? All women deal with sexual assault." Opal retorts quickly.

"I didn't limit it to one issue. Men are sexually assaulted as well. I was completely peer pressured into losing my virginity, and it's been a downward spiral with women since then. She initiated, wanted it, and took my virginity, then said she was moving across the country the next week because of some issues with her family. What about what men go through?" I ask.

"You're a guy. You'll get over it." Opal sucks her teeth.

"You're a chick. You'll cry it out, right? How do you sound? Women are just heartless. All the lies and illusions men think about you all. That's the only reason I've been successful with them. All those other men want to worship you. They have no idea how insecure and disconnected chicks are. They have no idea what chicks are really like, so they fap themselves about chasing tail. That's why they can never date. You're human too, you sin too, and you fart and poop too. Women are no better than men, yet all you think you have this superiority complex from movies and cartoons." I throw my hands up, sitting forward.

"You're a misogynist." Opal cuts her eyes at me.

"I am a man. A man tired of being abused and punished by society for being a man. What the hell kind of world is this

father and mother, who are both married. My mother is a Chemist, has three children, lived during the Nakan and Erdun Civil Rights era. She acts absolutely nothing like the chicks I date. Maybe one day she used to, but you mature and realize most of those ideals were sinful and selfish, I guess." I reflected.

"Who cares about your-

"Whoa... do not cross that line with an Ecrun man." Mya raises her hands, "Major cultural boundary. Do not finish your sentence. I apologize for her, Chris."

"Don't apologize to me. I meant it. She's one woman out of many. What about the rest of us who are still trying to get ours?" Opal puffs her chest out.

"Like everyone else our age growing up right now without anything of their period?" I scratch my head tightening my eyes.

"Shut up. You make everything so freaking small." Opal crossed her arms over her chest.

"Empirical." I correct.

"Shut up!" Opal shouts.

I chuckled, shaking my head.

"You're so cocky. Chris, you know that? Maybe that's why you get into so many fights with her. You just don't know when to stop, do you?" Opal's words cut through me like a knife.

sighed, bowing my head again, feeling unable to make eye contact or stare.

"I'm sorry... I didn't mean it." Opal offered, holding my hands, "I don't know how to back down from a fight either."

I gulped, my eyes rising, getting a full view of her breast before meeting her eyes. I opened my mouth, unable to speak for a moment as my brain tried to move the image from my head. I smiled dreamily, nodding my head contently, then leaning back in my seat.

Opal smiled, satisfied, "I'm glad I didn't lose a friend. You're on some other stuff right now, Chris. Why do you have so many issues with women?"

"Trying my best, and it still not working. Like what the hell? When I'm doing everything right, they're afraid of commitment. When I'm not at my best, they want to possess me. I swear a girl only wants you when you're beneath them, or they think they can control you. I need someone to help me elevate." I explain.

"And there are women out there like that. Maybe it looks different than what you're looking for or what's falling in your lap." Opal continues.

"You would be what I was looking for, bud. I would clarify. I don't expect to find it inside a girl my age. I expect to be the person. Well, become a better person than attract her, not attract my partners, not by law, but literally. I am their type when they date me. I wish I didn't, you know? I wish I sustained, maintained, and became more myself instead of finding someone who tries to control me, be me, or have my skin for a rug. I want someone who genuinely and honestly is seeking to help me get better." I try explaining further.

"You just said that, didn't you? Why are you making it so much harder than it needs to be? You either want it, or you don't. If you're dating girls who aren't serious, it means you aren't, which is exactly my point. Are you a genius? Probably the smartest guy I know for sure, book for book, debate for debate. Why the hell aren't you trying to help Nadia with something practical?" Opal smacks the table.

"My goal is practical. My people suffer from a lack of knowledge. I will educate them." I offer.

"How will you fund that? You could read those books any time, literally any time you wanted. You could study what's that thing your dad does, Mya? It isn't law, but it's in the legal field?"

"My dad and Uncle are both paralegals." Mya slaps her forehead, telling Opal for the 50th time.

"Yeah, word up. Attack the prison industrial complex head-on. You could filibuster them to death and set rights for prisoners." Opal waves her hands, "Do something practical!"

they were released to the public now without rehabilitation, they would destroy Nadia with what they learned. If you educate them before they reach seven years old, you will see the man they'll become forever. Instead, we're waiting until college to give information than one general perspective of it. I agree. I probably could have chosen something different. I was well-intentioned." I explain.

"You intended to marry Margot two months after dating her. Two years later, you can't stand her. You need to look beyond the big picture and focus on what works and what doesn't. You're making a lot of bad decisions." Opal remarked.

"Thanks, Doctor Opal Badu. I appreciate the analysis. Anything else you want to use to eviscerate me?" I ask.

"There's a lot more. We could talk over dinner." Opal winks.

"I'm a married man, remember?" I sigh, pained.

"You were so close to saying yes. You like crap like this, don't you?" Opal inquired, her cheeks blushed.

"I was not even close. I have a girlfriend. And Margot would burn us both alive on sight if she caught us." I rub my temples.

"Are you okay? You seem more tired than usual." Mya took my temperature with her hand, "You have a fever as well."

writing a paper for Professor Rakan Sameera regarding the history of the diplomatic allegiance between Ecru, Maya, and Esha." I yawned once more, covering my mouth.

"The skinny old man with the bifocals everyone calls some anti-regulatory extremist? He has you writing something like that? The world is going to miss his knowledge. It's a wonder someone could get through to inspire you." Opal chimed in her ever unwanted two cents.

Sameera was my favorite professor in my favorite class. You rarely get both. He wrote volumes upon volumes on Ecru. He has articles in every major journal throughout his lifetime learning Eshan and Mayan culture. He was the only one to use multiple sources throughout history and the world to teach. He had no plan or perspective. He ensured he gave us each perspective to form our own decisions. Every other subject was planar. One must be careful not to fall off the limited fable.

"You should probably go get some relaxation in to end your day." Mya's smile was radiant, and her curly sun-kissed brunette hair filled my nostrils with the scent of the strawberry-kiwi conditioner.

"Yes, ma'am," I say without delay, falling under her spell.

Opal pulled back her lips in a grin, "Have you two ever...knocked boots? The way you two look at each other. It's like you slept with each other before."

same bed. We have not literally or metaphorically knocked boots of any sort. No clogs, no galoshes, no combat boots, sandals, nor skins." I cross my heart and hope to die.

Mya punches me in the arm.

"You did?" Opal's eyes nearly fell from their skulls.

"I ground on him at a party, his hard-on was pressed upon me, but that's as close as we got." Mya blushed.

"You two are creepy, not together. Hearing your double-date story was horrific. You two haven't even fooled around?" Opal pushed.

"No, Opal, for Rakil's sake, let it go!" Mya was blushing.

"You're selfish with the sex, huh?" Opal stunned me with her remark.

"What?" I laugh, unable to process it.

"You are selfish with your cock. I hear rumor after rumor about you. Who are you keeping it from if you keep sliding into these crazy chicks?" Opal asked.

"He says the sex makes them crazy." Mya poked at me.

"I confided that in you, Mya. You weren't supposed to tell anyone!" I covered my face.

"It's like that, for real?" Opal bit her finger, "Tell me more, one of you, I need details!"

"I am not explaining my sex life to you, Opal." I cross my arms over my chest.

There's no way it fits inside any orifice I have. He's very blessed."

"You've seen it? Has she seen it? I can't even get a naked pic?" Opal flipped my book over, "Selfish as all get out with it!"

My jaw dropped, "I'm selfish because I haven't had sex with one of you?"

They both looked away with a 'You said it, not me' look on their face. Mya laughed it off, beginning to pack her things. Opal met my eyes again.

"Show me now." Opal insisted.

"We're in a library, and I have a girlfriend, Opal!" she was starting to test my nerve.

"I'm not going to do anything with it. It'll be so hot. I'll trade seats with Mya, and you can show me." Opal pressed on, pushing together her chest with her arms.

"Wow…" Mya clapped as my pants pitched a tent, "even the bulge is intimidating."

"I can't see it! Switch seats!" Opal began tapping the desk impatiently.

"Opal, you need to calm down. You're acting as you've never seen a man's junk before." Mya rolled her eyes.

"You think I have? Up close? Like a real one? Not once has a guy ever bothered trying actually to date me, let alone have sex with me. Men are intimidated by me. If they won't talk to me because I'm beautiful, then it's because they don't want a

here is more man than most. I want to see one, and I picked which one I want to see." Opal stood calmly, grabbing her chair to pull it around to our side of the desk, sitting on my other side.

"Happy?" I challenged.

"Pull it out. Let it breathe." Opal took a deep breath letting her hands rise and fall.

"I have a girlfriend." I repeat at my wit's end, "You don't get it to, do you?"

Opal pointed at it, "Come on now. Don't act like it's me. Look at it. It's scary. Stop being so selfish. This isn't about Margot. I want to see it, not suck it. I'm serious. I've done an over underwear thing once. Margot can have you."

"Better to let your imagination deal with the rest, huh?" Mya offered.

"When you and Margot break up, I want first dibs. I've been waiting." Opal enforced.

"What? How are you already calling bets on my relationship ending?" I asked.

"You cheated on a girl to get with Margot, but you won't cheat on Margot?" Opal rolled her eyes.

"Giulia and I had broken up earlier in the day, and I met Margot after. I admit I didn't wait long, but it was in the clear when Margot and I got together. When the hell did we start

temples.

"Go back to what you were saying before. Opal is just crazy." Mya covered her face

"Opal is serious. My eyes are on you, Chris Tor'jun." Opal took her two fingers, pointing them directly at my eyes.

"You need a hobby, Opal." I stare at her, "More than forums or blogs. You need an actual real-life hobby."

"Let's hear your hobby Mr. Activist." Opal muses.

"You were talking about the conquest of Ecru and Erdu by Naka. It's one of my favorite unspoken subjects in school. So, please continue." Mya insists.

I rolled my eyes, gathering my thoughts and closing my textbook.

"I'll fast-forward to the modern-day effects, so at least I can reach some conclusion in my thoughts. Personally, in Nadia, we have Nakans buying up property with Nakan money all over Nadia. No one is bothering to stop it or even do more than merely acknowledge it. Do you realize how hard it is to buy land as a foreigner in Esha? You at least need citizenship in Naka or Maya to buy land. In Ecru and Erdu, we never had or needed to set these laws. They never wanted what we had until they realized they had nothing. Our politicians and preachers are trying to suppress their people from reclaiming the land they lived on for centuries. They've become our very enemies. The

10,000 dollars. If a citizen tries to buy it, it's 50,000 or 100,000! Why are they handicapping their people and aiding their lifelong enemy? Self-hatred has taken control over our world. The Inner self-hatred all these people have for themselves eats them alive, and they learn to hate humanity, Gaia, and the future. So they allow all these people to destroy the world. It makes no sense to me. So, I'll teach history and recent history to save the future." I fume.

"Obatta and Bryon's death was the most recent tragedies to ever happen in Ecru, well maybe Nadia. Ecru has a rich history." Mya shrugged.

"Like what? Tell me more?" Opal bit her lip.

"I'll tell you a prophecy from deep, deep ancient Ecru. The one Obatta Sameera fulfilled. Before there was Tartarus, Eastern Naka, those lands sat opposite to the Garden of Eden. It was the central hub of the Ecru Empire, Jubilees. The leader of Ecru at the time was Jibril men Sah'ra. The Erdu had assassinated Jibril in a fake peace summit then attacked Jubilees. The Royal Family fled, and Jibril's youngest grandson became the warlord known as Naseem, who grew in the Stone Tunnels and changed his name to Formica. He led the Ecru Expansion absorbing those lands of Western Erdu, Maya, and Eastern Naka. Ecru stretched from central Naka to Central Erdu, all of Maya and The Garden of Eden. The people and Guardian of Ecru cultivated the majority of

before Sameera was assassinated, he signed a peace treaty with High Priest Tulip Qatar, The Godfather Gerald Knox, Dr. Henry Marvin Wright Sr., and Kismet of Esha to sign Ecru back into existence. Then, the priest, the don, and doctor, and Sameera all died out of the blue. History repeats itself when you don't learn from it. I had to read those books in an old library in Little Penah. We were never taught that in school. They never even addressed the deaths of our leaders." I continue.

"How is that a prophecy? Like real life or a fairy tale?" Opal asked, confused, "I don't know any of those names."

"They were world leaders. Tulip Qatar is the leader of the Qatar Family in Maya. They control the pure water flow throughout Gaia. He died mysteriously. Gerald Knox is the head of the largest organized crime families in Gaia, born and raised out of Exigo, Nadia. I'm not sure how you forgot Bryon Saleem of Kismet. he was the Director of Visions for decades. They were all students of Dr. Wright. Each died days apart leading up to the Peace Summit when we were still about 5. You forgot to mention that his son killed Lord Commissioner Maurice Gregor. Then two men rose to power the world feared more than death." Mya reported with expert research.

"Oh, Nakan and Erdun news, I heard all about The Gregors. Who doesn't know about the Gregors!? Alright, so Maurice Gregor came into power through the Regulator Regime.

years, he negotiated peace deals and ended wars that elevated him to the Regulator Regime leader by the Counsel of Generals. I think we were just entering The Academy when Maurice Gregor had his coronation into Lord Commissioner. Either that or my father took me. Everyone loved Maurice Gregor. Then, his son killed him and used the same Gregor customs to take his role as Patriarch. Then we saw a new coronation when one of my own, Ray Bradley Warren, stepped up to Lord Commissioner for mysterious reasons. The Gregors had more control over Warren than under Maurice, the Gregor Family, and the World Military leader. I had always been curious about it, but- how do you even begin researching such a thing?" Opal tapped her pen against her chin, trying to piece it all together.

"Maurice Gregor was cool to me because he was born in my town before his family up and moved to Naka. His death was a mystery to me. I have no idea what he had to do with any of it." Chris shrugged.

"Alright, so I pulled it up on Bingo. It says Jibril and Formica were both Sah'ra, that's the desert Erdu, it's also been uninhabitable for centuries. You said this is an Ecrun Prophecy." Opal noted, looking at her phone, "Wait... hold on, most of Erdu used to be a part of Ecru? Whoa, you're not crazy, ha it says here, commonly known as Ecru. Common? Widely popular in Esha and Maya, oh how chic."

"I still don't understand the prophecy… prophecy usually predicts something. I see dots connecting, but I don't see the story. So, what if these lands used to be Ecru. What does the past of Sah'ra and Jubilees have to do with today if both are gone?" Mya inquires with her investigator hat.

"Oh, I forgot to finish. Okay, so Foremica eventually fell into collusion as the Nakans began trading decades of personal advancement to build up an army to fight Formica. This was when they began their first alliance with Erdu to kill Formica. Formica had a son named Onyx men Sah'ra, known by most cultures after as a nomad, Onyx Black. Onyx was prophesied to be the Guardian of Ether, Ada. He fought off both armies single-handedly and wiped out The Major Hub of Ecru, Jubilees in Naka, to prevent the Nakans from ever entering Ecru again. Onyx disappeared from history. The Prophecy is that Obatta Sameera is the reincarnation of Formica, his political war set into motion the same process and reestablishment of Ecru. Sadly, when he was killed, most Nadians believe his son Leonticus was killed in the process. Leonticus was meant to be the reincarnation of Ada, the Onyx of our time. No one knows where he could even be. They did everything they could to stop the prophecy. That's when you see the mass incarceration of Ecru men because there were no longer real leaders protecting

tragedy the best I could.

"I knew a kid around our age in The Academy. He would respond to Leonticus but usually to beat the crap out of whoever said it. Do you remember, Opal?"

"Captain Ellys?" Opal asked, remembering but unable to make the connection, "I seriously doubt that guy is a part of any prophecy. Morgan grew up in the Warren Compound, too, with my friend, Leslie. He's practically the family of Lord Commissioner Warren. There's no way he's Obatta's son." Opal shook her head.

"I think it's worth investigating. No one ever had a chance to get to know The Captain. He was always in training, studying, or on missions. I would say he entered primary duty young. When we were in basic training, he was traveling for secret missions. The rumors were that he was an assassin, but he was our age. We never knew much other than he flew up the military ranks, then he disappeared altogether. Leslie hasn't heard from him at all." Mya held her chin, thinking hard.

"Onyx was separated from his father as well. He was trained in the Stone Tunnels under our feet. So, The Academy is the most likely area because that's where the only preserved area of the Stone Tunnels is kept. Leonticus Sameera was the boy's name. L.S... there's a very slim chance. If you can ask your

Chris sighs, slumping in his chair.

"I'm sorry, Chris. My sapiosexuality is going crazy right now. You seem to be caught up. I'm going to run over to Professor Hisaka's office and plead our case." Opal grabs my hands again, lifting them slightly.

"What are you doing?" I asked, suspicious as she raises my hands above her head.

"Opal, that's serious...." Mya notes out of great surprise.

"It's an apology gesture. It means I am going to fight a war on your behalf." Opal slowly lowers my hands into her lap.

"Huh...? Where you from?" I asked, unfamiliar with the idea of such a thing.

"My father was from the Warren Compound, the Mountains of Rockuta, my mother was from Western Erdu on the coast. Rockuta is 5 hours from Sah'ra, but they've never been to the city. I'm the 2nd generation to go through The Academy, and the first to go through university." Opal bows her head as she stands tall.

"That's amazing." I rub my chin, "A Warren bloodline member going to war for me? Holy crap, I better be ready for a phone call from Hisaka tonight."

Opal rolls her eyes, "I am going to win on your behalf, not get kicked out of school. I will be a lady and a professional. I'll fight like Sameera. I am off y'all. Text me later, Mya."

already packing my things to dip out, "Hey there, where are you rushing off to?"

"I want some alone time," I mutter.

"You do look pretty exhausted. Do you want to talk about it?" Mya offered despite my clear response.

"No, I don't." I groan.

"Well, I want to talk about it," Mya stated.

I looked around the library, "This isn't a good place to get laid. It's the worst place to talk about my life. Maybe somewhere else, but I'm not interested in discussing it with you at all, Mya."

"Let's go for a walk. We'll talk about whatever until you feel comfortable telling me what's on your mind." Mya insisted.

We found ourselves near a nice pond. Others were out along the green with blankets and picnic baskets. Some were sitting with their meals from the market with their dates—others with books sprawled out and about, in their notebooks and netbooks. Mya sat reading against a tree as I laid a few feet away, repositioning between staring at the water than the sky. My phone serenaded "Pearls for Pennies" by The Poynter Brothers, a group from Nadia. A new school R&B joint from their first album.

"My brother used to play this song all the time when it came out. I think I almost know all the words. Is it one of your

chorus.

"When it came out? That's a clear decade ago. I have to meet your brother sometime and talk music." I admired as I gaze into the sky.

"I could take you with me next time I go visit him. He moved to Esha to join Kismet when I came to college. I think he's stationed in Autorio, Maya, on a peacekeeping mission currently." Mya let her book down completely

"Sounds clutch." I yawn, unsure whether or not she was joking with me.

"Do you wanna know something? Of course, you do. This pond was the first place I ever saw you." Mya nudged me with her toe.

"Don't be touching me with your feet! And that's crap. We met in the food court during the meet & greet week. I remember it like yesterday. You nearly knocked my food out of my hands." I broke out laughing.

"I saw you before the food court while I was in my tour group. I was so pissed off I wasn't in your group. I saw you sitting here my freshman year completely alone, but you looked so happy. I know it's not too long ago, but it's scary to think you'll be graduating soon." Mya mused, looking off to the pond, transfixed on the glistening waves from the creatures below the surface.

mutter, remembering being woken up so many times to buy them alcohol because they couldn't get into the good parties.

"Oh shush, you loved hanging out with us!" Mya nudged me harder.

"I loved being your designated walker or buying you cabs. I liked it even more when you girls came knocking on my windows at 2 am telling me you just had to have wine." my sarcasm was sharper than a spear.

"I slept with you that night. We had to have wine." Mya's smile widened.

"You stealing my bed and snoring all night is not sleeping together. It's a major favor." I raise a brow.

"You're right. I was cuck-queen of the year with you and all your girlfriends. You never considered dating me once?" Mya seemed offended as if out of the blue, but it's a question she had been poking fun at for a while.

"I didn't ask for those relationships. And before you get a chance to say it, no, no, I didn't turn them down. I didn't know what I was doing, Mya. I barely even knew those girls. They just wanted someone to live their little fantasy with, nothing serious. I'm tired of being the story. I'm spending the rest of the school year in solitude, study, and meditations." I sat up, looking straight at Mya.

shakes my shoulders, "snap out of your depression."

"It isn't depression. I'm just focused! The last time I checked, I got us that. I'm trying to get better at all this crap. Not making the same mistakes until I die." I exhale but still felt the weight of the omission.

"Yeah, whatever. I remember forgiving you. Plus, you had a bomb presentation. It isn't your fault the world isn't ready for you." Mya squeezed my knee.

"I don't remember any of this forgiving." I rub my chin suspiciously.

"Yeah, well whatever. You weren't there for it. The point is I did it." She rolls her eyes.

"Argh, why do you play games like that? Just say how you feel! Stop hiding behind your eyes and express yourself!" I shout.

Mya stares at me with her lips gaped. Her cheeks ripened as she looked into my eyes. She bashfully looks away, moving her braids out of her face. She stroked her hair with a goofy smile on her face.

"You know… I would take care of you far better than Margot. I wanted you to know in case you ever wisened up and decided to date me for a change." Mya finally spoke.

"Date you for a change? No offense, girls like you are my problem. You're too casual. You come to me for advice on some messed-up situations. I would hate to be on the other side of 'is

Come on, now." I groan, beginning to laugh.

"Oh, shut up! I let him get a little feel, and he creamed himself. I only did it because he was talking a big game and my boyfriend was boring me. I'm still figuring out what I want, Chris." Mya crossed her arms over her chest, getting defensive, "What about you asking how to ask a girl for a threesome? You asked some pretty messed up things too. When you asked, I thought you meant me!"

"Which is why I want nothing to do with any of it. I want to let it all go. I don't want to have this conversation or go back and forth about our pasts. I'm trying to move forward with my life. I'm done with this conversation." I throw my hands up.

"You don't have to be so cold, Chris. I'm not leaving you alone so you can get over it." Mya looked away from me.

"I don't fear the solitude. I fear being misunderstood while being surrounded by people. You're always around people or doing something. I don't want to be around people just because I feel lonely." I try to explain.

"I don't understand... You're cryptic. I know you think you're poetic. You're just cryptic." Mya died laughing.

"You know that's exactly why I want to be alone. Terrance says right now it's him and his older woman. Aside from spending time with her, he gets all his time to himself and understands it. She trusts him and vice versa. Margot and I have

address it because we only call the other person out instead of saying why it's wrong. Rolling solo, I don't have to deal with any of that crap—none of the politics, emotions, and opinions backed by emotions and not evidence. I want clarity, Mya. I want the truth. I want to focus on finding solutions to my problems, not crying about them. I'm tired of explaining myself to someone who doesn't care!"

"I care." Mya tightened her grip on my knee, "My friends care. Jared cares."

"I am not talking about killing myself. I'm talking about not existing with your societal conditioning crap. Like Metatron." I exclaim.

"The robot car guy?" Mya said, confused.

"That's Megatron..." I slap my forehead, "Archangel Metatron, Enoch, Noah's grandfather. God took him and recreated him as a new man. He got tired of the sin in the world and wanted to be lifted from it. God gave him his wish. He walked with God and got lifted."

"What? Are you getting all religious on me, Chris? Why now? You think you're a saint now?" Mya groaned.

"Why do non-believers always act like that instead of trying to save their soul? No, I don't think I'm a saint. I'm not trying to be a saint. I am trying to be a better man. I would like to

neck.

She broke out laughing, "That's the weirdest thing I've ever heard. I mean, I've never heard it before at all. Why? That sounds dreadful trying to pretend to be perfect."

I rolled my eyes, "It's a practice of virtue, and you exercise virtue as you would exercise your mind or muscle. Through a life practice, you don't have to pretend. You become. And It isn't about being a saint! It isn't about pretending to be perfect! It's about choosing to work toward the good." I was getting infuriated.

"Margot ruined you, bro... before you got in your relationship, you couldn't care less about God or anything of the sort. I don't think you ever mentioned it."

"I don't believe in Rakil for Margot or anyone else! It's the reason why we're breaking up! I don't rest upon instincts or emotions. I am not afraid of death or hell. My belief in God has nothing to do with any reason you stay out of a church or mosque! Your limitations and reasons for not having faith are your things. Stop enforcing it on other believers and me. Your disbelief has nothing to do with my beliefs! Now, get off the subject before I lose my mind!" I fumed.

"Whoa, whoa, whoa bro... calm down you don't need to be so aggressive. I didn't mean to offend you." Mya raised her hands.

like people go out their way to misunderstand."

"Well, some do, but you seem all over the place right now." Mya raises her hands.

"To you. I am in one solid place in my mind because I'm trying to explain myself to someone who doesn't even think on the subject and thinks they'll immediately understand. I am fine, absolutely alone!" I shout.

Mya silently opens her purse and pulls out a purple tube. She pops it open, taking out a pre-rolled blunt, and presses it to her lips. She sparks it and takes a deep inhale before blowing it in my face. She gives me a wink then holds it out to me.

"You're so awesome," I mutter graciously, accepting the blunt and letting my thoughts go.

"I try, you know?" Mya shines her snide smile.

Most had arrogance, but she was confident and always willing to back up her tough talk. She always had a way of fighting to the top of leadership quicker than others. She didn't struggle with internal lacking or insecurity because she was so down-to-earth and well put together. She's an amazing friend, the form of a good person.

"I see what you mean. The more I study here, the more I feel like people at home have no idea what's going on. I keep asking my professors if people checked to see if these institutions and systems work before committing to them in

teacher, she said 'It works for the ones it's supposed to work for, and doesn't work for the ones it isn't.' After I asked her who it was helping and wasn't helping I reached the same dead-end with all the others. She told me a bit more but said it's private." Mya explained as she took the blunt from me. "I think we overcommitted to things we were meant to keep developing or completely abandon once we realized we were tricked."

"Don't make hints on my relationship," I mutter.

"I was not… I have no idea why the two of you even got together. All of us knew this had an expiration date, but you two keep fighting for it." Mya exhaled, "It's inspirational in its way."

"You all are so negative. If you try to help us instead of criticizing, then maybe it would stand a chance. Everyone has a bunch of insults and criticisms but no solutions." I reach for the remainder of the burning bush.

"Chris people see, people, talk, and then they assume." Mya sighs, taking another drag before passing it back to me.

I didn't want to respond. I would end up rolling my eyes going back to the same spill of my differences from others. Then people try to scoop you into this box of "other people don't think like you," as if some prefixed response. It was usually the anti-intellectuals who preferred the mental lethargy over any other stasis of existence. I swallowed the smoke, turning up my music as "First Fires" by Bonobo began to play. I exhaled as the beat

of sound engineering. Jared dreamed of working with him.

"You are freaking loyal… These songs are old, bro." Mya laughs.

"Time is a relative perception. A couple of years ago, I was apparently in this same seat, right? So, am I in the same place only physically or metaphorically?"

"You were sitting over there." she pointed to a rock behind us.

"Uh? That's a bit weird you remember that." I drifted off.

"I'm saying you've made progress. You're more in touch with your emotions. Ugh, just take the compliment and shut up." Mya blushed.

"Why do you remember so keenly?" I pursued my expansive curiosity.

"Shut up and smoke, Chris." she grinned.

"Mya, have you ever seen today and how it fades away? Another day with words to say. Don't hold it back. Let it go whether you need to sing it or scream it. Just mean it and believe it." I recited in a deadpan voice.

Mya stared at me with milky eyes, "that was so beautiful."

"Uhh… yeah buddy, it's a Somber Nights song. You said all my songs are old. This one is pretty new. Maybe I can find it." I look away from her, looping through my phone.

screams.

"It's a good song." I smirk, "You look like you're holding something back."

"Yeah, I don't want to listen to Jared Mitchell Wright singing at me. I want to see Jared go back to Kismet and lead. What the hell is up with you two and avoiding your destinies?" Mya asks.

"Don't know… believing in some higher power or purpose scares people off. They fear commitment." I sigh, remembering our conversation.

"And you?" Mya asks.

"I welcome it. I fear making commitments only to the wrong people or things. I want to be one of the people who are married for 50 or so years. I wonder and try to figure out what made those relationships work." I rubbed my chin.

"What about changing the world?" Mya groans.

"I can only change myself, Mya…." I confess.

"Our grandparents were raised differently than we were. The whole society supported marriage and the lifestyle. Now, we could care less, you know? At least I could care less. Now, we have nothing but ourselves to rely upon." Mya sighs, "Most of us are self-absorbed and short-sided."

"You think so?" I ask in agreement, wanting her to continue.

you to stay together. They told you different ways to make it work out or had religion and morality. She said how beautiful it was to see people falling in love and maintaining it for so long. The things people built and did together are inspired by love. Today, everyone is so negative and selfish." Mya recites.

"I want to meet your Grandma too," I note.

"Come home with me. I'll introduce you to everyone. They've heard A LOT about you and your friends." Mya rubbed my shoulder.

"Sounds good. When's the next time you go back? I'll have to save up." I pat her hand politely.

"Well, maybe if you two break up, it'll be more appropriate. They'll assume everything anyway. It would be so embarrassing if you weren't at least single." Mya groaned.

"You want me for yourself?" I ask, shocked.

"It's not even like that! If you came home with me, my dad and uncles might try to talk you into marriage on the spot. It would be intense. My sister brought a guy home, and they got married a few weeks later before going home. They didn't even have a ring." she covered her mouth.

"I wish Margot could think about marriage or something other than herself." I sigh.

"Are you breaking up? I'm visiting my family by the end of the year. It gives you time to save up and think about getting

he'll tell you his wife is his best friend. On second thought, you should probably go back to Nadia." Mya begins giggling.

"I'm detached from the outcome. I'm working on becoming a better person and learning all I can. I guess a father is supposed to be around for that. My dad is usually like a looming presence whenever I think of making bad decisions." I stretch out.

"I would hate dating you. You're so cold and distant. You seriously need to lighten up. Life isn't so serious." Mya warns me.

"Casual…" I tease.

"Old man!" she retorts.

"Respect the wisdom." I felt so clever.

"You need to make a choice eventually. Eventually, you're going to graduate." Mya warns me, trying to scare me.

"God decides not me. He'll make it clear for me. I've been reading a book on seminary. It doesn't sound too bad." I rubbed my chin.

"Chris, why would you do something like that? Margot got you confused!" Mya shouts.

"It isn't Margot. It's my choice as I already told you. Margot doesn't even believe in God!" I defend.

years to spend another 2-5 years in seminary?" Mya asked, bewildered.

"Why do people go to graduate school or take the Bar exam or become a doctor?" I turn to her as if the question made no sense.

Mya covered her mouth, "You are seriously thinking of becoming a priest!? Chris, you can't get married, have sex, any of that. Why would you do this?"

"I'm 30% joking." I shrug.

"That isn't a lot at all... You need to make the best decision for yourself. I guess your soul. I always thought you would make a great father. I guess you would make an even better priest. Then everyone would be your children. Plus, you can pray for me with the direct hookup!"

"I don't rush my important decisions. I'm debating about the vow of poverty. How can I fight for my people like that? I'm trying to figure out what my options are outside of teaching. I figured if I was to become a teacher being a priest would go hand in hand. I just don't want to become the enemy blocking my people" I shrugged.

"Have you talked about this with Margot?" Mya finally asked, knowing the answer.

"No, she would flip and try to talk me out of it." I relent.

"Margot would flip if she saw us together." Mya hints.

"What!? Why would she think something like that? What have you been telling her about me!?" Mya fumed.

"Well, you are bi-

"I am in college. I am experimenting. I don't need all your labels." Mya covered her face.

"College isn't an excuse to make bad decisions. It's a foundation to learn from them. We'll live with our decisions for the rest of our lives." I comment.

"I like what you said...." Mya mumbled, "I never looked at it that way. I always considered it the opposite."

"You have a whole life to make mistakes, party, and enjoy yourself. It doesn't stop with college leave that slave mentality and learn how to focus. It's rare anyone listens anymore these days. Unless you have a fat stack in your hands."

"Outside looking in, I think Margot is trying to kill your confidence. You've been down in the dumps lately." Margot held out the last few hits of the blunt before it begins to burn your fingers, "Make a wish."

"I wish for peace of mind and financial security," I say before taking a few hits then flicking the roach into the pond.

"I wish for a genuine A on this next presentation and a satisfying nap." Mya stretches out, "Where are you headed?"

"Back to my dorm to play Fallout or watch the new wrestling PPV. How about you?" I ask.

my dorm!" Mya begins to whine.

"You have your bed, and I want my space. I'll hit you up later to pay you back if I pick up more, bud." I yawn. A nap didn't sound too bad.

"You should hit me up regardless. Or bring me with you because I already have a bud on me. Your bed is big enough, and I can keep a secret." Mya holds up her purse.

I rubbed my temples, "I see why wanting to be a priest bothered you so much. You may try to call me overly religious, but it wouldn't be right. She sleeps there most nights. It's like her home, too, not just mine. Maybe if I was angry at her, now I just don't want any relationship at all with a chick."

"Sorry for suggesting then... you told me to let it out, right? I want to get you high and have my way with you. You've matured so much. It's hard not to find you attractive." Mya pinches my cheek.

"Haha, at least you're honest. I don't want to look at you that way. I mean, you're a whole woman." I tried my best to look at Mya like a sister.

"I know I make your relationship hard. I never imagined I could be jealous of a girl like Margot for anything. I never imagined being remotely attracted to you. I don't mind experimenting with you two. We could try hanging out altogether some time." Mya nobly offer.

intentions of trying to be your friend. She doesn't like you. I don't even want to put you or her in that situation because it wouldn't end well." I admit patting Mya on the shoulder.

"How do you do it? How do you put up with her?" Mya groaned, "At least I don't feel bad anymore."

"You want the truth? My sense of self-worth is wrapped up in wanting a real relationship. Actions align behind a goal. I want a real monogamous long-term relationship. As far as how I pray a lot, I meditate, I usually have to walk away, or I go berserk. I don't think I'm handling it well at all. I just want it to work because I want a relationship." I rub my neck.

"I think she wants to own you, not love you. Do you know the difference?" Mya asks me.

"Nope, I have no idea, and I just figured it's what women are like." I shrugged.

"This is why sexism hurts chauvinists the most. Love is supposed to be liberty. Having trust in your partner enough to let them be free and spread their wings. Having faith, they'll return. If not, then it's possession, jealousy, starting random fights, and ignoring your emotions." Mya edifies me, spitting knowledge at me.

"So, there's no middle ground?" I ask skeptically.

"Do you want to make Margot your ideal middle ground? If that's what you think of us as women, then we're all done for,

haven't found a middle ground with her, and she isn't looking for one with you. She- I won't keep talking about your relationship. Can you walk me back to my place? We could smoke more, and you can crash on the beanbag couch again. My roomie has a console. Let's stick together today, please?" Mya wraps her arms around my arm.

"Sure, let's do it." I toss my freehand up in the air.

Mya grins as she rushes to pack my things then takes off running in front of me. She waved my bag over her head, wanting me to chase her. I took a running start before vaulting over the trash can, leaping onto the railing, then running across it, rounding off onto the pavements in front of her. I could hear her heart pounding as I approached. Her smile widened as she played defense with my bag then took off once more in the opposite direction.

Mya laughed up a storm running ahead of me at a brisk pace for a girl in a sundress, but she wore trainers. We played cat and mouse for half a mile before it loses its fun.

"Dammit, Mya, stop running!" I bark out, stomping my foot.

"Geez, we're almost there. Are you tired?" she nudges me in the stomach.

"I'm tired of running after you! For what reason other than your entertainment? You crazy out your face if you think

and calm down!" I snatch my bag from her, which she finds uncontrollably funny.

"Ha, you couldn't catch me. Weren't you some athlete?"

"I was a freakin' mask. I ran rooftops and fought crime, hashtag *not the one*. Stop playing games, and let's get going."

Mya stared at me, biting her lip. She clenched her fist a few times then let it go.

"You're so lucky that makes me want to sit on your face. You're so lucky, or else I would fight you. Raising your voice at me like you lost your mind. I wish you would!" Mya jabbed me in the chest.

"You need to calm yourself down." I grab her up before she runs off with my bag again.

"Yeah?" Mya asks, giving up her resistance, "You sure you're not trying to sneak a feel? Maybe you need to calm down?"

"I'm not the one running like a lunatic! Don't try to flip it on me, Mya. Give me your hand. I gotta treat you like you're my daughter or something." I say, grabbing her hand and throwing my bag over my shoulder.

"You need to work harder than that if you want me to call you daddy. I can walk myself, Chris, thank you very much." she snatches her hand away.

ahead of her. Mya rolls her eyes and walks after me. She hopped, skipped, and jumped to catch up with me. We took it slow. We were listening to the music still playing from my cellphone. The commotion of the campus concealed us as our hands found the others once more. We were lacing our fingers, refusing to look at each other as we savored the fantasy of what if?

Moving out was an in-between situation. Bradley and I signed a 2-year contract giving me a lower rate of 50% of the monthly rent. We had to postpone our meeting due to a series of inconveniences, but he dropped knowledge in the office whenever we had a moment to invest. I had a few items delivered to the new spot, happy to finally make enough to replace some of my clothes and furniture. With the amount of money I made and saved, I was sitting on a lovely nest egg despite my investing money.

Still, I stayed on the low with my finances and fame. Whenever people ask about the Bass solo or Jared, I simply offer to introduce them. Jared loved telling the story. I loved my memories of it. The tour was over a year ago. It seemed distant. The Somber Nights were healed and better than ever. Maybe thanks to me, but ultimately, I made friends. I still need to find my pathway. Each member of the Nights had their own thing outside the band.

Jared was a Guardian of the Multiverse with amazing mind-control and aerokinetic powers. Jax owned a line of gourmet bakeries around Gaia. Miranda had a radio station and the size of a plantation. I was a student apparently at odds with the establishment. I don't know. I want to be more than just difficult to deal with or understand.

The freedom from my dorm was short-lived once Margot got my new phone number, a copy of my key then made herself at home in my dorm. All my belongings were in my dorm, and my empty apartment was paid off for two months. I had ten texts and more coming by the second. I was beyond angry, but I've reached a point of no true return. She's shown me in every possible way she doesn't want to get her life together nor respect me. Everyone has their past and their issues. However, it's hard to get over. You would think after two years, there would have been a progression. Nothing but drama, and fighting, felt a little different since the *breakup*. In Margot's words, she would decide when the relationship was over.

There was only lost bickering with Margot. I still have to move out of my things, find a roommate, and figure out my love life. I could use her help, but it felt like she preferred being an obstacle. Perspective is everything, and I feel like I'm in the wrong seat. I can't see outside my situation. I don't know what this looks like to others. I feel like I put so much faith in Margot, so much hope, but she had a different perspective entirely.

"Hey, you heading home, Torjin?"

had worked a double and felt exhausted. I closed on seven leases my first shift and another four during my night shift. I needed to be present in this place. Margot was a distraction at this point. I needed to stop dealing with women in general. Take some time to figure out what I can do with everything sitting on my mind.

"My last name is Tor'juuuuuun. Tour je Uuuuuu nen." I sound out.

"Okay, Chris... is that better? I didn't mean to mess up your name." she giggles.

"I'm used to it. It's not you. It's just the repetition. It's the repetition that bothers me, not her, huh? That's interesting." I sat back, rubbing my chin as I began thinking about my relationship.

"Excuse me, are you talking to me?" Opal asked.

"Huh?" I blinked as confused as ever.

"Where are you, Chris? You're acting like a nut." Opal sighed, being extremely patient and forgiving with me.

"I'm going through a few things," I mutter.

"Well, we're friends. I didn't know anything was going on. What's up?" Opal asks.

I stared at Opal for a moment as my stream of consciousness ran wild in my mind.

Margot was in my dorm waiting like a bat out of hell. I haven't even seen the texts, but I knew it was trouble. I also knew Opal had a crush on me through a mutual friend, Mya Harik. I always worked or been with Margot. Before dating Margot, I was infamously preoccupied with drugs and female attention. Drugs never gave me what sex did.

My first real relationship showed me the difference between love and lust. The true understanding and support that true love gave. I was immature and unaware of my flaws, as was Giulia. My relationships were my attempts to create some feeling I thought I should feel. A true partnership between love and joy was never created. It isn't cells being sanitized and reconstructed in a laboratory petri dish. Nor was it cake and ice cream every night or even candlelit dinners once a week. After dating Margot, I realize all I want is to be truly understood, for my good and bad. Not accepted and cherished for my flaws. Someone who knows they're there and knows I'm working on them. I'm tired of my past life being used as a gun pressed to my temple.

Margot was my infatuation, but I'm not sure I can go home to her again unless I love her. Do I? Have all these relationships, heartbreaks, one-night stands, and rejection made me numb?

Here, likely the most beautiful melanated woman I've met stood before me—the last two people in the office. I was struggling to leave a relationship I felt so deeply invested in. I'm

this point. Even my girlfriend was exhausted. We fought ourselves in the reflection of the other. I've seen it too long, too many times, with too many different women. All ends the same. Smiles, hugs, and find fun elsewhere.

"Chris..." Opal sighed.

"I'm sorry, there's a lot on my mind. I don't think I'm mentally available right now." I sigh, rubbing my neck.

"Well, we're alone. It leaves another option, ya know?"

She giggles as she shuts the office shutters. Opal began locking the doors with a skip in her walk. Her eyes kept glancing at me.

"I've been waiting all night to get you alone. Let's celebrate your new apartment. Do you have furniture yet?" Opal rubbed my cheek.

"Opal, you need to chill on all that. I have a girlfriend. I'm sorry, I'm an introvert, and that's probably the biggest issue my girlfriend has with me. There's a lot I need to work on and get over. I'm not dragging someone else into my drama." I raise my hands, not about to go into details about my situation.

"Yeah, whatever, now you have a girlfriend. Maybe someone is trying to save you from Margot?"

"The only person who can save me is me, if not me, then God. No woman can save me. And no man will help outside of what's needed. I just need to be left alone."

saying.

I grew irritated being laughed at, and It's one thing to be yelled at or fought with. It's very different from being laughed at and mocked. Neither was an option I would bother with a new relationship. I'm not sure I can go home to anyone. I don't take myself too seriously, but I can't stand being seen as some joke. Especially not by someone who wants to *love* me.

"You're so intense, Chris. You need to calm down."

I smiled, "Thanks for the dose of reality."

"What?"

"Opal, I have a really bad relationship, but I'm a reason it's bad. I get you to want to 'save' me but regardless, you can't save me from myself. My girlfriend deserves major credit for putting up with me as well."

"You're so intense, Chris..." she didn't care or understand.

I blame Mya for that. She's always filling this girl's head with the fantasy that Margot and I will break up any day for any reason. For the entirety of my relationship! I felt so deeply invested in this relationship, waiting every day on my ROI. We were supposed to get married. I could have tried to make it work instead of walking out on her. I'm supposed to be the leader. Not a whisky wispy stoner slumped, going through the motions. I failed. I'm not ready to fail again.

infectious laughter, warming me up slowly from the inside.

"I would like to know what on Gaia you have planned with me!" I raise an eyebrow.

"Well, I've been telling my friend Mya how much I like you. She told me I should go for it. I think we would be a good match. We have great chemistry." Opal was encircling me, licking her lips like a starving she-wolf.

"Why are you and Mya talking about me?" I inched along with the desk, creating an escape route.

"We're fans... You're not even trying to recreate our fantasies of you. You were supposed to be my office boo. This is our moment, carpe diem. It's like you're in space 24/7. I don't get it at all!"

"Yeah, me neither..."

How could two people so different sound so similar?

"That's why you're so attractive, you know? I feel so comfortable telling you. I just know despite your objections to my proposal, you're listening to me. That's so rare. I'm heading to get a few drinks with Mya. You want to come?" Opal swirled up to me with the grace of a ballerina throwing herself in my arms.

"I have to catch a bus or an uber home." I catch her and let her bounce back to the balls of her feet.

back and finally see your new apartment." She took out her cellphone, pressing play and setting her phone on the desk.

"I made a playlist for tonight." Opal smiles deviously.

"When did you find out we were scheduled together? I usually work this shift alone..." I began putting the pieces together in my head.

Opal's smiled faded into a look of pure determination. Something the military taught her was never to accept defeat. I wasn't looking to lose. She didn't know how to take losing.

"I can walk too. I want to get off my feet and rest up. I still need to study and-

"We weren't scheduled together. You see, I asked Bradley to schedule you and Terrance together on Saturdays. Using the logic that Terrance is the only one who knows how to clean the pool. Bradley agreed. Terrance leaves for home every weekend to visit his girlfriend. So, guess what happens when Terrance finds out he's working every single Saturday until next month?"

"He comes to you...."

"He comes to me! Hey..."

"What?"

"Dude... I'm doing this okay. You sit there, be handsome and delectable. Mama's rewarding herself for a job well done. Months of acting like I don't even know you all in this office paying off at once! Every Saturday, this will be our closing

the lights, close the shutters, lock the door, blow Opal's back out, turn off the TVs, then exit out the back, understand?"

"I like how you sprinkled it in there," I say wearily.

"Mya and Margot don't get along at all. You know going back to Margot wasn't a good idea. You don't think it's a good idea. So, you've been single in reality. Let's keep that streak going. Let's celebrate!"

"Mya has no jurisdiction over my love life, nor do you. I am not back together with Margot. It's just confusing. Mind your business. Let's keep our pants on, and you go catch up with Mya. I need to figure out how to finish moving." I had so much on my mind to think about now.

"I've been cool with Mya since we got to college. It'll never be like that between you two. You'll never have to decide between us."

"I'm too sensitive to be with Mya. She's mean. One of the most insensitive women I've met. Now, I know she tells my business to other people." I smack my face. I can't believe I let Mya even get so close to me, to think I trusted her.

"Ha, she's a mama bear. She's super sweet-

"I'm aware. Sometimes being nice isn't enough." I sigh, trying to keep my emotions distant.

Mya told me everything you wanted. I fit your description perfectly."

"What do you want from me, Opal? You can have all the feelings you want for me. I still can't reciprocate them. I don't want a relationship with anyone right now. I haven't even really had sex in a while, so I can't promise good results. I've been focused on myself lately. Not to be selfish but to heal. It's been a silent and serene summer. I don't know what I can do for you outside of friendship, honestly."

"Well, since you ask. I haven't gotten around like you or Mya. I haven't dated in a while, so I understand. I only want a kiss." Opal shrugs, raising her hands in the air.

"You already told me your plans for me as your office husband. Opal, a kiss gets consistent and usually leads to some sex. I've played that fool already, today I am only pennywise and a quarter-pound foolish."

Opal cut her eyes at me as if I shot an arrow straight through her long-term intentions. She rolled her eyes, crossing her arms over her chest. Opal was pouting as if all her options ran out. I knew what came next and was prepared as tears fell from her eyes.

"I just completely put myself out there for you! I offered myself trusting you. Now, I feel like some cheap slut! I bet you're used to this!" She turned her tears to anger.

Before I knew it, I was arguing with a woman who isn't even my girlfriend about being faithful. I sighed, the worst thing I could have done.

"YOU DON'T EVEN CARE, DO YOU!?" Opal explodes.

"I do, I do. Please trust me. I care. I must have misspoken by being silent. I do, I do. I'm trying to do the right thing. I do see what your soul has brought you. And I'm flattered a good friend like Mya saw you're perfect for me. But I'm not ready for a relationship! And I'm always going to try to work it out until it's over. That's how I'm wired. I want what my grandparents had." I hold up my hands, slowly approaching Opal.

"She doesn't appreciate you at all! You know that isn't what Margot wants from you!" Her bag was clutched to wield like a Morningstar.

"Her grandparents never had what my grandparents had, neither did her parents. She's never seen a good relationship in her life. I'm not everything you think I am or want me to be. It wouldn't last between us. I need more time for myself!" I try explaining to an emotional wall of water, and the tidal wave recedes. The undertow had me by my legs, unable to escape before drowning in the torrential volitions of a young adult woman.

"Yes, you are, but your self-esteem is too low to see what you want and need is right here on a silver platter, in front of

now, when are you going to settle? You want to go home and have some makeup sex with her! Couldn't you even consider a date with a friend? You can't hang out with me without sex?"

I frown and shake my head, "I'm sorry, I didn't say any of that. You did. I don't confirm any accuracy in what you're saying. I'm not there yet, period. I don't want to disrespect my relationship by rushing along. I don't need attention. I need my peace of mind and some silence. I'm trying to be nice to you. We've been friends for a while, for sure, but I have never had a one-on-one about my relationship with you. Bite your tongue on it before your mouth cuts the bridge. There's nothing you can offer me I don't have within myself."

"A woman is supposed to be complimentary with her man, not in competition. There are plenty of areas I can help you in. Including pointing out, you say you're trying to be nice, then put in no effort to be nice. You're a heartless man." She wiped her eyes.

"Yeah... I guess that's why I'm better off alone, right?" I clutch my knapsack feeling a strange surge of sadness.

"Chris... I- I understand. The last thing you deserve to be is alone. I- I respect your relationship, okay? And when we do eventually date and get married. I rather see how hard you worked to fix those things, so I don't have to deal with Margot than her be some reoccurring issue. Get your closure and find

to say on the issue.

"I don't need closure. I'm going to make things work out." I grit my teeth.

"Is she?" She giggles, "I'm sorry. I couldn't resist."

"Thanks... I think being alone is a personal choice rather than a necessity. I'm going to walk back to my dorm, get my things, and figure out the rest." I start to walk.

"If you're going back to campus anyway, you might as well come. At least get a ride." Opal suggests.

"Just a ride turns to just a kiss. That turns into sex. I don't feel like being around people today." I shrug, knowing the game better than most.

"Chris, that's exactly why you shouldn't be alone. Don't you understand?" Opal says sternly, "Mya wouldn't forgive me if I knew something was wrong with you and I didn't bring you to her immediately. You know that. At least get a good time in before you go home."

"Whatever..." I bit my tongue thinking about dealing with Margot and Mya, angry I rather live alone. History teaches most wars are lost fighting on too many fronts.

Opal smiles, "Let's go. I'm meeting her at a friend's."

"Where would you be taking me?" I inquire, crossing my arms over my chest.

Village," Opal said coyly.

"So, we can walk there?"

"Well, no, because someone else signed a lease here, so we're taking the party elsewhere." Opal sighed.

"Who could be so bad you're not going to celebrate where you live? Why doesn't everyone go to your apartment?"

"Well, I didn't realize who you were dating until I closed on her lease. Her roommate came in and brought in the two leases. I had no idea, I swear to you." Opal sighed.

"What? When did she move here?" I cut my eyes, remembering a good number of Opal's signings. I would know if one of her friends moved in, especially Margot.

"All my girlfriends moved her after I started working. I dropped a few folders off with a lease tucked inside during one of our paint n sips. Discounted rent, plus I get a signing bonus. It's like winning twice. Most of us did that. I guess word got around if you had the green, you could send a lease in, and she took advantage."

"I don't have friends," I state, satisfied and at peace.

"How could you talk like that? First off, I'm your friend."

"You are Mya's friend, and I'm friends with Mya. We don't talk alone or on the phone."

"I would be open to it. We don't because you act like I don't exist. You feel entitled to sex. Like it's always there waiting

you're blasé at best. I'm a good woman, and I offered to take this all away from you. You don't want friends."

I grinned at her deduction. It's not that I don't want friends, I don't want fake friends, and those are far more plentiful than real ones. Suppose it came down to be popular amongst sycophants or being alone. Well, it's clear which side of the fence I sit on in my kayak built for one.

"Ooh, I caught you!! I knew it!"

"Don't sound too proud. What type of man do you think I am?"

"Well... I heard you were a pimp and a player." Opal shrugged offhandedly.

"I'm in recovery. What type of man do you think I am NOW! What type of man do you see me becoming? I want kids one day. I might have a daughter. I can't raise her with the ideas I learned in college. I don't want a woman who only sees today and herself. I need someone to match my vision."

Opal gleamed with adoration, "You're so intense, Chris."

It sounded flattering for once in my life.

There was no doubting Opal was genuine. She wasn't hurt by this world or rejected by it. She was at home living her dream. Enjoying her day and life, she didn't need to recover. I'm sure she has her stresses and struggles that I couldn't endure. Military life is not a joke.

peace, not someone else's.

"I'll come. I want to see Mya and tell her to stop having those conversations about me."

Opal smiles innocently, "Oh, that wouldn't help much. She's the one who tries to dissuade us from a recurring conversation. She always has your back."

I learned not to touch the subject with a twenty-foot pole. Mya tells me so much of my girlfriend and vice versa, but they never really knew each other. It was difficult for me to entertain either of them, just spewing hatred about two women I loved so much. I guess that's what bothered both, how strongly I felt for the other. My relationship with Mya creates a rift whenever I speak to her. Mya has lost many boyfriends under them speculating me, and she had been involved on the low. I don't know. We're friends. I never wanted to ruin the friendship. She never wanted to date me, ha.

"I'm sorry to hear about your relationship. You should try being more tender with her. Maybe she won't fight you as much if you show you love her. Being so intense is very intimidating, intoxicating but intimidating." Opal sighed, beginning to move for the door with me in tow, "I don't know. Mya is the only one you ever seem to be yourself around. I want

and passion with us."

"We both deserve better."

"Um... well, we can build better. Gotta start somewhere, where we're at is always nice."

"You're very persistent..." I rub my neck, not wanting to start another fight.

"You can't have faith without persistence." She started schooling me. "I respect your relationship until you're officially single. Then I expect to be first in line after your period of solitude."

Why do these women keep predicting my downfall rather than my success? As if my success is contingent on being with them. Or is the end of my relationship so apparent to everyone but me? Am I the only one who believes things with Margot and me can work?

Opal holds out her hand, and she waited for my agreement for the end of my relationship.

"I can't shake on that but-

"Kiss me on it. We never have to tell Mya or Margot." Her severity caught me off guard, matching my own as if we both knew it was the only way.

I asked to see what the outside looking in felt like. I was a lamb tied for the sacrifice on Margot's pyre, and everyone smelled the home cooking.

staring dead in my eyes.

"That's still cheating, Opal. I don't want to be that man anymore!"

"It'll be a secret." She reassures.

"I hate secrets... I'm too sensitive. They just torture me. If it's not one of my secrets, then sure-

"Then it'll be my secret. Mya won't let any of us date you without informing the others, so kissing risks a lot for me. It's not just a kiss. It'll be a secret."

"Opal, you keep looking for these loopholes, but regardless it's wrong. And if I were your man, you wouldn't understand me telling you I was kissing other chicks. And I would be hurt if you went behind my back kissing other men! I had enough of those secrets and schemes. I want something sacred, not secret."

"That's why you're so obstinate? It's not like you're happy in your relationship Chris. It's not cheating if you're unhappy. You're scouting."

"If I broke up with a girl, I would hope she would wait a while and find real love. I would be crushed if she already had a new man set up."

"Where was this morality your freshman year?" Opal sucked her teeth, picking up the pace again, "I respect your wisdom."

"Can we be friends?"

"So, this is what the friend zone feels like..." Opal sighed, being extremely patient and forgiving with me. "Talk about unrequited love. You're so cold, Chris. I'm sorry for whoever hurt you."

"It's always been like this." I clicked my tongue, alerting her of an "out-of-order" sign on the door.

"We make a really good team, Chris."

"Then we're Teammates, great." I smile.

"Okay, okay... no, I meant partners. Well, whatever. I'm happy your curve game is so strong."

"Why did I agree to this crap?" I groaned.

"I CAN'T WAIT TO TELL OUR KIDS ABOUT THIS. True love always prevails! Only if you and Margot work out, then I'll know I wasn't supposed to have you. However, if for any reason you try to date some other woman, I would never forgive you."

"So I either work things out with Margot, or I date you?" I scratch my head.

"Or you can be alone... But it's better to date me." Opal rolled her eyes, "I truly can love you."

"I heard you the first twenty times." I groan.

Opal turns to me as if her hand was trailing to swat the taste out my mouth. She stared me deep into my eyes. Her brown eyes matched my severity, cutting through my very soul.

happiness, then others wouldn't have to pick up the slack. You're responsible for making you healthy and happy. Staying in your relationship out of pride will not bring you any closer to stability and success. Do you understand?"

"I wanted to be a husband since I was ten. I thought Margot was the woman I wanted to marry. I've been faithful, and I've been improving. I worked hard for my relationship. I had to let it all go. I am not trying to be cold. That's how it feels to lose someone you love."

"Baby Boy, I know. It's painfully obvious. But the keyword is painful. She's killing you, man. And the way you're acting isn't healthy. She isn't the one for you." Opal said plaintively.

My lip twitched as the glum grimace settled on my face, faced with the realization I'm blocked by myself. My ambition and aspiration superseded my reality. I would have to wait a lifetime for Margot to become the woman I saw her potential within. I didn't intend on waiting a lifetime to become the greatest man I could be. I wanted to start now and enjoy a life of significance. I've been working so hard to bring my dreams to manifestation. Margot is always so far from her mark, blaming anything but Margot for it.

"I love your vision and you. I'll learn to respect you. Just kiss me, Chris. At least know where you left your heart."

thing I want is a new girlfriend. I'm going to marry Margot, or I'm going to live alone. There's no in-between." A tear fell down my eyes.

I quickly wiped my face and looked away.

Opal smiles innocently and grabs my arm, leading me to the elevator. She rests her head on my arm. She's so soft and warm. Her perfume was floral with myrrh. I didn't need to kiss her to know how good she could be for me. All she had to do was stand by my side. The elevator shaft opened, and Opal led us inside.

I reached for the first-floor button after the shaft closed. Opal stopped my hand, slowly approaching me. She looked up, kissing me as she worked at my belt. Her perfume filled my nose. I reached for her waist, pushing her aside. Opal stared at me with renewed determination. She wagged her finger-licking her lips as she displayed her rich curves.

I pressed her against the wall. She moved on her toes, wrapping a leg around me. Her hand held my manhood, rubbing it so gently with her palm and fingers. She moaned quietly in my ear as I kissed her neck, grabbing two handfuls of her beautiful butt.

My cock hardened to her touch. I was sobered from my lusts as she stared at me with the same offering and wanting as so many other women. She shuddered to my touch, like

Her juices had their rich scent. A tropical sweetness sat on my tongue to her scent alone.

"So, you changed your mind?" She giggles.

"Maybe..." Or just experience kept bringing me back to the same point with women. "I... I'm sorry."

"Excuse me?" Opal says sternly, "We are not stopping."

"We already went too far."

"She'll be just as mad you kissed me as if you let me have my fun. Let's at least enjoy ourselves."

"Opal, that's been your logic this whole time?"

She shoves me away, fixing her skirt and crossing her hands. "My lipstick is all over you." She handed me a few napkins from her purse. "You're a good kisser."

"I've heard. I want to be appreciated for more than my body, though. I want to be appreciated for far more than money or anything material. I truly want to be respected for who I am and what I do. I'm not sure I'll get that from any woman today. I already made my decision between Margot and the infinite. I rather enjoy being alone."

"I understand..." Opal rolled her eyes, crossing her arms over her voluptuous breasts, squeezing them together before me.

I grabbed her waist, pulling her back over. She giggles, not understanding what I wanted, nor did I. Her body was so was developed and shaped like a real woman. I let her go relenting, repenting, and regretting the past few minutes.

Opal turns to me, rubbing my cheek.

"I can see you're very confused as to what you want. I want to be angry at you, but you tried warning me. You're completely right. You are Margot's, and I should have respected your relationship instead of tempting you. Now, I see what you meant. I respect it and forgive you. I hope you forgive me, and we can honestly just be friends."

"I have to think about it, Opal."

"I was teasing you. Can we kiss until we get to the car?" Opal tugs roughly at my collar, "I know you'll find something to tell her. I get you're trying to become a better man. I know you have a lot of experience with this, and I know you'll find something redeemable about love with me. Why not just finish?"

"Because there's a world difference between love and joy, and that's the difference between coitus and conversation. I rather limit my lies and regrets. I'm not that man anymore. You honestly just keep pressing me!" I raise my hands. "You're an incredibly attractive woman, Opal. I'm only human. Can you please stop?"

"Stop me." Opal smiles innocently.

Her bright smile shows she was brimming with confidence. She moved back for my crotch, and I didn't even

listening to my heartbeat as she ran her fingers softly along with my hard-on. She looked me in the eyes as both her hands began stroking.

"It's so much bigger than I thought. Like thicker." She started moving her hands faster. Her grip tightened as moans left her lips. "You're completely different than the first guy I dated. You're so relaxed."

"A hand job isn't too much for me."

"Do you want me to suck it?" Opal's jaw dropped.

"I wanted you to let me leave with my willpower and my dignity, but I can't stop you. I am not strong enough to resist a woman as beautiful as you. I wanted to be a different man, but I guess I'm no different than I before. I guess I was lying to myself the whole time." I frowned.

"Every time I start getting what I want from you, you make me feel so bad about it." Opal sighed, beginning to slow down, "my ex would have been excited if I even touched his penis over his briefs. You're so jaded."

"Ha, then you should leave me alone, but that does feel too good." I submit, unable to pretend anymore.

"You like it?" She was curious, "I've only ever done this for James. He wasn't as big as you or cold. I think sex would be different too."

after you." I elucidate.

Opal looked up and kissed me. "I meant because you're so big. You would split me open like a cantaloupe. I don't mind doing this when you need it. You've been adamant about it, but you're stressed out regardless. I could at least help you out when you're single right?"

"This is a one-time thing. We're never even speaking about it again. You said it's a secret. I cannot do this ever again. I cannot be this man anymore." I declare.

"That's fine with me... as long as you promise we can do more when you're feeling better."

"I'll always be friends with Mya, so... I guess you're not going anywhere."

"You're like a rock." Opal groans waving me away.

"I guess that's all I ever will be to women, a hard rock, a wounded heart, and a will to break."

Opal rolls her eyes, not letting me go after all, "So much it spilled over in your ego, I see, do you have to be so sad about me getting what I want? Why can't you view this as mutually beneficial?"

I couldn't even look Opal in the eyes, my lip quivered, and my heart sank. It's not as if Margot was the most loyal. For some reason, me giving up the life of being a gigolo felt right. It felt right to be faithful. It felt good to know no matter how terrible

balance, guidance, and leadership, but now there was nothing left at all. What could I ever tell Margot about me hanging out with Mya or Opal again? I can't even face Opal. How would I ever go back to Margot now?

"It's the first floor!" Opal abruptly turns her back to me, giving the cover and time to put myself away. "Are you all covered up?"

"I'm decent again," I muttered.

"Good sounds great!" She claps her hands, bending down for her purse pressing her butt against my waist as the elevator begins to close again.

"No, no, no!" I stick my hand in the door, and it begins opening back up.

"Haha, sorry, I like seeing how far I can go." Opal giggled.

"You're trouble."

"I don't want to be. I expected you to be into this, Chris. I didn't mean to disappoint you."

"I am into it. I'm only human. You're beyond beautiful, Opal. It was incredible, but I keep telling you-

"You're not ready. I see you're not just trying to brush me off or play coy. I didn't know you were so serious. When you are mine, I'll know I can completely trust you." Opal pats my chest, "You're not even trying now, and you're still a good man. Others would be exuberant to be all over me or to cheat. I didn't know

admirable, but regardless this only strengthens my crush." Opal grins, "now let's go!"

"You're trouble, Opal."

"I'm your future!"

"I still don't think you heard a word I said!" I call after her as she picks up her pace toward the parking garage.

I stopped heading to clubs as soon as I started drinking. I believed we were going to this lounge, none too far from campus the girls frequented—good enough food but more a meeting place. Josephine's is a beautiful Nadian restaurant from Graham spread to a stellar location in New Haven. Opal turned right past Josephine's and kept driving. I turned to her in shock as she smiled, taking a glance at me. She kept peeking at me whenever she got a glimpse.

"You should focus on the road," I comment.

"I keep checking to see if you're still handsome." She smirks, "You are, don't worry."

"Shut up..." I mutter.

"Mr. Grumpy, why are you acting so mean?" She giggles.

"I am not. I just have to find a way to explain this to Margot."

"Tell her you found someone better, and Margot should be on her ps and qs before she loses you. Simple enough for me to explain." Opal groaned, "we could have at least enjoyed ourselves if you're gonna bother feeling this guilty."

"If I did more, I wouldn't be able even to look myself in the mirror. I love Margot."

functionality. We could-

"Opal, I don't care what could be right now. I want what I have to work out! Can you lay off it!? I want to be faithful."

Opal rolls her eyes, "raise your voice at me in my car again. Lucky, we're going to get married eventually."

I scrunch up my face turning away from Opal. It was all some joke to her. I imagine she and Mya thought my relationship was long over. My pride wanted me to fight to prove them wrong. Mya's been a good friend, never made a move on me, gender never mattered, and we just get each other. We were always honest with each other. If she says it's over and she's trying to get Opal or all women with me. She must have been right.

We drove up to a huge house about three stories, likely twenty rooms with a huge amount of acreage. It looked like paradise on earth.

"Our girl Eliza lives here. She just broke into the fashion industry, and everything she designs sells. They're about to start a movie about her." Opal says with a bit of swagger and smugness. "We've known each other forever. We always knew she would be successful. Everything she touches turns to gold."

"Who else is here?"

"It's just the four of us. Why?"

"Margot won't like this at all."

You're already one foot out the door. You even have a bag packed. You might drop off this and end up with Eliza tonight." She rolls her eyes, "stop acting as you care so much."

"I'm sad because I do care. I just don't show it like most people. I don't do the whole emotional thing."

"You brood and brood and brood then act like you're not sensitive. Cheer up, please. Even if you're going to stay in your relationship, acting like this must kill her inside. I'm not even dating you, and it hurts to see you this sad. It physically hurts me. Please act like you're happy about hanging out with three beautiful women, k?" Opal gives me one last kiss before she turns off her car.

"I told you would be kissing me all the time now!"

She claps her hands.

"Here... You need this more than me." She slaps a gram in my hand with a pair of wraps. "This is my gift as your future girlfriend. Eliza has a bunch more. That was for me tonight and you if you wanted to come home with me. You're going to wear yourself out being so grumpy. So it's for you now. Enjoy."

"Gee, thanks!" I genuinely smile, "there are so many places to spark up here."

Opal giggles, "You're so easy to please."

"Sometimes, I have ridiculously high standards."

flinch. If I knew all I had to do was give you some weed, I could have saved myself the embarrassment. That's why you and Mya get along. Y'all smoke instead of sex."

"I knew Mya before I smoked..." I began but let it go, "What are you trying to say?"

"I'm trying to figure out why you're not trying to smash. I'm better than most girls you've been with, and now you're in this crappy relationship. I expected some more attention, Chris."

"I- Have- A- Guuurl- Friiiiend!!" I sound out for her, "If I were your man, you would appreciate this curve game."

"I do..." Opal rolls her eyes, "it's just so hard to accept. I get what Mya meant now."

"What!? Mya does not feel that way about me!" I was shocked.

"You won't let her. Liking you hurts. You're so focused on dumb things and dumb people. You won't even look in our direction the way you look at those hoes." Opal rolled her eyes as we approached the door, "you are the picture next to unrequited love. I feel bad for Margot, just a wee little bit. It must be hard to get a guy like you to commit. I can't imagine what it takes to keep a man like you faithful. Does she pay you?"

"What?"

"You're in a laboratory of your mind like all day. You act as if you don't even really see people. I'm not sure what to tell

must be hard to get used to someone being so distant if you could ever get used to it. High standards, abstract critical thought, you're lazy and talk to a lot of chicks. That's scary, bro."

"You think she's scared of me?"

"Well, I don't know your relationship like that, but it intimidates me. You being lazy just pisses me off though, try not to waste your potential."

"I'm not lazy."

"Okay, Mr. Three Hour lunch break comes back smelling like weed and beer." Opal rings the doorbell.

"For your information Ms. Opal Fulani Badu, Brad gave me a three-day vacation, and I came into work regardless."

Opal smiles, "I like intimidating. Just keep your hands to yourself because you have a temper, and I have mace. You make me want to be better. I think it's a lot of pressure on your girl."

"Gee, thanks, Opal."

"Do all you can for her, rest up for what was it a year or two? Then we're getting married." Opal says with confidence and poise.

The oak French doors swung open at the hands of a young woman barely taller than 5 feet in a purple silk dress with a long train of flowers. She wore three-inch royal blue heels. She looked older than twelve, but I knew Eliza had to be at least 22, natural beauty with skin darker than an eclipse. A tropical

the Mayan beaches.

"Daaaarrrling!" Eliza opened her arms to Opal, hugging her in close, "Hey, gurl!"

Eliza looked at me a bit confused, struggling to find words. I knew of her but was never too close to her. She was one of the friends Mya knew before we had met. Opal usually floated with the group, but Eliza did her own thing. She was quite successful.

I muttered, "she probably didn't think I was going to come."

"Which you weren't if I didn't force you!" Opal nudges me, "he was going to sit in the house and pout all day about Margot. We were both stags, so I invited him with me. Neither of us heard from Mya. Is she here?"

I caught Eliza's look of despondence out the corner of my eye. My shoulders dropped, and I buried my hands in my pants. I fixed my mouth to say I would go realizing there was nowhere to run for miles. I took in a deep breath, staring up at the ceiling, trying to think of the polite time to beeline to the tree line.

"Stop slouching!" Opal jabs me in the hip, "where's the food? I'm starving!" Opal grabs my arm.

"Oh, everything is in the kitchen. There are some beers outside on the patio and a bit of wine." Eliza opens her arms to Opal, "you look better every time I see you!"

you look beautiful. Is this your design?"

"No! Get this, a girl from my class made this for me. She says she had been watching me and liked my figure."

"I bet that'll be creepy if a dude did it." I scoff.

"Not if he looked like you. It'll be awkward, but I would let you try a comeback before I called The Regime on you." Eliza extends a hand to me.

"I'll find a way back to the city if you were gonna ruin my night up with that nonsense."

"I wouldn't call The Regime on a Nadian. You're rare. I would never be able to live with myself if I was responsible for you being hurt. I'm sorry, it was a bad joke." Eliza squeezed my hand with her secondhand.

"I'm chill."

"Yeah, he's my office fling. Chris Tor'jun." Opal introduced me far too honestly.

"Oh, hey there, how are you?" Eliza loosened her grip on my hand but wouldn't let it go.

"I'm better than yesterday." I smile uncomfortably, looking at Opal for help.

Opal defends me, "He's enlightened, with enough of that old school misogyny to make him adorable. He's like a grumpy 70-year-old with twenty years of life experience. And again, he's mine."

finger.

"Oh, yes, but we should all know about prior commitments. Shouldn't we, Eliza? Sometimes we agree to be with someone before we're ready. Isn't that right, Eliza?" Opal gently took my arm away.

"I'm gonna go find a place to roll this up," I mutter, leaving the girls.

An instinct told me to find Mya. Instincts got me in this situation. I needed to soften my edge and finally relax. Life was starting to get the best of me. There was no control to be had. I needed to let go and be at peace.

I glanced at my phone to find 25 texts and five missed calls. Magically there were seven voicemails. Margot was always a clever girl. After so many messages, I imagine she found a way to go straight to voicemail to avoid being ignored. Too bad, didn't work. I'm not letting any woman ruin my night ever again.

Eliza and Opal spoke at the door, chatting up a storm until they found me in the living room breaking down the weed.

"You are not smoking that in my living room, and you're apologizing to Opal." Eliza marches up to me with her long train.

My natural inclination for beautiful women gave Eliza my full attention. My dedication to my home of Nadia gave her my respect. I took my time to respond. It may have seemed as

in front of me, deciding to take it easy.

"I thought we weren't speaking about any of this Opal?"

"Why wouldn't I tell her you left me for three hours at work to go smoking and drinking?" Opal rolls her eyes. "You had a job to do."

I don't have time for this crap after all.

I roll up quickly. I was licking the cigarillos sealed.

"Where's Mya?" I ask with a sigh, too well-versed in the ways of angry and volatile women not to tread carefully.

"Back deck..." Eliza pouted when I wouldn't return her emotions nor entertain them. "Chris shares with me. It's my home!"

I bite my tongue, "This is your home. I will share it with you two. But I also need some time to myself before I can socialize. I'll give you one, and I'll take the other one. You need to stop being so aggy. You're not my girlfriend or my mother. I just met you a few months ago."

Eliza and Opal spoke at the same time, "We wanted to smoke with you!"

"What? Why!?"

"He's dim," Eliza mutters.

"When it comes to women, yeah, he's confused." Opal grabbed my collar, "come on, you're just gonna have to be unhappy."

or Margot Hoska?

"Hoska." Opal answers for me.

"You two are still together? Ew! Why would you feel entitled to live in misery like that?" Eliza held her chest, "He passed up Mya for Margot?"

"No, Mya doesn't want him. He passed me up for Margot!" Opal abruptly begins to cry.

"What is going on?" I say, confused to hear her sobbing, "Why are you all so emotional?"

"They all have their little crushes on you. I told them any woman who falls for you was out of her mind. Does anyone want to listen to me?" Mya came to my rescue wearing distressed black jeans, red low-cut chucks, and a white t-shirt. "I warn them all the time to stay away from you. Now, they can see how deranged you make women, and they want you more."

"I do not make women deranged, do I? Was it my fault this entire time?" I asked.

"I thought you and Margot broke up?" Mya asked, "Opal said you looked depressed like a boy who lost his mother. I knew it was Margot drama. Let him be. This boy will drive you over the moon and then move to the sun. Leave Chris Tor'jun alone."

Opal crosses her arms over her chest, "Yeah, Eliza. Back off."

that sign-off from Mya. I'll leave him alone."

"Opal," Mya asks.

"You're not my mother. Let's just smoke. I'm done talking about it to anyone." Opal raised her hands. "Chris, share my weed with us."

"As long as we drop the subject of dating me in my train wreck phase," I sigh, "alright, let's go. I can't wait to check out this deck. Your house is beautiful."

"Ha, it's my parents. They're out of town." Eliza covered her mouth, laughing, "It's alright. Way too much to manage. My dad's getting older, and it's about to get cold."

"I'll help... well, I'll work. It looks like y'all can afford to help a young brotha out." I chuckle, looking around to see spots needing patches or painting. "How's the roof?"

"The hell, I don't go up there." Eliza laughs, "You go from being rude to trying to make a buck?"

"I'm trying to be helpful, and sadly help in a Nakan world requires an exchange of goods and services." I shrug, "I'm not a fan of capitalism either but-

"So, if you're not a fan-

"Y'all will probably pay some North Mayans a mint for this job and the work to be done. All of you will take a loan out to have some Nakans in here. But you want me to do it for free?" I look up, feeling disrespected.

Mya and Opal break out laughing, grabbing me by the arms and taking me to the back deck. Eliza marches behind up, holding her train as she puffs out her chest. She sat across the table from me. Mya and Opal sat to our sides, arranging the ashtray and sparking up a blunt.

Mya took a long pull before Parisian inhaling, her little fancy technique. She always says it doubled the effects. I told her the majority of the THC was already burnt. That's why there's smoke. She told me to stop being a smart aleck. She just likes how fancy it makes her.
I chuckle.

"What's so funny?" Opal asks, beginning to giggle.

Mya looks at me as she takes her second to inhale, beginning to do it again when she starts coughing as she tries not to laugh.

"You're not funny, Chris! Stop thinking about me and get me some water!"

"How'd you know I was thinking about your goofy inhale!?" I laugh even harder as I snap one of the water bottles from their wooden crate.

The families who could afford it had water bottled and shipped from Mayan. It's the cleanest and purest water on the planet, straight from Baat's fountain itself.

be loaded."

"My mother is Mayan. Our cousins and family send it. Not that it's your business." Eliza smiled smugly. "My father is an engineer. My mother does interior design. They both come from money. The house was built 70 years ago, and the land was 100 dollars. Now, the house is worth seven million. We're smart, not rich. You're looking at seven decades of extensions and renovations. And we still own the land for five miles in each direction. We're also very, very to ourselves."

"Why would you come from Maya to Nadia?" Opal asked.

"For your information, this is Ecru. And my family has lived in Ecru since the beginning of time. We are where we have always been. I don't know where all these others came from because this is my home." Eliza slaps the table. "Neither Naka nor Erdu have any power or right to try to steal and claim rights to our homeland."

I applaud in my head, smiling boldly as the blunt came to my hands in the rotation. I closed my eyes and let my body sink as I realized I was in my slice of heaven. Our little kickback, this was the most partying I've done in a year since the party. Good conversation with beautiful women was worth far more than gold or dollars. This is all I needed a blunt and a good view.

I kick back, letting the girls discuss their classes, lives, and ideas. The whole while staring far out into the horizon as

deep wisdom and intuition I very much needed.

"Hey, Chris, I'm heading out. Do you need a ride?" Opal yawned.

I looked over to Eliza and Mya. I was mulling the idea over in my head as to how I wanted to spend my night. Did I want to leave my great time to go home and fight with Margot?

"Can't you hang for a bit?" I pushed.

"Bwoi, I'm tired." Opal groaned.

"You can stay in my dorm." Mya laughs. "My roommate is in Esha. By the way, hashtag squad goals, let's go to Esha sometime. We can travel through Maya. The mountains between Erdu are too big. And she verifies. God's Gulch is real."

I rub my chin, "What's that?"

"Oh, he's from Exigo. He's never heard of it." Eliza raises her hands.

"I was born and raised on an ancient border city. I'm from The Garden. We call the area between Nadia and Esha, Oblivion, the actual name of it. Most people forget they know nothing about Ecru. I spent a lot of time exploring the old halls and the ancient temple city."

"What? The city still exists?" Eliza covered her mouth.

"Yeah... it was like a five-day hiking trip. I ran away from home and spent a week exploring in the woods because my mom got mad. I would I disappear, and she couldn't find me."

"You give every woman who loves you a heart attack. You think it's cute, but it's not. Why the hell were you in the woods? Sit down and watch TV!" Opal abruptly begins poking me in the head.

"Well, I would never have seen the ruins or garden if I didn't explore. I did it all the time. But it's high key illegal. The Nakans and Erduns made it illegal. But ever since that one guy killed all those Rottweilers, they left the towns in the center of Erdu. Most went back to Nadine and Exigo."

"I guess the Brotherhood was effective." Eliza shrugs.

"It wasn't a whisper in the wind." I yawn, "Some say Bryon is still alive. I thought I might have seen him in ruins."

"You were a true Ecru Kid." Mya smiles, "You were so weird freshman year. I get it now. You're what an Ecrun would have been like, well, I guess it if you lived in The Garden. So you're like a real Ecrun, not even a Nadian."

"I guess there's still a lot I need to learn about myself. Well, it's decided. I need a break from my relationship. The emotional exhaustion is too much, and there's still so much to learn. I'm going to make things work as best they can for one more week. Then if they don't improve when I get paid, I'm going to crash on someone's couch until I get my new apartment then live alone for a while."

rebellious hate it. It's best to make it work instead of walking out. However, if you don't plan to marry her, you'll only waste both of your time."

"What's make you say that?" I ask Eliza.

"My dad taught me. He said if a man doesn't intend to marry you, truly spend his life with you. You might have sex or have fun. But you're essentially wasting your time. You're going to break up and have to start over again, or always have that weight on your heart and bind on your soul. It's better to wait because he wishes he waited till he met my mother."

"That's beautiful." Mya coos, "I love that, Eliza."

"Me too... my parents are divorced. I guess that's why I'm better off just waiting until I'm ready for marriage. I had to slow down because I'm not ready even to consider having a kid. I have so much growing left. Finding a good wife would make it easier."

"My parents are a big help. I do have to say that's weird when I hear other people talk about not having parents or being divorced. It's not beneficial to be single. But that's that Nakan culture influence Chris was saying." Eliza waves her hand, doing her best to relate to me.

"I would like to speak to your parents," I say.

Eliza throws up her hands, "They're just going to tell you to go to Rakil. They don't take credit for any of it. I admit I'm a relationship with Rakil or my dad is good."

"Rakil, huh... many people don't believe in Rakil anymore, only Baat, Enshishi, or Anki. I don't remember the last time I had a real conversation or smoked a blunt with a true believer."

"You're one of those atheists?" Eliza scoffed.

"I'm not an atheist! I believe in Jah'Ada, after what happened in Graham with all those Rottweilers. All of Qatar's prophecies came true. I believe in all this, but I guess I practice it differently." I shrug.

"Hmm... my uncle would love you. We have a big party once a month, usually a networking event, mixers, or church gatherings. You should come. Be around some different people." Eliza offers.

"Thank you, Eliza."

"A princess must be generous with her friends, or else she's a witch." Eliza wags her finger.

"Did your dad teach you that too?" Mya asked.

"No, my mom did because I never wanted to share my toys. She would spank me and tell me I would turn into a witch if I didn't learn how to be nice and share." Eliza covered her firetruck red cheeks, "My mom would go crazy if I told her I met you and didn't invite you. Did you take pictures of the ruins? My dad loves stuff like that."

"I was seven. I didn't have a cellphone." I rub my neck.

Mya says in disbelief.

I grin, "Well, it didn't seem so extreme. There are beaten pathways and old roads that go to it. Most animals don't bother you if you don't bother them. And the predators were preoccupied elsewhere or with something with more meat on its bones."

"Were you alone?" Mya leans in further, never having heard the story before tonight.

"Yeah, I never had too many friends when I think about it. I never fit in. I thought I would just live in ruins. Then when my food ran out, I realized I wasn't the survivalist I thought." I shrugged, "I got back safe—a few bruises. Then I got picked up from my grandparents when I got out of school after that until I stopped running off. My grandparents lived even closer to the pathways in The Garden, so I went a few more times when they lost sight of me. By then, I knew the way back and forth to make the trip in a single night by the time my mom or dad came to pick me up."

I yawn once more and much longer starting to get tired.

"Do you want me just to drop you off?" Opal asks, "You don't have to sleep with me. I do have a couch."

I sigh, looking out to the stars.

"WHAT DID MARGOT DO NOW?" Mya hits the table, "We're going over there right now and kicking her door in."

Then she got at me for something. I wasn't listening. My body was on autopilot, and I just packed some clothes and dipped."

"You pack your things on autopilot?" Mya says, disturbed, "I don't remember ever hearing you being happy in this relationship."

"When have I ever just been happy, period, Mya? That's what I mean by I have to be alone. The only thing I learned with all these girls I've been with is no one, and nothing can make me happy but me. And no one can make me successful but me. I might get money and opportunity, etcetera from the external, but the real thing is me."

"Is he high, or is he usually that insightful?" Eliza asked.

"That's why he never speaks. Most people get turned off by the depth. I'm proud of you, Chris. Do your thing and let me know how I can help."

"I'm going to let Mya take you home. Let me know if you need anything." Opal hugs me bye then gives her goodbyes to her girls. "I'll see y'all later. I'm going to be buried in work and projects all week. I expect to see you all Friday for a much-needed trip to Josephine's for drinks."

"I work Friday," I mumble, trying to get out of it before the plans formed.

about you." Opal smiles, pinching my cheek, "I'll see you at work all week. We could do lunch or breakfast sometime."

"Sounds friendly. I like pancakes." I smile, accepting something more my speed.

"I make great pancakes if you wanted to swing by my place before our shift." Opal jumps, "Blueberry or strawberry?"

"Opal, will you leave this crazy boy alone?" Eliza asks, "Please do you a favor."

"I was going to bring him breakfast. He doesn't have to be my man yet." Opal pinches my cheek again.

Mya looked on quietly, uneasily but quietly.

"Bye ladies, see you tomorrow, Chris." Opal heads off to drive back to the city.

"When did you two get so intimate? I thought you had a girlfriend?" Mya steps up to me, poking me in the chest, "already picked your next girlfriend!?"

"Mya, I told her I had a girlfriend, and I just got done telling all my plans. That's all Opal. We've never had any real relationship beyond mutuality to you before today. It's like she smelled blood in the water and came at me like a shark."

"Poor thing likes you a lot. You probably sent her over the edge with all that talk. Once she sets her mind to something, she's resolute. Chris was marked."

eyes, "What the hell happened with you two? I demand you tell me now!"

"Relax, Mya... I'm not worried about any young girl." I sigh, "I still have another rolled. Let's just vibe."

"I need an interlude. This dress is getting uncomfortable." Eliza stands.

"Why don't we just let you go?" I ask.

"Oh no, I want to smoke again. You two can stay here if you want. We have enough rooms for when my family visits." Eliza waves her hands, "and I make amazing pancakes."

"It's up to you, Chris." Mya sighs.

"If we pass out, we pass out. She has more than enough room. Margot didn't feel the need to come home last night. I'm not going to run home."

"Just move into your new apartment...." Mya groans, "How many times do I have to say. You have other places you can go. You're not stuck there."

"You're gonna have her screaming at you longer the later you come home." Mya runs her fingers through her curly fro, "I don't like Margot at all, but you two need to focus on each other if you're ever gonna work."

"Alright, I can already tell I don't want to be a part of this conversation." Eliza raises her hand, "Wait for me in the game room. I'll be right there." She rushes off.

kids." Mya grabs my hand, running off for the game room, "You'll love it."

Eliza went to change, leaving Mya and me alone in their playroom. Down in the basement with a projector TV with all the video games hooked up to a single remote for push-to-start access. A collection of DVDs functioned the same way. She said her father was an engineer. He could patent and market his TV stand and buy a second house like this with the profits.

"Like it?" Mya asks, sitting on the sectional couch and lifting her feet on the table. She waves my offer, "It's my favorite room in the house."

"I do. It looks like Nadian nerd heaven." I cheer, snatching the remote from her.

"Ew!" She sucks her teeth, throwing her legs in my lap.

"Yeah, yeah, you weren't going to do anything with it. Probably watch some B.S. reality tv." I sneer, turning on the Xbox console with a grin, "I don't even have one of these yet."

"Cuz you're about that broke life."

"Not anymore, gotta fix me up and manage my life better." I yawn, flipping on Dragon Age Inquisition. "I want to be well off and work less. I'm serious. I'm becoming a better man."

"I know, you've been like that since I met you. You're focused on the inner man. I appreciate it. It opened my eyes to

soul or personality?" Mya confides.

I shrug, "I don't remember saying all that."

"Well, no, because it's my idea now." Mya cuts her eyes at me, "Miiiine."

"I like your spin. I want someone who's a good person first, then all that other crap. I'm tired of dating rollercoaster." I stretch out, picking my character's hair. "I know you wouldn't understand, still out in the fields."

"Oh, shut up. I enjoy being single. I avoid your crappy situation."

"I cry about one girl in two years. You been crying over how many guys? Stop letting guys have sex so easily. It's a bad decision."

"I'm using them like they're using me. I have needs too." Mya rolls her eyes, not wanting to hear it.

"Shouldn't have relationships like that, to begin with..." I didn't want to get started, "I'm sorry, let me leave it alone."

"You know I'm listening, Chris... just tell me what's on your mind." Mya opens herself up to me.

"Well, I feel we stayed together because I held us together! We stayed together because every time she was weary, or she second-guessed, I pulled us back whole. I carried this relationship on my back!"

shoulders, "Doesn't sound like any relationship I want."

"What?"

"I mean, dude... She made it clear she wasn't the one. Everyone around you told you to leave. You were the one forcing it to work. You were the one who chose to stay. I'm not saying you could have left, but you should have. And now you know it. But you're upset and regretful with her over something you knew wasn't going to work, and you knew she wasn't ready for."

"So you're saying I should apologize to her?"

"No, she's a toxic person. What she did and put you through was horrible. There's no excuse for that. Being in a relationship, explainable, but the stories you tell me about what she put you through. That's just messed up. What I'm saying is that it's horrible, but you chose it, dude. You can't blame her for your decisions." Mya rubbed my knee. "As you would always say, it isn't your fault, but it's your responsibility, right? Your girlfriend had serious issues. I get it. You had the best intentions you wanted to help. You wanted to show her love. You didn't want to end on a bad note. You don't owe her anything, but you're blaming her for a situation she tried to get out of, and you kept putting yourself back into, I get it. The things you were asking for were simple, simple. I would hate to lose someone I care about because of the basics too. But she wasn't you. She doesn't have your perspective, and you can't force her to."

cover my face trying to find words, but instead, I sobbed. Things sounded so different from her mouth. So many of my own words and wisdom I didn't listen to these years. The whole relationship replayed in my head.

"Why didn't I just leave her? I'm so stupid thinking I could have made things work!"

Mya rested her head on my shoulder, ", no, no, you're right! You- You tried Chris. Many men don't stay. Many people don't anymore. Your relationship wasn't ideal. I wish I had a single ex-boyfriend who fought for me as you fight for Margot. I've been wrong trying to fight it for a while. I think I need a break as well. It's just hard to consider the long-term with some of these dudes."

"Then don't entertain these people." I say simply, "boys only want sex. Sorry to tell you that."

"Yeah, they do... It's about who you have sex with." Mya sighs dreamily.

"Eh... I think it's about having as little sex as possible and seeing what remains. If, without sex, the relationship dissolves, then you know where you stand. If you don't have sex and have a good relationship, that's what you're looking for." I finally get to start the game pass the tutorial, "oh, this is not like the last games at all."

over my shoulder, awaiting my response.

"Yep, friendship," I reply simply.

Mya rolls her eyes falling back on the couch, kicking me with her bare feet, trying to get my attention.

"Hey... have you ever considered a roommate? You know I can stay out your way. I want to get out of the dorms. You're the only person I could consider living with."

"I found a new place today, where I work. My boss offered me 50% off rent. You can be my 25%. We'll barely pay anything!"

"Aren't you worried he'll think you're using him?" Mya covers her mouth.

"I think he just respects the finesse. He's the one who changed my perspective about finances. I feel like I've been using a whole new section of my brain once he broke it down for me. I love that feeling."

"Using more of your brain?"

"Exactly, unlocking my full potential. It's so empowering. You know, babe?"

"Yeah, I do. Thanks for letting me move in with you." Mya acted as if she didn't hear what I said, so I didn't bother bringing it back up. "Do you think Eliza fell asleep on us?"

"Nah, she's probably picking the right footie pajamas to match her eyelashes." I grin, "I don't think she would fall asleep hand clutched on her mace."

"I won't be surprised. Eliza has a boyfriend she's dated for three years. They're madly in love. But he doesn't have your charm." Mya gives me a serious look, "please don't have sex with my friends without asking me first or at all preferably. I hope you're honest in wanting to be single?"

"There's nothing a woman can offer me. I don't need to provide for myself right now." Mya reaches over me, grabbing a blanket from over my head. She pushes her weight in her legs, weighing me down. "Don't move. I don't want you roaming around here, Chris."

"I am not going to sleep with your friend. If I wanted to, it'd be Opal, and I turned that up." I cross my heart. "You don't trust me?"

"Of course I trust you. That doesn't mean I shouldn't be tough on you. I'm worried about Eliza. She would lie up and down if you two had sex tonight. I can only trust you on the matter." Mya explains.

"Your girls are like that?" I was shocked remembering all that Opal told me in the office earlier tonight.

"Not for anyone but you. Opal doesn't even give other men attention. You're her infatuation. She doesn't know much about you. You would both have a rude awakening if you rushed into a relationship. I rather not get caught between you and her with knowing what's up with you and Margot. I don't wish that for any of my friends. You're too much."

"Yeah, I agree. I've been trying to say this to Opal all afternoon. Margot and I technically broke up today. I walked out. She put the pieces together and decided today was the perfect day to tell me how she felt. I couldn't focus on anything else but how much my life is destroyed."

"I expected you to argue me on that. You agree?" Mya brushed her braids out her face.

"I'm tired of arguing with people, Mya. I'm sorry for involving you in my relationship." I let out a strained groan.

"No, no... I'm happy to help. I just know none of them will understand you as I would. They'll think they're saving you from something but the reality is that they'll only be falling into the same deal." Mya hugged me, lifting the blankets over us. "I'll rest up until Eliza comes down."

"You're blocking my controller. I can't play with you all curled up." I tried maneuvering my hands around her, but there was no use.

"Then watch something. I'm comfortable." Mya decided for both of us.

I had no choice. She was already falling asleep, and she slept like a brick. There was no way she would be getting up so I

Mya lay in my arms.

"Oh, I want to watch that!" She points to some kids' fairy tale show before yawning. "It'll be good for you. You won't be as grumpy."

"Whatever. I'm just going to go to bed."

"Ha, sore loser... You should have respected your relationship instead of being a child. You might be home getting some head, watching whatever you want. Now, you have to deal with me!"

"If we room together, you better share. Understand?" I pinch her hip.

"Okay, okay, you know I'm ticklish!" She hits my hand, "You're not getting any blankets."

"What did I say about sharing?" I pinch her again.

"Okay, okay, can you please just stop?" Mya whines, "Let's be peaceful, an Erdu and Nadia truce."

I accept her peace agreement stretching out long on the couch. There are like twenty rooms in this house. Why am I sharing a couch?

"Mya, let's find a bed."

"What? No, I don't want to do that!" She flips on me, "You think I'm just going to bend over for you just because your boner is pressed up against me! You need to control yourself!"

"I just want to sleep in a bed, okay?"

turning off the TV and standing. "Let's go find a bedroom. I still don't want you roaming around. So, I'll share one with you."

"So, you want me to yourself?" I chuckle.

"Of course I do. I like being your favorite person. You even like me more than your girlfriend." Mya leads us up from the basement.

We head up the second floor with a selection of rooms to choose from, and she at least chose a bed with a Queen-sized mattress—enough room to have some space.
When we got to bed, Mya began taking off her jeans. Her butt looked like a rising cupcake as she shimmied out of her denim. I knew she had voluptuous c cups she showed off often. I never spent too much time behind Mya to realize she had cake. Mya dropped her jeans by the side of the bed without folding them, touching her toes and giving me a full panoramic view of what I had been missing all these years.

"What's wrong with you?" Mya asked me as she slowly rises knowing what she was doing.

"You and Opal will be the death of me," I mutter under my breath, sitting on the bed trying to catch my breath and sense of self.

"Weren't you tired, Chris?" She slips into the bed, watching me.

against my will. If I hopped into this bed in my briefs, I feared for the worst. I was already at full mast, wanting to give into my past self. Opal had opened a hunger I thought I sated long ago. I realize now the hunger is bottomless. The hunger would only consume me and never be conquered. It's up to which beast I feed.

"I think I need a cold shower." I shift away from her so she can't see my massive erection pushing against my jeans.

"Chris, we can shower in the morning. You think you're running off to see Eliza with that monster?" Mya laughed, jumping on my back.

"Whoa, it is not a good time for games." I try wrestling her off my back, but she was relentless.

"I know what's going on, and I already saw that slugger in your pants. Boy, how'd you fit all that in them jeans?" Mya laughs, placing her hand on my crotch.

"Man, I wish you could handle this thing." I groan.

Mya didn't respond. She gulped, not letting go at first but let me go, moving back to the pillows. She sat like a model waiting to be painted. Her tanned mahogany legs led up to a plump butt, a slim waist, and beautiful breasts. Mya tossed off her shirt, letting me see her in her matching lacy purple panties and bra.

her cheeks flushed red.

"You're so beautiful I could cry...." I whispered, backing away."

"Wait, where are you going?" Mya asked as I ran out of the room.

I snagged a second blanket from the perfectly available bedroom next door. When I came back, she was tucked in bed with her arms crossed across her chest. I draped the quilt on top of her and slept on top of her blanket and under my spare. Mya refused to acknowledge me, turning her back to me and sleeping. I was watching the TV in the bedroom 'til I passed out.

Mya's phone started ringing about an hour or so later. I reached over, grabbing it from her charger on the nightstand. It's Eliza.

"Hello?" I say, confused, seeing it was nearly midnight.

"You pick up her phone?" Eliza was shocked.

"Who is it?" Mya asked, rolling over and holding me, "it is Opal. Tell her how jealous she would be right now."

"No, it's Eliza," I tell Mya.

"Where did you two go?" Eliza asked.

"We're in the guest room, on the 2nd floor by the bathroom," I instruct as Mya goes back to sleep.

"Why did we need so many bathrooms on one floor?" Eliza groans, "I wanted to smoke before bed."

"I was matching my teddy to my nail polish and panties, then I sort of fell asleep." She yawns, knocking on doors, hoping one would be correct.

"Ha, well, we fell asleep too."

"Together?" Eliza giggles, "Did you two have sex in the guest room? Is that why your girlfriend acts like that? She knows about you and Mya sneaking off together?"

"What are you talking about? We are only friends! We're not even sleeping under the same blanket!"

"What that's so weird?" Eliza breaks out laughing.

"Tell me about it." Mya bitterly mutters.

"You two would be perfect for each other." Eliza rattled off, "Hey, wake up, and then I want to smoke. I'll roll in the morning. I was looking forward to it." Eliza was already moving through the hall, opening doors. "Where are you two?"

I groan, grunt, and grumble as I get out of bed, opening it up for Eliza, who was a few doors down. Eliza was in a pink teddy matching her nail polish and a silk robe matching her toes. She walked up to me, pinching my cheek. She opened her robe, letting me see her full form and the pink thong as she passed by me. I pulled Eliza back a moment, and she didn't resist letting me hold her waist and grip her booty. Eliza held my hand, letting her robe drop, spinning herself to give me a view as she went inside the room to join Mya.

could have chosen any of them. Then you say you two aren't in a relationship?"

"Shut up. I wanted to make sure he didn't go off to get with you." Mya groans, "Why are you waking us up?"

Eliza looked at me, standing in the door frame, enjoying the two models in front of me.

"Are you going to join us?" Eliza giggles.

"If I'm not careful, I'll probably go against everything I believe in, and I'll come back in a second." I shake my head, unable to hide my grin, letting my hard-on die down.

"I do care if he isn't in here having his way with you. I heard the rumors too. I'm not worried about him. I would go for the big booty out in the open and then go after the homeowner." Eliza says, sitting on the bed holding an ashtray and a purple lighter out to me. "Spark up!"

"I've been trying to tell Mya I'm done dating. She won't believe me." I say, lighting up the blunt, taking a long pull, "I told Opal, she won't listen either."

"They listened, but they don't want to hear it. A man uncontrolled by sex is intimidating. You lose a pull and power over him." Eliza informs me taking a long drawl, "My big brother says there's just a bunch of children chasing money and hedonism. There are few adults and just older people. Mostly the old folk, but they know so many people."

that perspective before." I comment, lying back down. "I get it, though. Everyone only cares about pleasure. No one truly cares about what's right anymore. People act like right is whatever grants the most pleasure, but I feel like what's truly right usually has some sense of personal sacrifice for the whole."

"You two would be perfect for each other." Eliza rolls her eyes, "He doesn't smoke, though. He's 35 and married. His family lives in Graham. His wife stays with their two kids. He might be a good mentor. My dad and brother are two men I met whose wives want to be with them. Ha, many married couples act like they were forced together."

I shrug, "You're taught to wait until sex after marriage. So, if you start having sex, there's some sense of marriage there."

"I understand why people think that, but it's still wrong. Besides, you don't fit that description at all. If so, you wouldn't have the body count you do." Mya comes at my neck.

"It's only been like 21 girls. It could have been way higher. I went through some rebellion, but then it all started making more sense why we wait. I appreciate the wisdom." I defend myself, "I'm not saying I'm an ideal guy or anything of the sort. I'm saying I need time to become him."

Eliza smiled, "keep your eyes on him, girl. They're the type of dudes who get rich or successful."

manifestation." I joke, getting under my blanket already baked like Mya's sweet cake.

Mya rested her head on Eliza's shoulder with a wide grin. Eliza made no comment giving her girl her moment. Mya crawled under my blanket, giving me no quarter. Kissing my cheek as she lays with me as if it's what she wanted all along.

"You two would make an amazing couple." Eliza notes, standing up, "I'm pretty high, so I leave the rest to you two. Good night."

"Night girl!" Mya yawns.

"Thanks for the hospitality, Princess Eliza." I lift the blunt in a toast.

"You're welcome! Good night all!" Eliza gives a royal wave as she departs.

Mya looked at me the whole time as we finished smoking. Her eyes were intent, but we didn't speak. We both had so much to think about enjoying smoking in bed. The ancient wisdom floats between my ears. All in all, it was an incredible day. The first day without Margot and sex felt life-changing. I had so many opportunities, but I only needed a good conversation.

After spending two years of life with someone, it becomes impossible to imagine life without them. You've done everything with them. You've adjusted your entire life to accommodate them, their needs, and their quirks. You change yourself, and they have changed for you. You're not the same person you were five years prior, for better or for worse.

I always questioned why people stayed in dying relationships. Why was it when you knew things weren't working, you don't part ways and move on? Then I realized. I never truly loved someone before. Not in a romantic "oh, you're so wonderful" way. It honestly feels as if I found my other half. We have a great time together despite us fighting, and there's no one I would rather be with. She was there for me when I felt most lost and abandoned. How do you not owe that person at least attempting to work things out?

But nothing dies randomly. There's always some predetermined cause. You didn't just have a stroke or heart disease. It was a life of inactivity and poor diet. Wear a seatbelt and keep your phone away when you drive. No. That isn't fair. It isn't true either. Sometimes shit does just happen. That doesn't mean that you can't take some preventive measures. Sometimes shit happens even after those preventive measures. That's

you in its gaze.

Sometimes relationships just fall apart. No. Occasionally certain relationships weren't meant to work. You attempted to breathe life into a cancerous being and were surprised when it became malignant. Spreading until it infected how you speak to each other, the way you see each other, your attraction.

Then it's been only a month, and your girlfriend refuses to sleep with you. I mean, just lying by your side. They deny there's anyone else. They deny that they don't stay because of your dying relationship. It's work, or a friend, or visiting their mother. But after a month, how many excuses can you take? This marks the beginning of month two.

"Good morning. I thought you were going to sleep at 14:00 again. Good to see you amongst the living." My roommate and best friend Chris Tor'jun greeted me.

He was in an unusually chipper mood, smiling and affectionate. I was stretching out from a deep sleep, falling asleep rather late, stuck on ways on how to make things up to a man who wouldn't even speak to me.

"Ha, well, I've been a bit sad since you stopped speaking to me." I said meekly, still in my teddy as I moved to go to the kitchen, "Are you hungry?"

Chris comes up behind me, wrapping his hands around my waist pulling me back.

"What are you doing?" I asked in shock, and it was all so sudden.

"Sshh..." he hushed in my ear.

"Ooo..." I moaned as he began shoving me as if he couldn't wait to get inside me.

His warm hands moved under my vulva, pushing up my teddy.

"I knew you weren't wearing panties." he snickered.

him freely.

"What are you going to do about it?"

His hand was replaced by a fat mushroom tip pushing into my folds. I bit my lip, choking on my moans as my body contracted.

"Ooo... Stop, you're too big." I pushed back against him as he tried to thrust back into me.

"I'll just slow down for you." He held my hips, pulling me back against him. I held his hands as my butt began slapping against his hips. He squeezed my waist, bending me over to ease in and out of me. "How's that, girl?"

"Mhhhmmm daddy, right there." I lost my sense of enjoying my surprise. He lifted my leg, held it on top of the kitchen counter, and let him get a better angle. "Oh, I'm about to cum, baby..." The admission came with some weight as my booty sat right in his lap as he slammed from behind. He was holding every inch inside me as my juices began running down his length.

"You came so quickly." He smacked my butt.

"I did... I've been waiting for you, baby." I turned my head, looking for his lips, his touch.

His hand cupped my breast. His tongue danced with mine as I squirmed on his big shaft.

the kitchen island. I kissed him on his neck, stroking him in my hand. "You're so wild today. I thought you lost this side of you."

He grinned, biting my ear. "You have to go to class."

"What?"

He opened his mouth once more, blaring in my ear, sounding off like a siren.

There's no way.

"Baby... Baby!" I called in vain.

There was no fighting my alarm clock.

I sat up in bed. I felt around the bed for Chris, but he was nowhere. He's probably in his room practicing his bass. He doesn't do anything but study and play these past few months. He didn't even consider me an option. He got some freedom from Margot, not enough, it seems.

I hit my bed, pounding my fist and crying on my pillow.

My legs felt like they ran a mile. I was soaking wet down to the blankets and sheets.

I fell over, covering my face, my cheeks flushed red. I can't believe this is from a dream of him. He would never let me hear the end of this. I have to wash my sheets! It's not even laundry day. Maybe he has extras, and I can stow these until Saturday?

be my roommate. Well, my best friend. My girls talk about it but-
Wow.

"Yo, you gotta get to class, girl." He drawls outside my door, knocking out loud, "You can't be sleeping all day like this!"

"Do you have extra sheets?" I ask, covering myself up with my blanket.

"Ha, you wet the bed?" He pokes his stupidly handsome face in my room, "Ha, had a scary dream?"

I smile automatically, "No, It was a pretty great dream. I- I spilled some wine in the bed, and I need some new ones."

"Told ya, drinking in bed is depressing."

"Ha, yeah, you told me from your personal experience." I giggle.

"Touche... I'll grab the sheets." he chuckled, "You sure you good, need me to come in there and help you out?"

I froze, unsure how to respond. I fixed my lips to say yes, but we were not on the same page.

What the hell was that, Mya!? Oh my god, this cannot be happening right now. I wouldn't honestly just let him grab me up like that and just-

I crossed my legs one over the other. Oh my god, I totally would. I'm such a hoe! No, no. Get your head together, girl. You're not a hoe. It's Chris. It's him! He's gotten so sexy over

incredible. It felt so real.

"I have Crimson sheets and red ones."

"Ha, you have Crimson sheets? I didn't even know they made sheets of Masks. You're such a nerd." I covered my mouth, giggling up.

"He's my hero. I want to be like that but a lover, you know? Less punching in the face. More creating amazing things for people." he stretched out long, "so you good?"

"You'll be better than Crimson." I stretched out seductively, "You're my hero, Chris."

He smiled, blushing "why thank you."

"Come sit with me." I patted my bed.

"On your pee sheets?" he looked grossed out, "No thanks."

Pee is not the bodily fluid you caused.

I crawl out of bed and climb on him.

"What the hell are you doing?" He laughs as I push against him as hard as I could against the wall. "You need to calm down before I lay the hammer of justice on you."

"You're gonna give me the hammer, baby?" I bite his ear, kissing down his neck.

He shoves me off, checking his neck, "why did you bite me?"

shrug, "come on, don't be afraid. I know I'm rough. I thought you liked it rough."

"Ha, you're adorable." he even pinched my cheek, "You can have the red sheets. I'm going to put the Crimson ones on my bed!" He tosses me the red sheets in his hand.

"Let's go to your bed then if you don't want to use my bed." I try to grab his hand.

"What are you up to today?" he looks at me sternly.

I shrug, "Class... I still have time."

"Which class again?" he cupped his ear.

"It's just microeconomics. I could use your help before class with something more intimate."

"You need that class to graduate, Mya. You're always late, or you skip the class. What's your grade even?"

"You want to get on me about my grades, but you're not trying to get on this butt. I only need a D to pass, Chris." I lift his chin.

"You're kidding me. A D means you didn't learn anything! You need to learn how to manage money so we can get rich!" He throws up his hand. "These Nakans are killing us with those fields."

"Why don't you learn it?"

"I'm the talent... I don't need to know that stuff, but I do because I already took the class! I got a B+ and would have

out the bones cracking in his back. "It's fun stuff." He rubs his neck. "I'm going to go stretch before my jog. You wanna come with me?"

"I do..." I did not, "Give me a minute, okay?"

He throws deuces leaving the fresh red sheets on the edge of my bed.

I made sure to hear his footsteps down the hall before I slipped out of my panties, arching my back. I bit my lip, finishing myself up. I began moaning uncontrollably, closing my eyes trying to recall my dream. How he grabbed me and slid inside me, hoping for God's sake the reality wasn't far beyond.

I finally got out of bed, changing my sheets, feeling muuuuch better. I danced out of my room into the bathroom, where Chris was brushing his teeth. I grinned, hugging him around his waist. He chuckled as I cuddled up to him, kissing his shoulders.

"What are you doing, you weirdo?" he laughed, spitting out his toothpaste.

He handed me the tube of fluoride-free paste. I made him pay for it since it cost an extra four bucks. He didn't mind. I guess I did feel better. I never dreamed so intensely before we moved into together and all his life hacks.

"Nothing..." I reached down for a different tube.

kissed his cheek, holding his hard, warm cock in my hands. His dick was one of the biggest dicks I've ever felt, not so much to my surprise as to my delight. We were both silent as we looked on in the mirror, his cocoa skin flush against my midnight black skin. I kissed his shoulder, stroking his wood. I looked into his eyes in the mirror as he took a breath. He probably didn't know the last time a woman handled his manhood. I was too busy pulling his manhood out of his basketball shorts to notice him objecting to me. I never really had a guy turn me down before. I leaned over the sink, bending at my hip, bouncing foot to foot, waiting for him to fulfill my fantasy. I was beginning to brush my teeth lightly, pressing my booty against his meat.

"Are you trying to tell me something?" he stroked my ego as he eyeballed me, dancing in front of him.

"I am. Hit it from the back real quick." I suggest as if offering what to eat for breakfast.

I lick my lips, hoping he was as gung-ho for this romp as I felt.

"What's gotten into you?" he began second-guessing, taking a deep breath, "What

are we doing?" he begins trying to laugh it off, "You're usually a joker, but this is a bit much."

I washed out my mouth, laying flush against the sink with my hips presented to him, slowly shaking my booty.

"Sssh... push up against my booty. Come fill up my yoni before you go jog, best friend. Give me the hammer." I enticed him.

He looked down at my hips. My teddy was peeling up, revealing my vulva and booty. He bit his lip, pulling me closer as if we were on a dance floor. He jerked my teddy toward him, grinding against his hips, dancing to the tune in my head as I hummed. I began brushing my teeth innocently as he tugged my hair back into a ponytail. We moved in sync. I met his playful thrusts, getting wetter by the second as my honeypot moved against his manhood, dripping my nectar along his length. My eyes began to roll in my head, feeling my lips trying to gobble him up.

"You like that, baby?" I moaned.

He didn't respond hardship etched all over his face. He didn't even seem conflicted, just uncomfortable. His hard shaft pressed to my labia's lips, and he looked like he wanted to bolt.

"Just have sex with me!" I turn to look at him, "What's wrong with you all of a sudden?"

"Ha, no, this is too funny." he broke out laughing.

"What? Are you laughing at me?" I stand up, my cheeks burning up as I looked at his stupid grin.

"Well, I thought we were laughing together until just now." he refused to stop laughing.

bathroom.

"Get out, Chris! Don't play with my emotions!"

"Ha, I'm sorry. I didn't think you were serious, best friend chill. I thought you were joking!"

I opened the door glaring at him.

"Joking!? I offered myself to you on a silver platter. Is it so hard for you to believe I'm attracted to you?" I snap at him, "Have you looked in the mirror recently?"

"I wasn't paying attention to my reflection, no." he rubbed his neck. "It's not even like that, Mya, for real. I am just not that dude anymore."

"My Chris, you've humbled yourself." I bit my lip, rolling my eyes and slamming the door once more.

"Ow, ow ow!" he yelped.

I tugged it open, "Oh my god, are you okay I'm so sorry?"

"Ha, just messing with you. I wanted to see you half-naked again, beautiful frame and great curves. Never noticed how nice you looked in lingerie." he was genuinely enjoying my nudity.

"I'm going to kick you in your chest, just you wait. You think you're funny, playing with my emotions. You think you're funny. You're not!" I stabbed him in the chest.

"Have you looked in a mirror recently? Do you think I'm lying?"

my emotions seriously!" I shouted, feeling so embarrassed.

"I don't because you magically manifested these feelings last night. Be real, Mya. If we had sex right now in a week or two, you'll be talking about how this wouldn't go right and how much you want your freedom. And how dating isn't your thing like you do with every other guy you've been with when you want some sex." He sighs.

"I want to make love to you! And I haven't been with anyone in months! It's nearly a year. I was speaking to this guy all summer. Nice guy, lame dude. His game was whack I couldn't vibe. You're different, Chris. You're the total package. I wouldn't want anyone else to have you."

"That's possessive." he groaned.

"Chris, why don't you believe me?"

"Ha, I'm not in disbelief per se. I'm refusing you because I'm your best friend. I know you. If we had sex-

"Would it not be great? Why would I leave you if the sex was as good as I know and have visual evidence for how good it'll be?" I tried lightening up the mood.

"I can't have another relationship revolving around sex." he shook his head, rubbing his temple. "I'm sorry, Mya. I don't know where this is all coming from. Believe me, I'm tempted, I'm flattered, I'm horny as all hell, but I can't fuck you. You're my best friend!"

AROUND SEX! WE'VE NEVER HAD SEX!" I shout, throwing the tube of toothpaste at him. "I don't like your accusations!"

"If we don't have one, why are you trying to change a good thing?" he picked up the toothpaste and gently put it on the counter. "You're flipping out over nothing. I'm not even your man."

I held my chin, wondering if a dream would allow me to sacrifice my friendship for sex. I was frustrated because my yoni was so wet, and he refused to push my act right button.

"I'm horny, Chris, and I want you to take me right here, right now! I don't know what else to do, to get you to see me as more than a friend." I threw my hands up.

"I don't want to see you as more than a friend. Even if we were to start dating if we weren't friends, how could we get married or anything? We would have zero longevity. I know that from experience." he sighed, "Not to mention this major emotional outburst, you're going crazy for what reason?"

"I... I don't know. I thought we would have to choose. Do you think about it?" I ask, beginning to calm down, not letting my sexual frustration and natural aggression control me.

"Well, we were a cloth away from the deed. And the way you're acting, I'm going to have to make a decision or hear some other guy humping you. I don't like ultimatums, Mya. That's not cool at all."

changed my standards entirely, Chris. Not just now, but for a while. I've considered it since we met. You wouldn't date me. You picked Margot and got pissed off at me. I thought maybe you had some revenge sex lined up after you and Margot broke up. I wanted to let you do your thing. But you didn't. You didn't want anyone. My girls have been talking about dating you for years, so the idea has always been there. It isn't something I'm just thinking up or raising. I've felt this way, but- I'm just honest with my feelings and the opportunity. I wish you would do the same. I'm your best friend. I have always been here for you and have always been willing to do whatever for you, now I'm including giving you some good loving."

"I guess that means a lot more for you than it does for me. I'm lost in the vernacular. That's modern romance?" he rubbed his neck, "I'll have to think about it."

"Chris! Why can't-

I began throwing a tantrum, but I wanted to show him I was becoming mature as well. I could accept being patient while he made his decision.

"Okay..." I said silently, "You can enjoy the view if you want."

"No, I think I'm going to go ahead and get my jog in. You should get ready for class. I need some time to myself." he

money so we can be rolling in dough."

"So, you're already thinking about us?" I ask, feeling hopeful.

He simply chuckled and headed off.

I was relieved. I was only going to go jogging to be with him. I hated running. Ugh, but he made me want to be healthy and care about things. He was a real man, with real concerns and worries only a year older than me. There was something sexy about calling a man daddy who could carry himself as my daddy. Maybe a bit oedipal, but it was the truth and exactly how I felt.

I've known Chris Kirin Tor'jun since my freshman year. He lived right down the hall from me until my sophomore year he was off the grid in some love-lock. We've always kept in touch but moving in together was way different. At first, it seemed like a dream.

There was so much pressure from my friends to know what it was like being with Chris Kirin Tor'jun. After his break up, he was untouchable and unavailability. He was backed up with ideas about why he was even with her or why not be with Margot? They expected the worst from us, but nope.

It's as if I never crossed his mind. I don't know how I ever could know what happened.

We moved in together after he and his girlfriend broke up. This is about nine months or so ago. He slept in the empty apartment for the week. His now ex had left on a trip, changing the locks to his dorm room and making it nearly impossible to get his belongings. I was hardly listening to how things were between them. The moment I met Margot I didn't like her nor did my friends. Two years ago, they would argue, he came over to my room for a day, and then they dated again. There was trouble in paradise, and he wanted someone to share in his

disappeared, he stopped reaching out, stopped visiting, and never spoke about his relationship.

They broke up nearly a year ago. He'll be graduating by next semester and had a job lined up for a year contract in New Haven. He asked me to move in with him as a friend. I don't mind a friend because it's far less expensive than the dorms, and living with him has been a treat. Though, we had to adjust majorly to each other's living standards.

The very first night we moved in, I had an endless amount of questions about their breakup. He didn't want to hear it. I guess it was comforting in its way. He was stubborn like that, and he called it loyalty. I called it stubborn. Loyalty is nice when your partner and lover had been loyal to you. We found out she had sex with other dudes while he was out of the district last year on tour.

I had little sympathy, and I had told him to break up with her before he even left town! She refused to support him and tried to have the tour cancel. He waited nearly a year to take my advice, dump her, be free, and enjoy yourself, at least have nothing to worry about while you're gone.

Do I get credit for it? Nope!

He trusted her and came back, and she lied about it. And she didn't tell him until he moved in with me. He sure wasn't sharing any with us, but her cookie was up for grabs. He doesn't

To do it while the man was on tour with his dream band seemed petty to me. I don't preach, and I like sex as well. I also enjoy being single, not to cause waves or hurt feelings. I couldn't understand why you would wait until your boyfriend's highest point to do something so foul with nobodies.

In my opinion, they were far too young for either of them to be worried so much about love, marriage, and the works. I respected him and took his advice because he was far more mature than I think I could EVER be. I think even when I'm 50 with a husband and kids, Chris will still have two lifetimes of wisdom and experience ahead of me. He's heard it all, thought it all, and didn't want to hear excuses because that's all he ever got outside himself. I could never handle the news of being cheated on as casually as he did, especially when he tried to stay faithful.

I suppose that's why we fought so hard our first two days of him moving in. I wanted him to be as furious and worked up as I did. Her straying wasn't his issue.

He claims it was everything leading up to it, the lack of honesty, no real loyalty, her views of him, and their lack of commonality. Mostly, reasons I would never let a man into my life, nor my bedroom, nor share my time of day. Yet, he dated this girl he had zero chemistry with outside of combustibility for over a year! For the wizened genius I thought he was, he came to my doorstep with some dumb problems. It all seemed like no-

realize how distant we had become. And how much he grew, he wanted his relationship to work so badly, but she just didn't have what it took.

I called myself his good friend, and whenever I was asked about him, I had a story to tell, but after our first two days of living together—talking, going back and forth. I realized how little he shared about himself, his views, or his life. I didn't even find out about her infidelity until five months of living together. To me, it seems their love predated any mortal attraction or bonding they may have had. It was a karmic lesson he had to teach.

She made an excuse, "I didn't think you loved me, so when you left, I had sex with other men to move on." and his response was, "Forget about me. If you loved yourself, why would you let another man, let long, other *men* have you so easily?"

He said she had no real response.

It's been about nine months since we moved in together, over last-minute housing disputes and his relationship finally imploding. Besides, he had a sweet deal on rent and two bedrooms.

Nearly a year later, we did less talking, more smoking, and enjoying each other's company. I realized how easy it is to feel he doesn't care about my existence, sharing my own home

around. He was unresponsive, inexpressive, always working, and lost in his new hobby as an illustrator. My friends looked to me for answers, but I, too, was on the outside. I asked him what was on his mind to learn rather than rant at him. Without Margot, it was easier to see him. That's just his personality and a critical part of his identity and survival. His solitude had become something he would defend voraciously. I loved him for it while she couldn't even understand or accept it. How could you trust a man who can't be alone?

A man like him made me realize how much I've settled, sold myself short, and straight-up hoed myself out as he called it. He even says it about himself when he played the field, prompting him to fight so hard for his relationship with Margot.

It was far less about me in my mind than my selection of men and where I met most. I didn't want what he had at first, but he made it seem incredible. We have slept in the same bed a few times after hanging out. I lie close to his chest and heart on those nights. We wake up and smoke a bowl or blunt. Say our goodbyes as we both left to do our thing, then the feeling of having someone to come home to coming home to him felt incredible.

I had enough of watching this man go to waste. He would rub my naked body down once I took a shower after work. He could talk about anything on the planet without penetrating me.

caring! Toilet seat down and no hairballs in the sink. Well, mostly my curly locks. He cleans up after himself and me. He even cooks dinner and buys me wine after long days. Not that he had much money, to my knowledge. He just says, "I keep the weed lit. I keep my glass full." Then he pats me on the head to continue with whatever he was doing. He refused to accept compliments.

It was nine months, and he still wasn't over his relationship, to my dismay. I kept quiet about this after telling him he should just forget about her. He just smiled and told me I wouldn't be able to understand how he felt. I don't think it was the love he felt. I believe he's still recovering from the damage she caused him. If he wouldn't date me, I had plenty of other friends who would be willing.

We were watching a movie. I was sprawled across the couch with my head in his lap as we do every once in a while when I push the issue of not being comfortable. Honestly, just wanting to be cuddled up with him.

I was curled up with him, watching "Men in Black 2." He could have bought a real copy by now for $5, but he faithfully kept his collection of bootlegs.

"You know, you have that Will Smith body going on. Not this one, the buff 'I Am Legend.' Will Smith. He and his wife are such a hot couple, you know? They are so lucky when they get to

"Not the relationship I want, ha." He grinned.

I smiled at his perspective of being 'redeemed' in his mind, far past his years of running around with his flings.

It was strange. Since we moved in, there were never any girls over. He never really talked about any. And whenever I had my girls over, he completely faded their attempts at flirting if he did hang out. Or he would roll us a blunt and find an excuse to leave. He would conveniently pop up once they left. He claimed he wasn't interested in women anymore. And I knew for certain he didn't magically turn gay. He had no issue enjoying us. We could be down to our panties or bikini. He would look and never touch. I assumed this whole time he was sneaking around or had some booty on call, but nope. He had given up on relationships and dating. This was not at all fair!

"How are you?" I asked, rubbing my chin looking up to him, feeling investigative journalist hat firmly on my head.

Mya Harik was on the case. I needed to get to the bottom of this big unused third leg I needed in my life.

"I'm good... Why?" He muttered with a sigh, "I don't like how you're looking at me, Mya." he chuckled, "What's wrong? Do I have a solemn look again, or you just feel like being a bug?"

"I was just wondering...." I took a small pause, "Why aren't there any chicks all over you anymore? You could have a great girl if you wanted."

"I'm not even interested in that either right now." he seemed distressed. I knew who came to mind as he slapped his forehead and tried to look away, "Yo, check out the alien."

"Yeah... I heard you give that same line to Rebeka the other day. She didn't like that. She digs you. It hurt her feelings."

He shifted uncomfortably, "Look... I'm not trying to get involved with anyone right now. I just-

"Spill! Tell me the real reason. We're friends, and you have to! It's friend code, them the rules, boyo!"

He chuckled, "there's no story to tell. I just- I had my fair share of girls. They aren't worth my time or effort. Each thinks they're some special snowflake, but they're not. They're the same. Some are dope. Good for them. They're usually not my type. And there's a crowd of others I just don't seem to meet or who are taken. My theory is they're too fickle and selfish at this age, and I'm waiting until I'm thirty." He shrugged, "I suppose the right one will find me. I don't want to get bothered with a woman not looking for marriage."

"Marriage, you're completely off the market?" I was admittedly a bit intimidated, thirty and married. That's not fair at all.

He sighs, "I'm just not interested right now, alright? Maybe sooner, who knows, I don't, but after my last relationship, I can't see myself getting too attached or opening myself back

"So, you don't know?" I say with a bit more hope.

"I honestly don't think about it too often anymore. When I first decided to abstain, I used to, but after a while, it got much easier to ignore these chicks. I watch other dudes chasing hoes or wanting a girl underneath them. I just don't need it, the sex, the emotional drama, and the attachment, none of it."

"You gotta stop talking to those hoes, ha." I busted out laughing.

"I've dated nice girls. I was the hoe, but I invested a lot of time and energy into my last relationship for nothing. To the others, they're all gone, or I moved on. I keep in contact with a few, I guess but not interested. Why can't you all just accept it?"

"Yeah, sure they're nice... But they're in college looking for sex like everyone else."

"I understand this very well, and I'm not interested in dating one of these chicks. In a few months, they'll get bored and move on to the next. I'm not with it. Most see absolutely no issue hopping man to man. I get it. I guess I've been there, but I'm done with it. I want what my grandparents had." He sighed, "After my last girl, I just- She messed my head up. I can't trust a girl after that. It'll always be in my head."

"You just watch too much porn... I saw your browser history. You already know if you needed help, you wouldn't need to watch that crap."

than my actual relationship experience with women?" he rubbed his chin.

"I don't think the porn is helping. I have scientific facts to back me up on that. It would be much healthier for you to let me help." I say, trying to lighten the mood.

It wasn't as if he gave up females, just trusting hoes and little girls. I could respect it.

He rolled his eyes, "whatever, I'm not going with on this conversation."

"Come on! I didn't mean to offend you. Tell me more. Spill all the details!" I wrap my arms around him, "tell me!"

"Bug off, Mya," he warns.

"So, have you spoken to Margot recently?" I asked Chris.

"We met for lunch a month or two ago. That's how I found out she was getting spit-roasted," he confesses easily.

"Oh..." I paused, knowing how good that felt after a long week from my freshman year. I was trying to find my head before I continued. I swallowed, feigning a smile as I choose my words, as if I wanted an answer, "what did you two talk about?"

"Well, she wanted to plead her case for us getting back together. She offered to let me get even with a few of her friends. We spoke, and then she asked if there was a future for us." he stopped with a heavy sigh.

intermission before he ran back to Margot, hard cock between his legs. And I'll be here waiting for them to fall out again. To nurse him back, for her to steal him again.

I hesitated before asking, "well, what did you say?"

I was afraid of his answer.

He wraps his arms behind his head, staring up to the ceiling, "what do you think I said?" He sounded genuine enough.

With no reason not to trust his sincerity, "I think you told her that you'd think about it."

He smirks, but he doesn't speak. He takes a breath before sitting up, "you know me well!" he chuckles, but his smile fades, "but no, that's not what I said. I told her that it would be unlikely, if not impossible. Getting back together would be unfair to me. I let bygones be bygones, but I would never date Margot or anyone like her again."

I was relieved but confused, "don't you mean unfair to her?"

"No. I meant unfair to me!" He says defiantly, "To go back to the same broken relationship, too blind to realize how sick it made me. I deserve better. I want to be respected, not to be discarded like trash. To be loved unconditionally. I deserve to be someone's man, not their plaything. I deserve maturity, patience, someone who will grow with me but not marriage just as people, friends, and lovers. I deserve you. You'll be fine without me.

deserve to have some happiness in my life."

I can't fight my smile, leaning to hug him tightly. "Ha, I couldn't see how you turned her down. Her friends are pretty cute. Especially not by choice, you used to be addicted to Margot. I feel you, though, all these man-children running around. It's hard to find someone who can just stay home."

I looked up at Chris. He was home every night, with his fine self. Single as could be, and not even interested. I was looking forward to one of my girls telling me how it was. We lived for a good Chris sex story. None of them ever stood a chance, from what it sounds.

"Rebeka thinks a lot of you, and she's mature, beautiful, a redhead. She loves reading."

He shrugged off effortlessly, "Cool."

I smiled, thinking of another girl in my crew who could break him out of his dry spell. Good head would change his tune. Good kitty would change his life.

"Well, Opal likes you as well-

He hesitated for a moment. "I'm not interested, Mya. How many times do I have to tell you the same thing?"

"I refuse to believe a man as handsome as you just don't care about getting laid! Especially not one of my girls. We're way thicker than her friends with better personalities. And we keep you focused."

girlfriend. I want something serious. I could get laid or get some head if I wanted. I don't want that right now. I want an actual relationship."

"Me?" My smile was absolute cheese, with my Shirley Temple dimples. "I didn't know you were feeling me like that."

"Didn't know you thought I was handsome." He winked.

I paused, blushing and getting some distance before I filled my head up again. How can he be single?

Flirting came so naturally to him. Why did he have to be single? His wife is going to be so lucky. If he ever goes out and plays the field again! He may never find a wife. And he's so comfortable with sitting around here, doing his work, and keeping to himself.

"Do you have any other questions?"

"I have many!" I raise my finger.

"Jah'Ada save me...I was hoping you would say no." he slaps his face.

"So, does your penis still work? Do you still get hard? What do you do when you get horny? Is there still a chick on call?"

He only laughed, shaking his head, "my equipment didn't just break because I'm abstaining. That question was crazy." Chris's chuckles were deep and grumbling. "Naw, No side chicks, and I tell myself no. Self-love is everything for me right now. I

my energy. I don't think porn is the issue because I stopped watching it seven months ago. Once you girls began using the apartment as your lingerie parlor, porn didn't do it for me anymore."

"Mhm... Mhm..." I rubbed my chin, evaluating his answers. "So, you don't want women anymore? Are you not attracted?"

He laughs, "I don't get what you're missing. I just don't want to have sex or date or get involved. I'm tired of being hurt, mistreated, and ignored for someone else's selfish desires. There are just more important things going on in my life than being some girl's doormat. I don't think a girl will add much. They just think of themselves."

"We do not!"

"You're a cut above most, Mya. Or I wouldn't even room with you. You respect my choice and my space. At least I used to think you did until that stunt you pulled in the bathroom."

"I still think we're halfway there, lying in your lap during movies, we sleep together. Not to mention you've seen me naked more times than I could count. Ha, Yeah, I guess I respect your choice, but I wish I understood it." I giggle, unable to keep my naughty thoughts to myself. "So, is there a religious reason? Did you join a cult or something?"

"I hope you aren't associating religions with cults... And no, it's a personal relationship with God. I just don't want to get

this movie?"

"This is news to me! You're celibate!"

"I'm not celibate, and I'm not defining it. I've chosen to wait until a nice woman enters my life. I probably wouldn't wait for marriage. But I want to be with someone I could marry, not just a fling or an expiration date. I want something serious. Make each other better, you know?"

"I don't hear many guys talk like that... Most are still barely keeping a girlfriend." I rubbed my chin, "What's stopping you from dating?"

"Eh, I couldn't do girlfriend again. I don't even know where that idea came from, and I want something real. Not because of my future or my looks, not for the sex. But, for me as a person. I feel like I deserve someone who would love me even if I followed my dreams and aspirations rather than this secure life. I want a woman who wants to be with the actual me, not my reputation or their fantasy."

"Tag along for your fantasies, but will you support their fantasy too?"

"That's not what I said." he said defensively, "I have aspirations that require a great deal of internal fortitude. I haven't met or dated a girl ready for that. I'm prepared to go alone. If I can help others along the way, of course, I will. And I doubt I could ever be attracted to another woman without

"Some girls fantasize about being with you. Is that a crime?"

"I don't do the same. Aside from the chosen few, even then, I don't fantasize anymore. I'm over day-dreaming. I don't know. It just seems human, and dudes do it too. But I want more than to be a hard stick and some money. Be here for me and with me, not a plan. These girls don't even care about my thoughts or ideas. They don't even have thoughts or ideas. They only care how good it looks holding hands down the road."

"I sort of understand that. That's deep, bud. I didn't know you felt that way. Guess our generation dropped the ball."

He shrugs, "Two generations ago. Everyone's having sex, but no one wants to procreate. They have no idea what love is anymore."

I bit my lip, only nodding along.

He's single.

And worst. He thinks he needs to be because of these little hoes running out there! That's a crime! It wasn't fair. Good guys being ruined because of hoes. I can't stand for this.

"If you ever need to talk, you know I'm here, right?" I kiss his cheek then take my place in his lap. "There's no reason, and you should feel how you do. I know there is a literal reason, but the type of women should change. Not your dealings with

"You jealous of my alone time?" he was a sharp cookie.

It's why my infatuation was growing. So many men acted as if I was so confusing, but he saw right through me.

"I can deal with your alone time, and I'm more jealous of your hand." I yawned.

"What?"

"I said all things have a plan," I repeated more clearly.

"That is not what that yawn sounded like, but I'm not gonna pry." He turned up the movie and leaned back.

He watched, cool and calm. I kept fidgeting, being inches away from his unused penis. It was a shame. I paid it no mind earlier out of respect and friendship. I couldn't process anything else but him and the giant alien on-screen. Having seen this movie a few times, he took precedence.

"Mya, can you stop?"

"Did it get any smaller since you stopped?" I rubbed his thigh, licking my lips. "How long has it been?"

"You're one of my best friends, Mya. Chill on that. It isn't funny."

"I was trying to be sexy, not funny. Friend-zoned by my Friend. Hmm. It's going to be hard moving out of this box. I understand those boys better now." I back off a bit needing to respect him.

bets they would have gotten together. Maybe that's our issue. He's tired of being the story. He just wanted to be successful.

What am I thinking!

There's so much working against me. He's my friend and roommate. Despite how bad I need it, he doesn't want sex! Plus, I would never hear the end of it from Opal. She had a crush on him, even if it won't be reciprocated anytime soon. They had gotten closer, but she was at the same distance I sat.

"I have to head to the bathroom." He adjusted slightly, and I could feel the hard-on unexpectedly brushing along my cheek as I let him stand up, instinctively getting on my knees.

We made eye contact for a moment before he went off down the hall. It seemed the conversation was getting the best of both of us. I may not get another chance. I held his waistband and licked my lips. Holy crap, all that is out the window. I need to feel him inside me. At least see it. God, no! I'm a hoe!

I let him go, rolling my eyes, needing a full deliverance to get through our lease agreement. My body was burning with the need of him.

Rakil, He's just supposed to be a friend. Why am I feeling this way? Especially when he's the one fine being friends! He's the guy. He's supposed to chase me! God, that hasn't been true since we were kids. I would have to go for it if I wanted anything

friendship? Do I seriously have to marry this guy?

Calm down, Mya, calm down. It's been a while for you too. You're just horny. I can't let my yoni take you down that path, no sex for sex's sake. He's right. Why would I even bother if not just to tell my girls? Then he'll be even more hurt, and Rebeka sure wouldn't forgive me.

I let out a sigh, feeling pushed against the wall.

I don't want to tell them. And, we're roommates. We're already a couple of steps ahead of the game. We've been friends for a minute now, close to a couple of years. Maybe I don't need to have sex with him. But I want to be considered. I mean, time is finite, and there aren't many other guys I would date but Chris. I'm sure he feels the same.

"Dude, I should get some food." He yawns, coming back sans hard-on, "I'll be back in a bit."

I frowned, rolling my eyes. There wasn't temptation or tension anymore, boring.

"What are you in the mood for, babe?" I asked.

I was expecting a lecture, but he acted as if he didn't even hear me. His face with a static smile, eyes glued to the TV.

"Did you hear me? We should get something to eat." He stretched out, kicking his feet on the coffee table.

"I asked what you wanted." I sat up, leaning against him,

He chuckled. He looked me over and licked those lips before turning back to the movie.

"What's so funny, punk?" I jabbed him in the ribs.

"Ha, stop. I'm ticklish. Chill!" He jerked away from me.

"Tell me!" I continue.

"You need to relax before you catch the People's elbow. Tickling is dangerous business."

"Ha, whatever. Tell me!" I leaned on him, threatening to continue.

"Well, I was entertaining the idea of why we haven't done anything before—not even kissing while drunk. I've done more in less time with the worst chicks. Seems weird, you're my type, but I never even considered making a move."

"Now, I'm your type? You never go after what you deserve." I sigh.

He shrugs, "you're my girl."

"What if I wanted to BE your *woman*? Like for real, solve your problems and come home to me after work?"

"Already do." He smiled, "it's also nice as is, right?"

"I don't know... Getting some neck after work would be nice, wouldn't it?" I remember feeling the weight of his girth against my face.

He chuckled, "you're funny, and that's why I like you."

This boy is dense. I'm flirting. How can you be so

knew but his curve game. How did his curveball get so strong? I was on the other side of his politeness. In the "no-fly zone," and he was watching me cautiously behind his smile.

I sighed, "You're making me feel weird for taking this seriously."

"Ha'naaaaw!" He laughs out loud, "Yooo, Ha'naw... I'm not interested right now, and we're friends. I'm not roping you into my trauma. Besides, you only want to shag. I'm not with it. If you need some sex, Mya, maybe, just maybe, I would consider it. Don't string me along as if you want more from me right now. I really can't play games anymore."

"Did you just reject me!? I don't care how polite you make it. At least let me hate you over not wanting to be with me." I sucked my teeth.

"Naw, just couldn't do it. You're my friend." He repeats for the 1000th time in the past year to Opal or me.

It would be a crime to take anything he said personally. I wanted him, and he knew it now. He wasn't the type of person to lead me on.

"Look, Mya. For real, I would love to do everything you suggested and more. I would. You could do better, and I could get something a bit more my speed. I am trying to live a life of faith. I need more than sex. I need a wife." He shrugs.

isn't your speed?" I ask in his ear, kissing his cheek.

"That's not it! We're cruising too fast for me right now. I think I need to get out your way and let you find your prince charming." He raised his hands.

"I'm not a freshman anymore. All I do is study, class, and chill with you. We're halfway there already, ya know? My girls always ask me how the sex is with you. It would be nice to tell them."

"Uh..." He rubbed his neck, "You're making me feel super uncomfortable right now. You're not serious, are you? Your girls talk about this?"

"You and your guys don't? They don't think you've hit at least once?" I raise a brow, "because I don't know any guys who wouldn't joke about that."

He laughs, "Terrance is practically married, Jared has Miranda, and Jax doesn't date. They ask if we're dating, but that's because I'm living with a chick. Your girls only care because it's me. That's different. You're not the topic of discussion."

"Oh my god, Chris, that's so arrogant!"

"You're just mad I told the truth." he yawned, "Oh, please, I am not remotely happy about it."

"Shut up..." I mutter.

He laughs, "the movie's about over. Imma head to my room. Try to find someplace that delivers."

before you got back from work." Show him it's real.

"Uh... Thanks, Mya. I didn't even know you could cook."

"I'M A WONDERFUL COOK!" I say defensively.

"Ha, I just meant... I figured all that was left were these modern chicks. Only cares about money and themselves. You surprise me."

"I'm full of surprises. Give me a chance to change your mind." I asked he didn't respond. "You're just going to ignore me like I didn't say anything?"

He smirked, "Mya, you know better than me right now. I'm still trying to figure out how you even got on this thought process. You're acting weird."

"I am not! I'm admitting to not only your potential but your great progress all these years! It's sexy seeing someone getting better while so many are still making high school moves. You're on your grown man." I nudged him with my hip.

"Ha, yeah, I guess so?" he was taking it in stride as he took everything these days. Compliments or insults washed over him. "Eh, if your cooking is gonna take longer, then I could just walk to Gary's Pub or Servo's, for real. It'll be nice to go for a nice walk."

"No... Sit your happy ass down. I'm going to cook for you!" I snapped, pointing to the barstools, "Walk to a chair, and watch me put this work in, got it?"

sitting on the barstool pulling out his cellphone to check his messages.

I was probably far more aggressive than any of the girls he's ever dated. My father taught me to be assertive, and my military training taught me back up my words. Most other guys couldn't call my bluff or know of my judo record. Chris wasn't afraid of me. Though, I'm not about to have him putting any hands on me to find out whether he can take me or not. I wasn't curious to see if I could fight him. I wanted something so different. He would never believe me even if I could articulate it.

I don't want what my grandparents had. Working day and night my whole life, I still send off all my kids to the military because I can't afford to feed them and then lose two out of five anyway. My parents were still married and happily married. They have rough patches, but my dad says love finds a way. I want what we have now to be what we do forever. Getting him to see me that way after all this time will be impossible.

It's why we got along so well. He was so, not passive but aloof and unmoved. Nothing ever really bothered him outside of the chosen few political issues and his ex-girlfriend. I was warm-blooded, outspoken, and usually always got my way. Except for with him, the only man who would tell me no and make me listen to good advice.

to realize his full attention was on me.

"Ha, yes, ma'am." He leaned back like he was used to the treatment or had long been awaiting it.

As I moved past him, he gave me a light slap on my butt. I would never admit to him how much I liked it while he's in saint-mode. I looked a bit stunned, unsure whether he meant it as he did or if I was about to get some loving tonight. I knew I was at least sleeping with him tonight. A quick change of venue to his bedroom, a blunt, some wine, and it's almost a guarantee how the night would end. I need to calm down, and his willpower is insane, especially lately regarding sex and intimacy.

I had a new energy about me, shaking my booty as I danced to the fridge. I leaned in, poking my booty out, looking at him from the corner of my eye to see if he was paying attention.

"I'm making some chicken thighs, spinach, and zucchini with linguini. Is that cool?" I ask, going through the fridge.

"That sounds way out of your field of easy-mac and pop tarts. Want me to help?" he teased.

He was an amazing cook, so I never really had to. I loved being cooked for by Chris, so whenever he ate, I always had a plate of food waiting for me. I wanted to give back.

"Ha, you're gonna want to marry me after this meal. You need to start appreciating a real woman. Pick a movie and roll a blunt."

yawned.

"That's fine... Can you be quick? I only need half an hour."
I turned to find him already behind me putting on his shoes. "Oh,
hey there, babe, do you need me to match, or do you need any
money?"

He looked offended but brushed it off casually, "Naw, I
met a dude who lives in 1077, he said he has a good bud, and
he'll give me a sample. So, I'll probably just run by and come
back down." he said as if it was nothing.

"You're always meeting new people." I smiled. Yet, it
never brought too many over. "How did you manage to pull all
that together? What did you two talk about?"

He shrugged, "My energy, I guess. He thought I was cool.
I'm just living. Acknowledging my fellow man, plus not a lot of
people has the amounts I need. He's a low-key guy but a little
sketchy."

"Good, good. Hurry on now." I say, beginning to chop the
zucchini into chunks.

His arms wrapped around my waist, and I leaned back to
kiss him. He pulled away from a moment, and I gently nuzzled
closer to him. I was embracing what could be if he would let
down his cool.

"Whoa... what was that, Mya?" he asked, caught off guard.

"Hurry back..." I say, kissing him once more without

Forget sex. I can get used to this. My friends will be so jealous. They think we've been waiting so long. They'll be so angry I never told them! And they'll never believe this was the first night we kissed but most importantly, we haven't been knocking boots. Imagining what it would be like was all too much.

The zucchini was boiling with the pasta. And the spinach pesto was heating in a pot. If he was only going up the hall, he should be back by now. I wanted him here to see my plating skills from all the Gordon Ramsay shows we watched faithfully.

I let out a sigh, "he's probably smoking there."

I roll my eyes until I hear the laughter in the hallway. Both the laughing voices sounded familiar. The girl's laughter was the little neighbor who floated around here all the time. The second was my roommate. I went up to the peephole until I saw him right back the door, recoiling, nearly falling over myself.

"It was good meeting you," she says, giggling as his key slides in the door.

"Good, to be met. Hit me up some time. I'm right down the hall." He was eying her all over.

I opened the door and saw some little Eshan chick. I hope he knows she's low-key stalking him. Whenever he gets off home from work, she tries to cut him off in the hallway. Like clockwork, whenever he's usually back from work, she would

hallways for about five minutes, then sigh and leave if she didn't see him. Every day he either got in right before her or after she went in. I low-key watched her every day through the peephole. I had an air of doubt she was looking for him, but this confirmed my suspicions.

I sucked my teeth as he came into the apartment.

"What did I do?" he saw my face.

"Glad you met a friend..." I join his side, claiming what was mine.

"Oh, you two live together?" She saw me, and her eyes widened, then she turned back to him.

"Yes, I'm his roommate. Is that a problem?" I ask.

"Upstairs, you said you were single?" She fidgets, biting her thumb.

"I thought you just wanted to smoke sometime?" he was oblivious, "I told you. I'm not trying to start anything with anyone, ya know?" he confirmed, letting my heart rest easy. "She's my best friend. We've known each other since freshman year."

I was still first in line way before you or any other thirsty thots lurking around to break his heart. And if not me, I had plenty of friends who would treat him better. I stared at her as if she lost her mind coming into my territory or trying to push up

didn't even know she existed before today.

The Eshan smiled bright, "oh, I get it... Yeah, hit me up. I'll be running over to my place with my girl for a bit. We should be rolling up at my place. If you come over, then I'll smoke you up." she brushed his arm with her hand holding on to his wrist, "Text me when you're on the way. She'll love to see you as well. Ha, I have been trying to meet you for a minute, but you're never around."

"I'm usually here. I work to pay my bills and rent. For the rest of my time, I just try to build up my skills. I haven't been as social as I used to be with my workload and schedule."

Her eyes flipped to me for a second, letting me know the competition wasn't disappearing anytime soon.

"I can't wait to hear about it. Please just come by as soon as you're free, okay?" she waved, heading to get to her room a few doors down.

"Peace." He threw her deuces and then turned back to me. "Hey, Mya, do you wanna go later?"

"I'm not sure I was invited, bud... She seems much more interested in you." I roll my eyes and bypass him. "Dinner's ready."

"Ha, I don't think so. I just told her I wasn't interested." He had such faith in women caring he was single, attractive, husband material, and off the market.

doesn't care. You just made a challenge." I explained the game to him.

"You feel the same?" he caught on quickly.

I opened my mouth, caught off guard. I laughed up, covering my mouth.

"Mya..." he groaned.

"Ha, I'm just kissing you. She's been trying to jump your bones for a minute." I shrug, "besides... I should be the one you're dating. When I suggest you date someone new, I meant me, not someone new!"

He coughed between laughter and shock. "Mya, you're hilarious. You've been off it tonight."

"Haven't meant to be or anything. Ya know? We're young hot coeds. Everyone expects it from us."

"For me, that's less reason to do it. Forget about other people's expectations." He shrugged. "Do you wanna eat at the table?"

"Can we go to your room?" I suggested eagerly, a bit more zealous than he wanted.

He raised a brow, "why?"

"Kiss and cuddle in bed? Smoke a bit and drink some wine. I've been thinking about it the whole time you've been gone. Dinner in bed sounds better than breakfast, doesn't it? Take care of each other. No sex, just Flirting and touching." I

He laughed, shaking his head, "that won't end well."

"Neither will going over there smoking with that airhead," I muttered, stomping into the kitchen

"Hey, watch it. She's Eshan, not a ditz."

I shrug, "100% Erdun." I run my hands along my curves. "We grow em strong in Erdu."

"Don't forget mouthy."

"Whatever." I roll my eyes and laugh. "So, can we go to your room?"

"That's not the best idea. Let's just pop in another movie. I got some good weed. Let's just enjoy our night."

"Are you going over there?" I swallow.

"She said to text her when I was free, and I'm not free if I'm having dinner and watching a movie with you."

My cheeks reddened as I giggled like a fool. I stood in the kitchen, licking my teeth as I made both our plates. He sat at the island rolling up a nice blunt for after dinner. After, he poured two cups of the fresh uptown he loved so much and rarely ever shared.

I swallowed my pride and desire, enjoying our friendship. Watching happy as he devoured my food, going back for seconds and thirds before sitting on the couch rubbing his belly as we watched Men in Black 3.

ate on the couch with our feet kicked up on the ottoman, watching Will Smith japing on old school Kay. I was in heaven, living my fantasy with the first man I've truly grown to love. Chris snickered low-key feeling on my booty in one hand, passing me the blunt with the other. I pretended not to notice but was overjoyed our night was going so well. It seemed he was considering we should get more serious about a relationship.

His phone rang from his bedroom a few times, but he was reluctant to leave. I was unwilling to let him leave my side without him first reconsidering the future of our relationship.

"What's on your mind, Mya?" he asked me, not hiding how he was kneading my booty.

"How bad I want you...." I leaned into him, giving him better access to my booty, "You say you don't want me but keep teasing me."

"I never said I didn't want you. I said I didn't want to be dating or making love. It's not you, Mya. It's me. You're an extremely beautiful, educated, and funny girl. I am not in any condition to have a relationship." he sighed.

He started to move his hands away from me, but I clutched his shoulder. I nuzzled his neck, kissing up to his neck, reassuring him I was comfortable. Our eyes met as I guided his chin down to me. We kissed far more passionately than I've been kissed before. His tongue pushed into my mouth as his hands

waiting all his life to feel me. I felt distressed, knowing this wouldn't end in sex. Did it matter as long as he felt we had a chance?

We're friends. It's fine. No one is going to find out. What we decided to do in our apartment was our business, right? This is between God Almighty and us.

He pulled my breasts from my bra, pinching my nipples between his fingers underneath my shirt. I tossed my shirt off, feeling my self-control leave my body when he began playing with my breasts. We never had so much as kissed today. He's been kissing me, slapping my butt, feeling on my booty, and he knows how badly I want to jump his bones. I'm going to have to get aggressive with him if this is going to happen.

"Kiss me." I rub his cheek.

He leaned in, and we held our tender kiss for a moment before I went in for more. I was not wanting to stop until we were naked and slapping skin on the couch.

"Better now?" He asked, beginning to sit up, "get it out your system?"

"Worst, it's much worst. You're in for a long night, buddy..." I guided his hands along my curves, moaning to his touch. "Feel how wet you make me. Don't you want to feel how badly I want you, bestie?" I whispered in his ears, inviting him to explore my body further.

answer. I moved in, wrapping my arms around his neck and kissing him. He pulled me closer. I slide my sweatpants down until my booty began pouring out, overflowing in his hands as I moaned softly in his ear.

"Ooo..." I moaned as I straddled his lap.

We kissed as lovingly rubbed my clitoris, and my juices dripped onto his fingers like a ripe mango. I was completely caught off-guard as my fingers pumped in my wetness.

"Alright, alright, we need to chill!" he caught his breath, holding his hands up like the Regime was arresting him.

I screamed as shivers ran through my body. I had been so close to an orgasm, but he stopped right before I could ride over the hill.

"What's wrong, bestie? I need you to fill me up. Just take it, Chris, it's yours." I rubbed the imprint of his hard-on, licking my lips.

"This isn't real love, Mya. You lust for me. I told you this would end badly!" he sighed, "How did we even end up like this? We're going too far."

"Can you eat me out at least?" I arched my back, rubbing my clit with my other hand. "I can handle it, but I want to enjoy myself and enjoy you, Chris."

"I can do that." His fingers continued to play with my wetness. I went weak, clinging to the couch for support as he got

"Yes, yes, baby. I want to." I sounded so weak to my horniness, a slave to my desires "taste me, baby."

Chris's face seemed so strained, but he had promised. My flesh was on fire, wanting him more than I could describe. It felt like my vision blurred, only able to see my fantasies of him taking me all over the apartment. I gripped his head, wrapping my legs around his neck and pulling his face to my sex. He jerked back violently. My vision returned, and I saw a look completely unfamiliar to me. He looked pissed.

"Let's head to my room. We need to slow down. We have all night, not to mention our whole lease and lifetime. If this is something you want to pursue, then we should enjoy the night at least."

"You mean as friends or as lovers?" I tease, trying once more to get some head before he slips under my legs, tossing them to the side, evading my triangle hold.

He sighed, "You're pushing this issue. I don't like ultimatums, Mya."

"No one is forcing you into anything, Chris. I want you to want me." I lied, knowing I had him for an entire year, and he needed to tame me if he wanted to be a holy-roller. He could be a saint for everyone else. I needed a taste of the Chris I once knew. To feel him once before what little remained of the old Chris was gone forever.

I've had men shower me with gifts or take me on dates in hopes of a hand job. I've been peer pressured into sex. I smoked up, and the next thing I knew, I was butt-naked with my feet in the air. Gotten drunk and rammed in each hole until my boy toy was exhausted or his friend wanted a turn. Chris refused me, and I could not understand why. Other men didn't seem able to control themselves, especially not the men who wanted to feel my gift from God between my legs. Recollecting the men who had their way with me, still hitting me up and telling me how badly they needed me. It felt so easy to go back to it. If getting sex from Chris would be this hard, I needed someone to give me a good orgasm.

"I do very much want you, ha. Or else we wouldn't have gone this far. I admit my part in things, but we can't blame this on the weed and good food. You deserved some love for throwing down. As I said, I don't want you running back and telling your friends. And I'm not trying to find another chick just for things to end in a couple of months."

"Chris… I said I understand." I was getting frustrated with how he spoke to me like some ignorant child.

"Then you understand I want to wait before we have sex. I want to wait, Mya. I can feel my balls ready to pop, and you look so sexy."

him preaching at me.

"Mya-

"Fine, fine, I'm going to take a quick shower, alright? Can we at least not pretend like this didn't happen? I know things will be awkward for you, but this is the direction I want to take, and I know it's what I want. This wasn't a mistake, Chris."

"I never said any of that. I enjoyed myself, but I don't know. I don't remember when a woman and I decided to stop and leave it at kissing or foreplay. Either I want what they have between their legs bad enough, or they wanted sex, then we rush into it or force a relationship to get there." he sighed, "It's not you, Mya, you're my type, and I want you, I want you. I just can't repeat the sins of my past."

"I can tell." I giggle, rubbing his crotch, "Let me at least take care of you, baby."

"Ha, I'm very used to going without. I'll be okay. Just take your shower, bud. Take your shower, I'll roll another, pour us some wine, and we can relax tonight." He smacks my butt, "Get going."

"Oooo... stop." I giggle, pulling my pants up, "I'm glad you enjoyed your dinner and dessert."

"I think I passed on dessert." he chuckled.

"Shut up..." I blushed, rushing to the bathroom with my cheeks flush.

remember the same memories flashing across my mind and cleaning a stranger's seed from my face, my hair, or from inside me. For some reason, this feeling felt so familiar. Having sex, having a man all over me, and still needing to cum. Things seemed to end after they reached their climax. I don't remember how many times I truly reached my peak. Often needing one or two men in a night to feel what I desired, and even then, I felt sick to my stomach.

In my freshman year, two upperclassmen got me drunk in their dorm. I didn't tell anyone where I was going. Once I was drunk, they had me suck their pricks to pay them back for the cheap liquor. I had a headache from the jungle punch. They called me every name in the book and kept the liquor coming as they took turns playing with my breasts. Drying humping me until finally, they couldn't resist themselves and ripped off my clothes like I was some hooker. It felt good. I had only had sex a few times beforehand with my boyfriend I had broken up with a few weeks prior. Once I was single, it seemed no man could resist shooting their shot. They came inside me. Only one wore a condom. The other I thought was cute, so I let him hit it raw. I let him cum inside me and again on my face as I sucked him off. His roommate had to wear a condom but had no issue coming between my breasts as I blew his friend.

body as the two laughed and joked about how they would do this to me every week. How dumb I was and desperate I must have been. The shower hid my tears, realizing these two didn't even know my name. They had only known my ex and had a grudge against him. I was some trophy they had wanted because I belonged to another.

Many of my experiences ended similarly until eventually, I didn't care who the man had been. I didn't care who I had sex with or care if we stayed together. I figured they were all the same. I wanted to feel wanted, to feel an orgasm, for each time to be better than the last. It didn't matter how attractive the man, whether or not he cared about me, had good sex, or even had a sizeable cock. It was a crapshoot. I was usually too drunk or high to care about any of it.

Chris had a point. He knew who my friends were, and this is the first day the idea has ever popped in my head. But I knew I was right. He never tried to take advantage of me. Even before he became religious, he advised me and warned me I was walking down a pathway to hell. I know I love Chris. He wouldn't believe I wanted anything more than sex or to scratch my emotional itch. That's just how things worked for me sometimes. An idea pops into my head, and it's just true. He and I would make an amazing couple. That's just a fact. He never seemed the romantic type. He suspected me, as I suspected him. Now, I'm used goods. No wonder he didn't want to have sex with me.

That was the past. I haven't had sex with a man in over a year. Opal was usually my go-to whenever I felt I could control myself and vice versa. It kept us from dating horrible men. It kept me from returning to my old ways. I hadn't recognized Chris and the man he had become. That freshman girl I used to be was long gone. I replaced with a girl who refused to be hurt or used and had no issue hurting or using men for whatever I needed. Mostly for whatever I felt I wanted. Sex, food, drugs, or attention used to fill my diet. I've been trying so hard to get Chris's attention since his concert. There hasn't been another man who could hold a candle.

I could have easily slipped back into the life I used to live. I could easily call up one of my old beaus, and they would gladly get a booty call in to brag to their friends. I would come home and complain about how men are dogs. The world keeps spinning.

No, Chris is right. Enough is enough. I know he can satisfy my every need. I have him exactly where I want him. There is no other woman in his life and no other man in my life. I'm not sure how long I can wait until we have sex. If he wanted me to follow him on his spiritual journey, then I'll gladly follow.

I enjoyed a nice warm shower, lathering up my body, letting my body simply be at peace from the pleasure. I had Chris

I let my naturally super curly hair go free as Chris always recommended not bothering to straighten it. I took out my braids last month and had a paycheck or two until I could afford to get it done again. A bit of olive oil, wiping away my tears, and I was walking to his bedroom in my towel.

I wasn't quick enough to stop him from being on the phone when I got back. I realized it was the Eshan down the hall. I groaned, making my presence known as I lay on his bed, hoping to have his attention and company to myself tonight.

"You said tonight? I misunderstood. Uh, my roommate and I are eating dinner. I already smoked a bit. I thought this would be later in the week, and I didn't realize your girl was there already waiting. I thought you were going to be chilling with her for a while. We have a blunt rolled up already. We could match if you want."

"I wanted to smoke you up. Dude, I legit asked you to come over here." she was audibly irritated, "No, I tried calling you like five times. I didn't want to knock on your door because I didn't want to seem too clingy, but if I knew you would stand me up, then maybe I should have kicked the door in!"

Did you call him five times after only meeting him today? You should have taken the hint and called him back tomorrow like a normal person.

of his nose, trying to figure out a solution.

"What time is later?" Her voice was seductive and sweet with a long wispy drawl. "Couldn't you stop by for a blunt and head back? My friend wants to meet you. She says you have a class together."

"Ha, if my friends can't get high, I'm not getting high. Dems the rules. Just come by in a bit. Let's just have a good time, Kay?"

"Fine... Text me when you're ready. Don't take too long. Or should I just come by when we're ready?"

"Eh, just come back whenever you two are set. I have some wraps if you want to roll up."

"Great! I mean, if that's what you like. I have a piece as well. Oh- what? I hope I'm not spastic! Sorry, we'll figure it out when we get to you. See you soon."

Chris sat on the edge of his bed, rubbing the bridge of his nose as if a migraine tremored through his skull.

"Hey, we're gonna have guests tonight." he yawns, falling back on his bed, "It's been a while. I don't think anyone's seen my new room."

I roll my eyes, "Tell her to stay home. It's just us tonight." I nuzzle his neck, speaking in my whiney voice. "She just wants to jump your bones."

"Ha, not getting the two of you confused, are you?" he

"Chris, I waited years. I thought when you wanted to be roommates that you finally wanted to get serious about us. This chick hangs outside our door every day to talk to you." I protest.

He smiled, "really? That's sweet."

"Chris, you said-

"Yes, I did after I told you a thousand times I'm not interested in pursuing. I don't want her either, Mya. You just need to have some faith in people." he sighs, falling back in the bed. "You're rushing me. I rather her come over. Get some space and slow this down. It'll be nice to meet some new friends."

"Play the field and see your options, now that you changed your mind." I was offended and intimidated. Men always went gaga for a new cookie.

"I didn't change my mind, Mya. You're just coming at me like a wolf. I don't know what to say, for real. It's like I turn you down. I have to deal with your attitude. If I say yes, I have to go against what I want. I don't want to be in this situation. So, I need to think before I continue. This will give me some time to think."

I didn't realize I was pushing him in such a corner. It seemed like he's been enjoying it up until this point. The way he's touching me and has me acting. Can I let him just do that with another woman after all this? Oh, god, I'm feeling him. God help me. This is what we were trying to avoid. Am I stuck? Am I

"You're right... We need to breathe." I pour him a glass of wine and take a sip from it before handing it to him. "What?" I asked, catching him looking at me sideways.

"You're about to pour yourself a glass. Why you sipping mine?" he laughed.

"Tell me... Are you just- not even remotely interested in dating me?" I knew so many other men that had all of me who didn't.

He sighs, "I mean... Yeah, I am, but- I like you, Mya Harik. I don't know. The last girls just weren't with it. It's like they didn't care, and they didn't want love. They just wanted a boyfriend. You're on me and whatever, but for how long until you want to be friends again? Girls are fickle. I don't want to waste my time or catch feelings. All of you like the sound of love but never the reality, especially not the work it takes."

"I understand... But I'm not caught up on sex anymore. This feels like how it should've been from the jump. And it's what we've technically been doing sans sex has been intimacy. We have everything that's ever been missing for both of us. Am I missing something?"

"In one direction, but I don't get caught on that. That's how you are. That's how I've been we're flirts. I like you, but I love my solitude right now."

"Yeah, with you! I'm not up under any guy. You're my

to room with a goofy who would be sniffing my panties. I want to be with someone a bit more mature and focused. We would be doing what we're doing. But maybe we'll get married and have a kid in a couple of years, not watching bootlegs and smoking weed. But we wouldn't have to stop that at all. That sounds like a good time until the grave. That's my point. I could spend the rest of my life with you."

He sighs, "I wish you didn't put that in my head. You're not even serious about kids."

"I would be with good men, focused, real men. They're so rare! Most of these dudes are man-children, goofies, or creeps. If you got me pregnant, I wouldn't be upset, and if we planned it, that's even better."

"Glad I moved past that standard." He was unmoved by anything I had to say.

"Look, if you were a girl trying to figure out who you're gonna be letting nut inside you, or be sweating on top of you or humping on your butt. And especially take around your family. Options seem short sometimes. I used to have my doubts about you. But I watched you get your life together. We were on the phone together whenever we had a breakup. You're my best friend. If you were the man, I married-

"Seriously, just stop... You're not even serious. You just want some meat! Actions speak louder than words. Yours spoke it."

"That's not it at all!"

"Yeah? Even if I did believe you, you're only thinking with your clit."

"That's... Partially true, but I want more than just sex. I have no issue with us waiting. I admit I've never taken it seriously until today. For real, Chris Kirin Tor'jun. I would love to spend my life with you."

"Please just go get dressed. If you're so worried, hang out with us. Let me know what you think about them." he rubs his temples, "Kira's gonna be here in a bit. I would like a night not being accosted by women for sex."

I roll my eyes, "I'm not playing you, and I've never said that to a man before, Chris."

"I don't think you are, but I know when morning hits, you'll be singing a different tune like every other chick who took me down the road of sin. I thought only men ran the game, but women are no different. My life isn't some game. I'm done being the story."

I felt so hurt being compared to every other woman he's known. I was even being compared to Margot of all people. I was grabbing my glass and knocking his blunt to the ground.

"Oops..." I roll my eyes, bumping his remote off the nightstand to the floor as I dragged my feet out the door.

he barks at me, snapping me out of my callousness.

"Whatever!" I scream back at him.

"What'd I say? Act like you lost your mind if you want to, girl." He raised a brow at me as if I lost my mind.

My anger was replaced with an even deeper wanting. I sipped my wine, letting my towel drop and watching his jaw drop as he looked upon me. I turn about-face, shaking my hips as I marched out of his room.

The door knocked, and I muttered. I wanted to let her knock until she went crazy. It would only piss him off, piss off the neighbors, and they'll close the door on me. Besides, I wanted to drink and smoke with my friend more. I never had a problem with any of his friends or girlfriends. They might have had an issue, and now I see why, from both sides, unfortunately.

I opened the door while Chris was straightening up his space. It wasn't too dirty, but he hadn't had company since we moved in. Something I never really bothered to note before today. He usually went to Terrance's or whatever nearby the Nights had. Those were so few, and between Terrance graduated early and moved back to Nadia. I doubt he'll ever be back out this way. Jared is currently in Esha in negotiations with Kismet for a college tour. There's no one else I've seen him with anymore. I'm sure he has friends, but he stood alone.

Her almond eyes met mine. She looked disappointed but handled it well. She mustered up a smile holding up the sack of weed, hoping to make quick friends. I wasn't impressed with the little eighth she was flossing. Between the two of them, they could have grabbed more. I remember the gesture from my

butt naked with a headache.

"Hey, what's up, girl?" Kira smiled, "this is Margot, my roommate."

"What are you doing here, Margot?" I push Kira aside, eyeballing the last person I wanted to see right now.

"Hey Mya, it's good to see you too. I believe I was invited. When they were smoking upstairs, he said her roommate could come. Chris and I spoke months ago and decided to let bygones be bygones. I was hoping to keep the peace tonight. How about we try being *friends*?" Margot's smile seemed like fake porcelain, pretty little white teeth but would shatter as soon as you test it.

I opened the door, letting them in. "He's in his room. He'll probably be a minute."

"Great, how was your day?" Margot asks.

"My day was wonderful, like living in a dream. What possessed you to come over here tonight? You haven't done enough?" I replied sharply.

"It's nice living with my man, isn't it?" Margot smiles with a wink.

"I bet you wish you knew." I give her a wink right back.

Margot's eyebrow rose as she fixed her mind for a response. I left them at the doorway and walked to the kitchen to pour myself another glass of wine.

His door crept open, and there was some whispering

Margot peeking into his room then waving Kira over.

"Can we come in?" Kira asked, pushing the door open more. "Hey!" She smiles brightly. "We picked up from a different guy. Damien is a bit of a creep. The NRA plaques and Mayan Resistance Flag were a bit off-putting."

"And he keeps trying to slide in my DMs." Margot chimes.

"So...?" Chris responded, dead as a doorknob.

"Are you okay? You look sad." Kira pinched his cheek.

"Just lost in thought." his eyes darted from Kira to me then back to Margot.

Kira swooned over his memorabilia from his mask days. He had a display of the Masks he collected and a story for each one. She jumped up and down, asking for him to share one.

I stood outside his door as Margot tried squeezing past me to reach her friend. Her girl raised a finger to her lip then looked over at me.

Don't look over here, hoe.

I was sipping my Cabernet Sauvignon the whole way acting as if I couldn't notice Margot struggling. Chris was sitting on the floor, leaning against the wall. Kira sat on the bed holding a gold and orange mask with a bright star on the forehead with an open eye. Margot finally gave up, waiting for me to walk in first. I'm not sure they're aware we're all enemies yet.

caught your full name." Margot says, extending her hand to me, trying once again to befriend me, "I'm Margot Hoska Dalio, communications major."

"I have no interest in talking to you, Margot. Smoke your blunt, get your closure, and move on with your life." I roll my eyes.

"Chris, I thought you always said we would try to be friends?" Margot whined from behind me.

Chris rubs his chin. "Sounds very familiar. I remember saying we would get married too. The only guarantee life gives us is that things change."

"I have rites to be here, Chris. Let me in." Margot's tone changed as she stomped her foot.

"Where does the name Hoska come from?" Chris asks.

"It's a family name about one hundred or so years old. My Grandpa always goes on about the Hoskas of old, thousands of years ago. They were pretty disappointed when I came to college instead of following the family business."

"What's the family business?" Chris asked, far more interested.

She sighed with a frown, "We-

"Maybe another time. It's not that important right now. I don't think it's one of the best things to lead with. It's a bit trippy. I don't know what's going on. Can we just be friends?"

know is Big Jacob Hoska, the cat burglar."

"That's my dad." She buries her head in her hands, "it's my senior year... How can they expect that from me? At least let me graduate first, right?"

"They've been doing it for years. They're good at it, ha." I chuckle. "Must be better breaking into banks than cramming for tests, right?"

"They're criminals..." Margot sighs, "There's a lot of places my father can't go."

"Jake the Fox is a legend!" Chris chuckled, "Probably not the best father."

"Nope! Not at all, Can we smoke? This stresses me out. I-I'm sorry, I didn't mean to be rude." Margot rushed things along, "I didn't expect you to be so interested or knowledgeable. Most have no idea."

"Eh, I have weird interests these days. I considered robbing a bank or two trying to pay for university." he sneered.

"Maybe I can finally introduce you to dad now that you know why I've been such a brat. I did a lot of thinking. Will you let me in?" Margot asks.

"I just want to hear about this mask...." Kira lets out a groan.

"What is happening? You said if my friends can't smoke, then you won't. Can you relax a little? It's alright to let down

her tone became more determined.

"Fine, Margot, go inside." I relent, tired of hearing her prattle on, "can he finally tell his story?"

Kira leaned against her girl. "Do you have to be so dramatic?"

Margot smiles at Chris as she sits on the edge of the bed. I curl up on his bed by his pillows, burying my head in the feathers of his cologne and musk. It must have been some sight for him to have all of us strewn around his room.

"You do want to use a piece?" Kira asks, reaching in her purse.

"This is a blunt house." Chris points to his nightstand at the cigarillo wrappings.

Margot giggled, "I love blunts too. Do you want to roll or me? I'm pretty good now."

"I have one ready. We can just spark this. I'm pretty tired." Chris raises his hand with the blunt meant for the two of us.

I guess it was just a blunt, but they offered to smoke us up, didn't they?

"I know, but I wanted to match, ya know? It would make me feel better." Kira takes out her small bag and sets it on the table. "I hope I'm not difficult."

"Not at all, you're fine. Margot or Mya can roll. I'm going

bottles."

"Oh, so now you like wine?" Margot grins.

"Oh, now you smoke?" Chris challenged.

"Well, you opened up my mind a lot. I hope you can be open-minded as well tonight." Margot confessed.

I let out a sigh, grabbed his grinder from inside his nightstand, and held my hand out to Kira.

"I'll roll," I say.

"I'll help you with the glasses." Kira stands to follow Chris, and a few seconds they were gone.

There wasn't much she could do between the kitchen and back. Besides, Chris is a normal Chris disinterested and friendly. He acted the same way with my friends when he wasn't feeling flirty. They were dividing us up. What were they planning?

"So... You two are dating or just sex?" Margot asks me straight out, "Since this is a blunt house, I thought I would just ask."

"Nope," I reply with a pop of my lips. "Doesn't seem like that even mattered or occurred to you or your girl."

"Well, she's smitten. They had a class together a couple of years ago. Then she found out we lived down the hall."

"Great..." I roll my eyes, "She doesn't even know him."

"But she wants to... Isn't that good enough? I know him pretty well." Margot laughs. "You sure you're not dating, you're

communication classes paying dividends.

"I'll punch a stranger in the face." I squint my eyes at her "don't analyze me."

"Oh, that was not an analysis. It is palpable. Kira swears up and down. You two are just friends. I don't know. Maybe protect your man better than I did?" Margot shrugged her shoulders.

I laughed, "He's not interested in anyone after the fiasco dating you. All he does is work on his projects. He's close, he says. Don't try distracting him, or else we'll have real issues. I know he wasn't perfect toward you either. Be friends if you're gonna be friends but don't come in here scheming on his heart."

"That's a shame." Margot bit her lip, "Seeing you up close, Mya. You're so beautiful. I was hoping for an orgy..." Margot sighed, falling back on the bed. "A girl can dream."

"Ha, what the hell?" I laugh as I seal the blunt closed with my tongue. "The hell did you just say?"

"I said I wish I were that wrap you're licking up. Ha, if he and Kira have sex, then we can get to know each other. Do our own thing. You're here and cute. So, why not right?" she bit her lip, hoping I was going to be along with the idea, "Ha, I'm joking, I'm joking."

"You planned on double-teaming my boy from the jump, didn't you?" I shook my head.

holding her hair back and kissing him while she did it. Maybe, we take turns. Maybe head isn't enough, and he decides he wants to take one of us for a spin. Knowing him one girl isn't enough. So, I would be willing to include you in on that." Margot shrugged, "you two seem like you're going through something. I just have a sense for these things. It comes with the whole being a cat burglar and whatnot."

I nodded, unsure of how to respond or if I wanted to. She seemed innocent, but she was a liar. Her little sundress betrayed her secret. Does she think I'm stupid?

I looked up, noticing Chris and Kira weren't back yet. Margot had finished texting someone on her phone then turned her attention back to me.

"Were you the reason he broke up with me?" Margot asked.

"He decided he didn't want to be mistreated anymore all by himself." I stare her back in the eyes.

Up close, I could see why he had fallen for such a girl. She was confident, beautiful, and direct. They seemed alike, but she had something lurking behind her smile. I felt so on edge around Margot. Every time I tried to relax, my shoulders tensed even harder.

Margot's brown eyes were mesmerizing. It almost seemed as if they were changing colors. My body felt paralyzed

wetness from earlier.

"Oh, Mya, you got yourself all wrapped up in my little plan. Don't worry. I'll make sure you at least enjoy yourself." Margot waved her hands over my eyes.

I was wide awake but unconscious, comatose.

"You wanted him along… I could tell from the café you would be in trouble. Well, since you couldn't beat me. You can join me, Mya. We'll be fast friends. You'll help me bring Chris back to his senses from all this solitude nonsense."

Margot pumped her fingers into me, claiming me with her gaze. My body felt so neglected I couldn't stop here. She quickly gave me what I had been craving all month. Margot stabbed inside me the way only hatred can. I felt myself beginning to squirt from the shock and excitement. I lost my voice, unable to scream or moan.

What came over me? I felt as if she had cast some kind of spell on me. As if I completely underestimated my opponent's fighting style. I had wondered for so long how she got Chris wrapped around her finger. She would never let me live this down.

In the kitchen, Kira was listening to Chris's story of the golden and orange mask.

thing in Graham, a little far from where I lived but began to make his presence known in Little Penah. I was with a squad called "The Midnight Patrol," we started at midnight and would stop a few hours before school to get a nap in before 2nd period."

"You were like an actual Mask?" Kira bit her lip, thumbing the material of the mask.

"I was something. TMP was definitely on the side of order. There is no real military or police force left in Nadia in the past hundred years. Some of us wore Masks to lessen the gap between chaos and order. Others hid their faces as they let chaos consume them. Morningstar was a bad dude. He developed a cult following after Sameera's death. People wanted a leader so desperately. Instead, they got a man who used gang initiations to break in recruits. So many died in the process, and the ones who survived were brainwashed, attending daily indoctrination meetings."

"How do you know that?"

"Word got around. A few of our people infiltrated the group. Only one came back. One was killed. The one who came back was Leo, who wore a lion mask. He came back with his mask in his hands, the ultimate sign of shame. Leo was a deeply prideful man. He wanted to replace Crimson one day. He was just a man when he returned, a broken man. Leo told us the

moving to the mountains in Erdu."

"Whoa…" Kira covered her mouth.

Chris nodded, his mood somber, "That was my last run about as well. First-time things ever got so bloody. When we got to his compound in Graham to end it all, after months of fighting and hunting them back to Graham, we found every person died. Everyone but Morningstar, who was in a summoning circle in the middle of the room, tried to summon the spirit of Enshishi to help him fight. We knew nothing about magic, spells, or religion. We just didn't want to see our home destroyed by our own hands. Morningstar didn't care at all. The Crimson Elite stormed the compound after we started the fight, and thank God. Crimson fought Morningstar one-on-one, and it was otherworldly. Crimson was a pyro-terrakinetic fighting a demon from hell, and it seemed like an even fight. If it persisted, then Crimson's mentality would break him. The turning point was when two locked up. The Demon was much physically strong, but Crimson bellowed out a prayer. He recited, 'Our Father, Who art in heaven, Hallowed be Thy Name. The Thy Kingdom come. Thy Will be done, on earth as it is in Heaven. Give me your will and power! Help me win this day in the name of The Heavens!' Then I swear a ray of pure ethereal light shined down and melted Morningstar to bone and boiling blood. Nothing remained but his mask. Crimson was wounded badly but moved as if he was

to remember the day that God prevailed and God always will prevail. A man may fail, and man may doubt, but God will always prevail. Then five months later, I was coming to college in Erdu. I hoped I would find Leo, but he's further east. I could only move forward with my own life."

"Whoa, so you're like a demon-hunter?" Kira was mesmerized.

"I'm a student, ha. My role in the fight was minimal. I fought some of the lesser demons and helped my own, but I'm human. I never had anyone teach me how to use my element. Once I saw the summoning circle open, I nearly shat myself. I prayed like it was all I could do though then The Crimson Elite came."

"I love spirituality!" Kira rubs his cheek.

"What's your religion?" Chris asks.

"Well, my parents are devotees of Anka, The Air Guardian. They say we have believed in him since the beginning of time. So, I guess I'm aligned with my region. We believe in all the prophets and study the whole history of Gaia. I enjoyed studying about Ecru."

"Whoa..." Chris says, impressed.

"I am just trying to get through without upsetting any Gods and enjoying my life." Kira laughs as she sips her glass of wine.

"Toast with me." Kira pours him a glass.

"What are we having a toast for, Kira?" Chris raises an eyebrow.

"Well, after your story, we should toast to how much your situation has changed. I mean, you survived. You're graduating. You're at the top of our class. And you're so handsome." Kira hands him the glass.

"How do you know all that?" Chris tilts his glass toward his lips.

"Well, I liked you before Margot even saw you. I talked you up so much the next thing I knew. You two were dating. She said she would introduce us years ago. I knew you were a great guy, but I never had my opportunity." Kira explains.

"That's nice… so Margot told you all about her ex-boyfriend? With intentions of what?" he asked.

"Well, you can have more than one girlfriend, right?" Kira said nonchalantly.

"So, you two would both date me…? How would that work?" Chris rubbed his temples and shook his head, remembering his freshman and sophomore year, getting a headache.

"Ha, we can show you if you want. She said you two got into a really bad fight. We want to make it up to you tonight."

between us." Chris shook his head.

"Of course, I didn't get all the details, but I apologize on behalf of Margot." Kira tries to tap his glass.

"No... Margot needs to apologize for herself." Chris says, coming back in the room. "I'm just not interested."

"What?" Kira nearly spilled her wine on herself.

"I would date you by yourself. Not with Margot whispering in your ears. I already dated Margot. I guess she's a great friend, but we are not compatible."

"Well... good, forget about Margot." Kira giggled.

"Why would you even allow yourself to be a part of that type of plan, Kira?"

Kira struggled to find her words. His disappointment made gravity feels three times as strong. Kira fell to her knees, moving to her last resort. She looked up for permission.

"Do what you must." Chris sighed, taking a sip from his glass.

Kira slowly began unbuckling his pants, watching his eyes study her. She saw the question on his face. I was asking why she was doing it. Kira pulled out his manhood, holding it in her hands, kissing up its length, trying to get a rise out of him. She managed it in her mouth, coughing and gagging as it pushed down her throat. Kira covered her eyes, trying her best not to cry, feeling like a total fool.

"Want me to help you up?" Chris asks.

"Please… a little more?" Kira wipes her eyes.

"Kira, I just met you today. What are you trying to prove to me?" Chris pleads for an answer.

"I thought this is what men wanted?"

"I used to want it. Now, I want loyalty, intimacy, someone who motivates me and gets me to the next levels of my life. If you need this, then I understand what it's like. I'll break you off real quick, but I don't think this will bring us any closer. Sex usually creates more distance if there's no love."

"That sounds so beautiful… did I ruin my chances with you?" Kira strokes his length in her face until it was erect, licking along with it to his head.

"I've never seen an Eshan as beautiful as you. You also look so good with my kielbasa in your hands. We could figure something out, but we're moving way too fast. Why didn't you just ask to talk or hang out by yourself? We could have done our own thing."

"Margot didn't think it would be a good idea," Kira said everything he needed to hear to figure out what was happening.

Kira struggled with his size more, feeling light-headed as she bobbed her head halfway down his length. She was drooling down her chin as she nearly suffocated, bringing herself down his full length, kissing his golf-ball-sized jewels. Chris ran his

passed out. Kira sat back against the cupboard, catching her breath, wiping the saliva from her face.

"Whoa…" Kira closed her eyes, hoping it would stop the room from spinning.

"Want to try your luck?" Chris giggles.

"I need to smoke. Do you have any mouthwash?" Kira covered her face.

"In the bathroom down the hall, there should be some." I wasn't moving from my post.

"I can't move… can you get it?" Kira asked.

"Yeah, I'll check on Mya and Margot as well. I'm surprised they aren't arguing."

"Wait, wait. I'll go. Just hold on, let me catch my balance! I'm on my way!" Kira screams out.

In the bedroom, Margot had me folded on my shoulders, my legs rag dolling in the air as she had her way with me. Until we heard Kira's screaming, then Margot relented to find out things hadn't gone as well on the other side of her battle. Her friend had failed, and her prize was returning. Margot broke eye contact with me. I regained some self-control. I grabbed her arm and hooked my legs around her neck, beginning to choke Margot out from muscle memory. The triangle-choke won me so many jiu-jitsu competitions. Hornier than ever as I released her, hoping I hadn't killed the mood.

Margot smiled, rubbing her neck beginning to laugh at me, "Are you going to tell on me?"

Kira came back blushing and disappointed. She sat quietly on the floor at Margot's feet. Margot combed her fingers through Kira's straight hair. Margot whispered something in Kira's ear. The girl shook her head.

"Wow, good thing we didn't make a bet. I thought any guy would be all for it." Margot was loud enough for us both to hear, "A bit disappointing. I thought Chris was a stud."

"I wish you didn't ask me to ask him," Kira muttered under her breath.

Margot smiled, "I didn't want to be left out. Besides, I thought it would sweeten the deal to know he had his pick of which mouth to enjoy. We don't mind you watching either." she made eye contact with me.

"He's a brick wall." I sigh, sparking the blunt. "You asked him for sex?"

"What? No, I could never do something so embarrassing!" Kira covered her face.

"What did you get done?" Margot asks quietly.

"I tried, but it was beyond me. I couldn't do it. It was too much." Kira's cheek turned firetruck red as she shared.

"Did you at least enjoy it?" Margot began to giggle.

seeming confused, "You said this would be easy, Margot."

"Nothing is sacred anymore, and I want something sacred." Chris sighed as he appeared with the glasses, "So, you two planned this after I told you I did not want you back and did not want to have sex with your friends to make up for what you did? Not only that but instead of you doing it yourself, you send someone else to do your dirty work?"

"Ha, we can be yours alone. We don't mind. We've never shared a guy before, but we share everything. I like sacred. That's so poetic." Margot replied as if she didn't hear a word he said.

"One woman is enough trouble. Rakil forbids I had two." Chris laughs alone.

I think Margot felt a personal insult. Girls like her didn't get rejected often. "Three beautiful women offer themselves to you. That seems like a yes, every time."

Three of us were pissed. The same guy in one night denied three women. And he was laughing at our expense and having girls throw herself at his feet. Even Margot was a beautiful girl. The dress fit so well, complimenting Margot's long raven-black hair and deeply tanned olive skin from a rich bloodline and plenty of sunlight. She is beautiful, young enough to be taught all his ideas, and mature enough in her own right. Kira had an adorable face. His phallus was big enough to split

never tried before but might need to try this plan with Opal. I definitely wouldn't mind seeing the two of them more intimate, and I never considered watching him in the act an option. The thought of having seen Kira try to fit him in her mouth thrilled me to no end.

Hell, considering, if we do stay friends. I wouldn't mind watching either of these girls at least give him neck. They seemed so ready for it. They would have to share him at once.

Margot lost interest, staring off into space. She didn't take rejection well.

"You all look so sad, and then you wonder why I wouldn't bother. No sex, and you're out of it?" he laughed, "This is exactly my point, Mya. Have sex with a chick, and yeah, maybe she'll stick around, but it's like all you girls care about is getting sex these days."

"None of this was about sex, Chris Kirin Tor'jun, are you daft? It's about showing you how badly I wanted you back. You're not even interested in me anymore. It kind of hurts me. It at least feels weird. It's been a while, so I expected you to move on. I was pretty excited when I learned you didn't have a girlfriend, and no one knew who you if you were having sex: the wine, weed, beautiful women. You're having a great time. Why not us? I wanted to suck your cock, not have sex. I wanted to

has missed you by submitting to you."

Just when I thought she quit, she had a new method of attack.

"I don't care. We're sharing the same space. Couldn't you ask me privately instead of sending your friend? And if we can't be friends in this space, then hell no, sex is definitely off the table. It sure shouldn't be the main course or a bargaining chip." he lit the blunt and took a nice draw before blowing it out his nose, "I'm so done with chicks. They just want money or your soul energy. I'm tired of it."

"Ha, well... How much more is there to life?" Margot laughed, "You have both and two girls who want to enjoy those things with you. I have money as well. We can share, I'll invest in your business or whatever your project was, and I could help you be successful. I didn't mean to offend you. All we wanted was to suck you off together."

"You should have gone into robbery than communications." Chris exhales his second toke.

"Ha, I just wanted to suck your cock, bro. Smoke and suck your cock with my best friend. Sounded like a pretty simple request." Margot rolled her eyes. This girl was a sociopath, but it seemed to be working.

I was getting pretty wet with how forward she was being. Kira bit her lips, hoping he would crack, ready at any moment to let the weed, wine, and Margot's reverse psychology do its work. But he was a brick wall. I know he'll reject her. I hope he rejects her.

Margot smiled wide, walking over to Chris and brushing his cheek. My lips jerked as I wanted to rip her off, but I wanted to know where his answer lay. Would this be my first time with him while sharing him with two strangers?

"I want you in my mouth. Just let me." Margot bit his ear, rubbing his chest, nearly sitting in his lap. "There aren't many men I'm offering to suck, and you're on all three of our lists. I think every girl here wouldn't mind a little taste of your fat dong. This is going to be a great night for you if you just let down the monk act."

"I have to go to the bathroom." Kira stood, "can you show me?" She looked at me, hoping I was down with coming back to see Margot's mouth full for the green light of her orgy.

If I left, it wouldn't be another random girl like Kira with him. It would be Margot, a woman with no boundaries and no qualms about taking whatever she wanted. She would never respect our home if he caved in. This night could have been the two of us alone. She was going to be getting my dessert.

"The bathroom is down the hall, to the left." I pointed. Besides, I'm next in rotation. And sharing isn't my strong suit. "Hey, baby, you don't need to. I know how you feel. I'm starting

bones at the same time, I would get out of that room ASAP."

Margot feigned her surprise and anger toward me. She smiled wide, hiding her scorn. She rested her head on his shoulder as she took the blunt from him.

Sociopath!

She probably just wanted to suck out for his life force. These young succubae were everywhere. I at least made him dinner first.

Chris just laughed, "You girls are a trip. You're more aggressive than men when you want something. I'm not interested. Look, I would love to. But we have to wake up tomorrow. I'm tired of the morning after. I want years, not a few nuts, for a good time. As good as it does sound to delve down your throats and to make little Kira gag again. I want more from my life. It's not that you women aren't attractive. It's like being offered a taste of each region. Believe me, if I was a lesser man living in my past sin, then I would. I've just been given a taste of something greater. I know if I give in, I'll lose it. My connection with God is more important than a couple of hours of sex with beautiful women who care nothing about my soul."

"I just want you more that you turn me down. You're just making it a challenge!" Margot joins his laughter but was deadly serious. "Can we at least see it?"

beyond belief.

Margot wickedly bites her index finger.

"Margot, he already said no, it's okay. He has a point. Let's just enjoy ourselves, maybe another time?" Kira shrugs.

Margot was past the point of caring. She ignored Kira as if she didn't speak. Kira left so she wouldn't need to watch what needed to be done for their nut.

So, this is why men are so aggressive when you turned them down. Rejection hurt. The failure only seemed to create more persistence. The desperation I was used to was before me in feminine form. Am I willing to watch her do this?

"You want to see my penis, and you'll leave this alone? I think when I take it out, you're going to make your move." he chuckles.

"Why did he have to make this so hard? Why must it be such a big deal for him to not just be like other guys and say yes?" Margot asks me, hoping I would side with her.

"We wouldn't want him if it was that easy. This is why we want it so bad." I groan, slapping my face, "You've never appreciated Chris nor been with a real man before. All you know are little boys who couldn't wait to get their little wieners played with. Well, you're looking at the real deal. He's run through girls like you for years. You're not a challenge or interest. Can you please stop? It's past embarrassing." I giggled.

herself.

Kira came back in. She let her hair down and loosened up her belt to slide her pants off. She expected things to be working. She was shocked when she came back to see us exactly where she left us. Not on our knees or backs. At least she got past the blunt. It was the only thing either of them would be sucking tonight.

If he went over there, it would have been a sealed deal. They could have kept it secret until they got him high enough or drunk. They thought I was like them, ain't that funny? I'm glad I kept an eye on these little thots. Even happier we got the home-field advantage. Over there, who knows how this would have ended.

"Stop..." Chris no longer laughed. He stood up, "It's getting late. It's time for you all to leave. You can take the blunt with you."

I smiled. Thank god. He ended it.

Margot furrowed her brow, "Why, are you a priest or something now? You're supposed to be the King. What's wrong?" she crossed her arms over her chest.

"You're not worth the regret. And fun isn't worth my time. It was nice hanging out. I think it's past time you two leave." Chris sighed, "Good luck, thanks for stopping by. I'm flattered by the opportunity."

strung along by her little friend.

"I just wanted to get to know you, and this was Margot's idea. I promise. We just wanted to have fun. I'm sorry. I didn't mean to offend you, and I'm so sorry. Please, can we stay?" Kira pleaded. "Here, please, keep some bud. I'm so sorry we didn't get along. We were drinking when we came up with this idea, please. I didn't expect this, I thought, I thought it would have been okay."

"You don't know me well enough to beg like this. Go home. Get some self-respect." Chris pats Kira on the head.

Kira frowned, "I think we're just a bit drunk and high. We're neighbors. Let's figure this out in the morning."

"We'll talk about this when we can. Not anytime soon. I need my space from chicks like you. I'm sorry, I wish things were different. I just can't deal with this right now."

"Chris, I... please don't be mad at me, Chris." Kira wiped her eyes, "I like you. Margot told me this would make you like me! She said guys like threesomes!"

"Please just go home, Kira." I yawn, "You're not making it any better. Take his advice, and don't follow bad influences."

Margot stood up, snatching her purse and handing out her hand for their bag of bud.

"You missed out." She said after snatching it, "I give great head ask your friend over there. I would have blown you until

313

suggest you take it before we offer another guy this opportunity tonight!"

"What? No, I'm doing this for anyone else! I only liked him!" Kira cried out in horror.

"I'm sure. Suppose I wanted to have a threesome. I could have made it happen in the past. I've had plenty of opportunities. I didn't want it then, certainly not now. Thank you for reminding me why I don't date." Chris escorts them out and then returns to the bedroom.

"Haha, I can't believe you're kicking me out!" Margot shouts before the door slams shut.

Chris returned. I was posed on his bed in my birthday suit, smoking the rest of the blunt. I tossed off my clothes, hoping he would want to finish up what those two started. I crawled to him on all fours with my butt shaking in the air.

"Leave." He points out his door.

"What? I didn't do anything!" I say sharply.

"Exactly, you didn't do anything. After all, we talked about, after what we just went through in the living room. You didn't do anything but stand by. I mean, you could have said Margot was at the door. Just get out, Mya. I want to be alone."

"Chris, don't be like that. I had no idea Margot was coming. She said you knew she would be here. That you two

myself.

"I had no idea Margot was coming here! Now, please get out and leave me alone." He barked.

"Chris, let's not waste this opportunity. We've already come this far. Let's finish up, then head to bed. Please." I begged my yoni felt like it was on fire. I had an itch I couldn't scratch myself.

"Now!" he says sternly, "I am not joking. Get the hell out of my room. If you're not going to respect my decision not to have sex, at least respect my half of the lease."

"Don't go there. I wouldn't have let it happen. I wanted to see what you would do!"

"You're supposed to be my friend. Not another test. So, what if I said yes, you would have been down for it? You would join in?"

"What? I- I don't know, Chris. I didn't think you would do it. I hoped you wouldn't. I wasn't going just to let her do whatever she liked. I wanted to know how strong you were."

"I don't need to be tested nor tempted by someone who calls themselves my best friend."

"Chris, reeelaax, we didn't do anything. Nothing happened. Baby, I wouldn't have let you have sex with those thots." I tried to cover up, but Margot had brought me to my first orgasm in months.

thoughts and feelings. You just sat by and watched while that girl said whatever she wanted to get my cock out of my pants. You just watched." he shook his head, "I can't believe you. I can't trust you."

"Chris, it's not that serious... even if you did do it, I would have understood. They're both attractive, and I'm beautiful. It's alright to enjoy our youth and have a little sex." I didn't see why I was being punished besides realizing my pants had been off this entire time.

"Maybe that's my problem." he said in a final tone, "Get out, Mya."

"Can we talk in the morning, at least?"

"I work in the morning...."

"Can we talk in the afternoon?"

"I'm working a double."

"At night...?" I say, frustrated.

"I don't want to speak to you at all. Please just leave me alone!" He shouts at the top of his lungs.

I sulked out of his bedroom stark naked. Relieved we were at least roommates, and I didn't have to change in the hallway. I took a final glance back at him. He looked as if he wanted to cry. I hurt him and abused his trust. We pushed him to his very brink. After all the progress he made, he failed himself.

door, hoping he would change his mind, but he was steadfast. I never realized how strong his convictions were on this topic. Not until this morning did I even realize he stood strongly for those convictions at all.

There wasn't just lust in my heart or a crush. I knew I was looking at the man I wanted to marry. My respect soared.

As I reached the door, I rubbed his cheek and kissed him softly on the lips.

"Thank you for being the voice of reason and being a real man. I know you're angry, baby. I respect you so much. I respect you so much, Chris." I kissed his cheek, leaving him to his thoughts and solitude where he found so much peace.

It was difficult having the door slammed behind me, but it made me reevaluate my decisions these past years. I don't know a single man I have been with who would have refused my friends and me, let alone those two offerings the same proposition. I also never given myself to a man I ever considered worthy.

I wish I could find a way to explain to Chris why I didn't try to stop them because I felt he deserved them. I thought he deserved my friends. I think the world of him. But I see the fatal flaw of having nothing to offer a man but sex and accepting little from him but sex and money. It wasn't a relationship, and it wasn't loving. It was hardly anything at all.

We shared the same space, but there was the same distance as when I first met him my freshman year. In his own work and world, he was off to himself, leaving us all to our devices, thoughts, and life. I just wanted to be in his arms or hear what was on his mind. Instead, whenever I entered the room, he hardly even acknowledged me. Even if I sat near him, he would take it as a personal challenge to focus far more. It went on for thirty days until he began to come around again. For the past month, every time he looked at me, his face twisted with anger or was writhe with pain.

Sitting in the living room waiting for him to speak to me became agonizing. I stuck to my room with the door open, hoping he would pop in. His door, however, was always locked or closed. I didn't want whatever he was going through to shut me out. It was all I could do to remain open. He had to walk by my door to the bathroom. We'll make eye contact before he would keep going as if I didn't exist. It was better than dealing with the pained expression when he meditates on the night. Still, he glanced in, checking on me, hoping his solitude didn't offend me. It's all he has left is his mind and spirit. I understood why he needed to protect it. Not even I understood what he was going

weed, he meditated on until the second coming of Ada.

Today I was sitting at my desk working on a new article for my political journalism class. I wanted to take our failed assignment from Professor Hisaka's class and turn it into an investigation. The topic of how Naka gained such a strong influence over the politics and economy of Erdu was specifically interesting to me. Speaking about Ecru was taboo, but most of my Erdun professors encouraged me to finish my assignment. This wasn't for a grade. It was for my nation's pride and catharsis.

I sent Chris emails, asking questions about his research and thoughts. Those emails were the only real communication I could get from him. He replied with hyperlinks, curt sentences, or videos but ignored me, telling him how I missed him and loved him. I kept sending them over the month, hoping he would realize how silly it was to ignore me. Then I realized he wasn't ignoring me. He only did what his blood commanded him to do.

My laptop flashed with a new email notification from Tor'jun. The subject of his email read, "Your Conclusion."

'My research led me to understand that Ecru was indeed the root of Naka's rise and Erdu's fall but most misunderstand why. Ecru was an isolated nation with all the world's major resources, natural springs, and wells, with two rivers coursing through its mass. It needn't interact with any other nation, and perceived as a threat or a necessity. Erdu has peace with Ecru for centuries but traded it for Nakan Currency and promises. The hope was to capture Ecru from two fronts, the west and the east. Ecru refused to be captured. After all the resources, lives, and time loss to the effort, the only thing Naka could do to regain its losses was turning its attention to Erdu. Erdu had betrayed its oldest ally of Ecru, it had no access to Esha, and Maya set up a trade and water embargo against Naka and Erdu.

Ecru was self-sufficient and isolated. This is what gave it its global power and made it such a threat to Naka. Naka had nothing of its own, and if it didn't capture Ecru or Erdu, it likely would have crumbled. The common belief is that Ecru had been captured and then Erdu. In truth, it was Erdu that had sacrificed its convictions, souls, allies, and people to support Naka's desperation. In turn, like a wounded dog, Naka bit the head off of Erdu and rewrote the political doctrines turning Erdu into a war-fueled nation controlled by its army. The army was funded entirely by Nakan currency and built upon indoctrination to protect Nakan culture. For centuries The Regulator Regime fought Naka's war, divided Erdu, and murdered anyone and any group who stood against it. This expanded the Erdun and Nakan borders into the once untouched lands of Ecru that eroded into what is now Nadia. Naka used the same tactics that conquered Erdu to destroy its longest enemy of Ecru finally.'

thesis so succinctly. I read it over a few times, beginning to realize more and more why I didn't understand him specifically. I prefaced his conclusion with a crunch paragraph.

"People in Erdu were so vastly different. There was a large pro-Naka populace. Most of the region supported Naka, The Regime, and hated anything not from Erdu. I have raised in the coastlands most of my life before my training in The Academy. My home was so far from the drama and turmoil. We didn't care about The Regime or other regions. We had everything we could ever need and more. I was one of the many children conscripted into The Academy, a requirement of 20% of each section of Erdu. I had never known how or why my homeland was so divided amongst itself. Why we focused so much on fighting, but Chris' conclusion laid it out perfectly. We had long lost control over ourselves. The majority of us were taught what to believe from Naka. The rest of us had to figure it out ourselves without Rakil, without guidance, and without any contact with the outside world other than through The Regime. There were still sections of Erdu without electricity, WIFI, or plumbing because they refuse to bend to The Regime. The Regime and The Academy have become the only means of modernization and industrialization in Erdu. If it isn't done for the military, then it isn't done at all."

of examples, interviews from my professors, and research. Now, all I can do is wait and hope he can edit it before I posted it online. The internet still wasn't controlled by Naka. From there, I would send it to each major newspaper, magazine, and activist to let it spread like wildfire.

I was exhausted after finishing the paper. It took an entire month, and since it wasn't an actual assignment, I still had to manage my full course load in addition to getting this done. So, lying down and enjoying the last scraps of my bud in my bowl seems like a well-deserved treat. As I began sparking up a few puffs, I heard his door unlock and open.

I held my breath, hoping he wouldn't walk right past me after sending him that email. Instead, Chris solemnly walked in and sat on the edge of my bed. His shoulders rounded, weighed down from a month of deep thought. His lips twitched, parting but only releasing exasperated sighs, unable to form his word. Chris ran his fingers through his fro, looking back at me from the foot of the bed.

I set my bowl down as we sat in silence for a few minutes until he finally spoke.

"You were right. I shouldn't have let them over. I had no idea Margot was her roommate. They played me like a fool, disrespected our home, and I feel like I lost all my progress. I felt

as his back stiffened from the admission.

I was silent. Watching the stoic expressionless look on his face turn to relief as the words left his mouth. At the end of his solitude, he only blamed himself. It seemed to give him his solace and relief. To know it was him, and he had to grow set him free from all of our sins.

"They were young and horny. I didn't know girls were as bad as men were. Sheesh, she was hypnotic. It was almost worst." I giggled.

He didn't laugh, sitting in his thoughts.

"Do you want to finish this bowl?" I held it out to him.

"Not right now. I don't feel like smoking. I just want to be alone." He didn't sound convincing, only rehearsed, as if he was only trying to convince himself he needed to be alone at this point.

I could understand him blocking out the rest of the world. Would he truly shut me out forever? I crawled to him on the edge of the bed, hugging him from behind and moving my hands under his T-shirt and rubbing his back, squeezing his muscles and soothing his joints. He let out an exasperated sigh as his tense body finally released a lifetime of stress.

"Thank you, Mya..." He closed his eyes. "I'm just tired of these girls, man. That's how they're getting? Guess that's my fault for my history. I almost did it too."

fantasized about it the whole time like a creep. But you had the reality, and you turned it down. I'm so proud of you. And I'm so happy to call you my best friend. I love you, Chris. You're worth so much more than sex, so much more. I'll respect your decision."

"I just wish we kept it like it was. Probably would have been watching Nakan Dad, smoking ourselves silly, cuddled up naked by now." He let out a sigh rolling to his back, letting me know he wasn't ready to be touched.

I lay on his chest, "ya know... It's only about ten or so. It's not too late." I giggle. "I'm sorry, but remembering makes me hot. I couldn't even believe that it was happening. They just straight up came out with it. That Margot has some crazy eyes. She looks at you, and it's like her mouth is saying one thing, and her eyes are singing you into paralysis. She's dangerous."

"Yeah, she'll stare you in your eyes, and you'll lose a day or two of your life." He shook his head.

"I almost left you alone with them..." I slapped myself on the face, "I was so angry with you for inviting them."

"I might have given in if you weren't with me. I thought about being with you or dealing with chicks like them. I put it in perspective. You were making a lot of sense earlier."

I smile, "I won't lie. Margot had her way with me. I don't think I was much help at all. I would have joined in if that got

be even more honest, I gave into Margot immediately. Though, I don't really like sharing. And I don't know those girls. I'll you what. Opal and I are going to make it up to you. You deserve it."

He laughed, "You're a trip."

"Baby, I'm your vacation." I grinned.

There's a moment of silence. He was looking good. And I knew I was looking good.

I shifted, leaning into him and rubbing his chest. It was the closest we had been in a month. I couldn't resist kissing his neck, kissing his shoulder, kissing him down his chest. He grabbed a handful of my booty as our tongues danced salsa and meringue. His hands were playing conga on my booty. And my vulva was singing the tongues remembering Margot's forked tongue.

I slid out of my shorts. He pulled me back to him, flipping me on my stomach. He moved my panties aside. His tongue joined my harmony. He might have felt like a piece of meat, but I felt like a feast. My nails dug into the bed. I cried and kicked, screaming to the ceiling.

"Oh, God, don't stop... Don't stop." I pushed my hips up higher, reaching to pull my legs apart for him. I had been dripping wet and soaked over, remembering when Margot was starting casting her spell. It was quickly replaced with my baby cleaning me all up.

forceful. Our mutual hatred was our passion as I let her pull me to an orgasm. Chris had already had me on edge. Chris's head game was skilled, sensual, and deliberate. He was strong enough to hold me down by himself, licking my vulva, my labia lips, and sucking on my clitoris what felt like all at once. He sent orgasms through my entire body. My toes curled, and my body felt so relaxed and loose. I had never come so many times in my entire life, let alone from only someone's mouth. I turned overtired and horny as ever, fighting between the two, but Chris won without question. I had never cum so hard before. I knew we could try to push that tonight.

He spread my butt cheeks, propping my knees beneath me as he continued feasting on my clitoris and labia from the back. I cried out in pleasure loud enough for the neighbors to hear as they knocked against the wall. I couldn't help myself as if I lost all sense and control. I rolled over once more, this time putting some distance between us, afraid I would die unable to breathe from moaning and screaming.

"What was that?" I asked, slowly rubbing my clit as he stood up and looked at me.

I trembled before him, realizing I had never had sex with someone like Chris before. I don't think I even had sex with a man lasting longer than his head session just now. Opal had some staying power with her toys, but we usually tapped out

with intent to punish me. He hadn't even gotten started. Truly I was afraid of what he would do to me. I wanted sex so badly I forgot who I honestly wanted to have with me.

"We had a deal, right? I didn't want to forget what I promised a month ago." The stoic expressionless tone sounded so matter-of-factly as if he wasn't impressed with what he had just done to me.

"Chris... I wanted to have sex with you but- you made me think about it. We could wait if you wanted." I gulped.

As much as it pained me to say it, it was quite true. I wanted him more than I wanted sex.

"I appreciate that." he sat down on the bed and flicked on the smart TV as if it was his room.

I laid my head in his lap as he closed his eyes. I unzipped his pants slowly, reaching in his jeans and stroking his manhood erect. My mouth watered as I took him out, his meat smacking me on my forehead. I giggled in excitement, rubbing my forehead from the brunt pain. I could get used to our new movie watching position.

I eased him in my mouth. I let out a sigh of relief as he eased against the back of my throat, making me cum from the sensation. I never felt someone's manhood fill every nook and cranny of my mouth. His hand wrapped my hair into a ponytail as he guided me down his length. I moaned and suckled him,

I tapped out and came up for air.

"Are you trying to kill me?" I coughed.

"You should have considered that before tempting me all this time." He was remorseless, but it didn't stop me from going to seconds.

I sucked and stroked him. I swatted his hand away as he reached for me again. I fit about half of him in my mouth, wrapping my tongue around his girth. I pulled up this time, feeling defeated. He was completely unfazed by my head, and I had driven myself to cum twice more, giving the best I had to offer.

"Get on your back." His tone was brusque.

I looked him in the eyes, ignoring his words. I wasn't done taking his punishment. I grabbed his cock, taking my time with his bulbous mushroom cap. I knew I couldn't handle his girth or length. I rubbed his jewels as I finessed on his head. He looked down at me, biting his lip until he leaned his head back, giving into ecstasy.

"Only Margot has ever given me head this good, and you're beating her by miles." he moaned.

The compliment made me soar, knowing how good Margot gave head firsthand. Thank my hard work, love, and Cosmo magazine.

I closed my eyes as his seed filled my mouth. I let out

took him back in, not wasting a drop. He tasted sweet and salty, like his personality. I loved his taste. I've never let a man nut near my face since my freshman year. I swallowed a mouthful of his milkshake and stroked him for more. He remained hard as a rock.

"I'll get on my stomach...?" I bit my lip, wondering if he had the stamina.

"I said get on your back." He rolled me on my back, pulling off his shirt as I pull off his jeans. He pinned me down. I wrapped my legs around him, kissing him wildly as he eased between my legs. The head of his hard-on rubbing against my wet lips, his grip kept me in place as he penetrated me.

"Chris..." I choked on the words, orgasming again from entry, feeling like a virgin giving herself for the first time.

I dug my nails into his back. A smile plastered on my face as I clamped him between my legs. The sound of the slapping of our skin was the soundtrack to our lovemaking. I had the greatest evening of my life having bomb sex with the only man I ever loved. And knowing I get to wake up with him any morning I chose. My life was perfect.

Our hips smacked together hard and fast, but his face lacked enjoyment.

"Chris, you don't have anything to prove. I'm yours. Get your nut, baby." I whispered in his ear, slowing him down with

"Thank you." He kissed my cheek, showing his relief to hear it.

He pulled me further down the bed. Grabbing my hips and easing his length in me until I felt him pressing against my guts. I lost my breath. My toes curled, my tongue hung from my mouth as I knocked on heaven's door seeing white lights from his slow, deep strokes. He was pushing in me wonderfully. Bless this man. He lay on top of me, lifting my chin. I wrapped my arms around his neck, kissing him sloppily as his hands squeezed into my hips, holding me down so I couldn't run from him like my body kept trying. I was instinctively pushing away. The pain from his big black cock gave way to pleasure. As he eased out of me, my walls gripped around him, finally adjusting to his length and girth. He was only able to take out a few inches still deep inside me. To my surprise, my yoni refused to let him out. His pace got quicker, his pumps even shorter as he proceeds to mold me into his cock glove. My walls tried their best to squeeze against him, but he had me stretched to my limit. I would never be able to let another man inside me again.

"I'm gonna cum..." He bit his lip, looking down at me.

"Go ahead, baby. Fill me up and make my yoni wetter for your big cock." I bit his ear.

The first time he came in my mouth like soft served ice cream. Now, he came inside me like a tidal wave. All the nuts tightened around him as I began crying in his ear, begging him not to stop filling me up. He felt incredible. I would never let another man have my body. I didn't want him to stop. He didn't need a pull-out game. He was right where he belonged. I imagined our wedding once he visited my home in a few months. I could already see all of the children I wanted to give him. There needed to be another generation of this perfect creature on the planet for someone else to enjoy.

He kissed my forehead. He kissed the bridge of my nose. He kissed my cheeks. He kissed my neck. Then I pulled his stupid face to kiss him on the lips.

"I love you, best friend..." I whispered, rubbing his cheek.

"I love you too, Mya." he grinned, "thanks for snapping me out of my depression."

"What can I say? I know what I know. I'm not always thinking of the greatest solutions to my life. I know, baby. I know how I feel about you. I know we can be amazing together, Chris."

"Let's do it, baby!" He clapped his hands, looking up to the ceiling.

I was completely exhausted, barely noticing he left the room and returned with a blunt between his lips. I could cry from joy seeing him take things to a new level of pleasure. He had his collection of bootlegs under his arm, two glasses in his hand, and a bottle of white zinfandel in his other hand.

without thinking, blushing once the words came out of my mouth.

He worked hard for it.

"Well…" he squeezed my booty, "I know my first course isn't too far away, but after that, we can head to Merit Diner. They have an amazing Friday Breakfast special."

"I've never been because it looks so… dingy." I cringed, hating that he didn't think I would cook for him.

"It's a retro place!" he says defensively, "I love it there, plus breakfast is 2.99," he chuckles.

"I want to cook for you, baby." I rubbed his cock, convincing him in my way.

"Fine… I guess I'll just have to rest up and bed and let you take care of me." he stretched out long, "To think this is what I've been resisting having you by my side."

"To think I've been resisting this in my life all this time. I can't imagine offering you anything else but all of me. Let's make things work. Even when we fight or I'm too much. Let's make things work."

He grins, "Well…. Duh, what the hell do you think I've been trying to get you to understand all this time?"

We lay in each other's arms until the sun rose. A day ago, this seemed so far-fetched. Four years ago, this seemed an impossible figment of my fantasy. Here he was, the man of my college. To think I met my soulmate so young. Right now, lying in his arms. Chris Kirin Tor'jun will be the man I marry and start my family with, and he's my lover, partner, and best friend.

Mya rested so peacefully. I reached under the blanket, fondling her breasts. She cooed, starting to shift in her sleep. She began rubbing her butt against me, giggling, giving away a clear sign she didn't want to ruin the moment. I pulled her closer. She turns into me suddenly, kissing me and holding my neck.

"I love you..." Mya says sadly, "And you're still emotionally abusive and unattached."

"I'm emotionally abusive?"

She laughs, "Most intelligent people are just listening. Didn't you say we wouldn't ever do this? Aren't you still in love with Margot? You're ignoring your own emotions. I care about you, and I know for a fact what to expect from you!"

"I knew you would pull this morning after story..." I groan, stretching out to get up.

"Baby, I am not like those girls. I have no intentions of leaving you, but I expect a lot from you. Please just talk to me." Mya crawls to my side, kissing my neck sending chills through my body.

"I know I can be... I guess neglectful. That's why I wanted to be single and figure it out before dating anyone. When I was young, that's what it was like, my parents were always busy. It

It's how we get to where we wanted to get, then we got it, and it felt empty to me, at least. I was raised differently. Probably the biggest issue is I think they're spoiled, sheltered, and overly sensitive. And they act like I'm the man on the moon."

"You act like you're the man on the moon. Now you smoke, and you're in the universe. I love it about you. But Erdu is a very strict and regulated region. Mountain-folk and farm-folk are hard workers and very ambitious. Our rich live in fortresses for the past few centuries. And we don't have poor people. Outside those old families, most people are provided for so, and I get the whole that's what truly prevails. But we also needed to open up our borders because there has been an abuse of power and government. So, there is a limit to how much discipline and austerity are needed. We did not know that until our ancient ways sold half our land to Naka and led to several water embargos killing millions for thousands of years. I see how much better you've gotten, babe. I need you to raise even higher, treat me better than anyone you've ever dated, and let me build a true alliance with you. I need you to treat me like I am the woman of your life. Like your Queen. Then, I will have no issue treating you like my King."

"Treat me like your king, and I'll have no issue treating you like my Queen. I'm not worshipping little girls. I worship

girls today don't know how respect works."

"You give respect to get respect, Chris." She sighs.

"No, you earn respect! I'm tired of having this conversation with a woman. I'm a man. We live different lives. There's a lot more pressure. I don't need you telling me to raise higher on the totem pole. It's never appeared in my life. Ain't anybody offered me respect for showing up, no you have to work, I know this despite the rumors, Nadians work pretty hard. Especially since I'm from the heart of Nadia, I know Ecru, and where I come from, I don't need some lecture on my potential. I earned the way I walk and carry myself. I'm not giving it away for free because it isn't given to me. I live by choice, not accident, either by choice or Rakil's. I'm supposed to love my wife. You're supposed to respect your husband."

"Look here, Mr. Heart of Nadia. I'm from Mount Sinai in the Askia district of Erdu. Now, I shouted out a place you've never been. I don't care where you're from, and I'm not worried about you worshipping me. I'm not trying to be another Chris Tor'jun Ex. I want you actually to try now! You need to see a therapist. You got some PTSD going on." Mya got up.

I grabbed her hand, tugging her back. She stared at me as if I lost my mind before relaxing, letting me sit her in my lap. She stared up at me, rubbing my chin pulling me in to kiss her deeply. I press my forehead to hers, overwhelmed with joy as if I ignored the woman who has been by my side all along.

"If I ever pursue the arbitrary path of dating you, I'm going to marry you, Mya."

"Ha, what? I guess I can bring you home because I am done dating." Mya pushes away from me.

"I promised myself. My next girlfriend will be my last or the one I will marry. I also promised I would never lose you as a friend. So the only choice is to marry you."

"You're so full of it." Mya began to tear, probably the first time I've seen her cry.

"What did I do now?"

"What are you talking about? Stop ruining the mood!" Mya slaps my arm.

"You're ruining the mood with your crying."

"I'm crying because I'm happy!" Mya wipes her eyes more.

"Who cries because they're happy?" He asks.

"A lot of people, you idiot!" She plucks my ear.

"Well... then I'm sorry for not understanding your spectrum of emotions."

"You're forgiven."

"Whatever..." I chuckle, "I'm happy you changed my mind."

path of dating, if we're honest. Outside looking in, you've been unfaithful to me, but we'll crack that up to you never popping the question. People think us saying we were friends was being polite. I've had these unrequited feelings for a while." Mya nudged.

"Stop that unrequited love crap..."

She breaks out laughing, "So, you've heard it before because this is definitely. It's my first time telling you that."

"Yeah... I'm sorry, I meant what I said." I grin, "It's a bit empowering turning women down. Now, I know what it's like to be an object of desire."

"Shut up. You've been an object of desire. You're mine now. Off the shelf, for my eyes only! There shouldn't be anyone for you to turn down." Mya pokes me in the chest, "Do you understand?"

"A bit possessive, huh?"

Mya smiles smugly, "well, you've given me plenty of reason not to trust you leaving the house without a tracker. Stay in the house like you've been doing."

"If that's the case, I'm not sure I want you out either, Miss One Night Stand."

"Oh, shut up, I wasn't even dating you."

"Nor was I dating you!"

hugs my neck tightly, kissing my cheek. "You're miiiiiinne!" She hangs onto me like a spider monkey, wrapping her legs around my waist.

"I have to piss Mya, get off of me!" I groan.

"Ha, carry me. I'll make breakfast. Roll a blunt and pick something to watch." Mya kisses my cheek.

"I have to go for a jog soon, or else I won't do it at all," I say.

"Well, you've been getting faster. Hurry home and do it when you get back?" She suggests.

"You're not coming with me? You just got done about how you don't trust me."

"I don't want to jog..." Mya, let's go and crawls under the blankets. "Ew, it's 7 am!? Get away from me, Chris. Go running. Wake me up in at least three hours. I trust you, bye."

"It's that easy, huh?"

"I don't like running." She declares.

"Let's lift weights."

"I have always wanted a squat booty?" She pokes her head out of the blankets.

"I love squats." I shrug, "Let's head to the gym."

"Why now? It's so early!"

"Get your butt up. Let's go. We'll jog there or walk, then we can."

hike or whatever you're doing. I'm calling an uber..."

"You're so lazy!" I laugh.

"Shut up, just go run. I'll get up in ten minutes and make breakfast."

"It's a deal." I chuckle, kissing her on the forehead.

"I'm going to need a nap..." She mutters, hiding under the blankets again, "I like your butt. Keep jogging, baby."

"Ha, you're just in space."

"No, you're in space, Mr. Heart of Nadia. I'll see you when you get back. Pass me my phone so that I can set the alarm."

I snap her phone off the charger and toss it to her. I was heading off to the bathroom to start my morning. Compromise, who would've ever thought of that?

Chris went off jogging. I never knew his running trail because I never went along. I had no idea of knowing when he would be home. If he offered to work out together, I usually met up with him at the gym after his route. He offered for me to catch up with him for a workout today, but my legs wobbled from his spine-pounding from an hour ago. I felt exhausted. We hadn't slept until 04:00, then woke up for another quick round. He ran off of a regiment, meaning if he didn't leave on schedule, he would never have gone. We were both tired, but I lacked his self-discipline he seemed to have manifested over a few months, likely years. He carved himself from stone with a plastic spoon. It was incredible to see what he made of himself.

I used to have amazing discipline via The Regulator Academy in Stone Harbor, Erdu. We woke up at 05:00 for training and drills then had breakfast shortly before a full day of classes. And if you came to class or the mess hall dirty with only a half-hour between the two, you were punished with more drills and jogging. I had an institution and strict schedule to support and direct me, which makes college a breeze. Without the Academy, I quickly fell into the habit of sleeping in until noon and stuffing my face with jelly donuts. I could never have

diet and lifestyle were so strict, and in the mountains, supplies were so specific. On the day I graduated from the Academy, I took a trip with my best friend Opal to New Haven and ate a dozen jelly donuts by myself, not to mention all the other delicacies and delights we had on our trip. When I came home, I had lost my six-pack, grew some hips, and went up a bra size. I don't live with regrets.

Chris baffled me. He had developed this internal spirit of discipline and growth without drill sergeants or institutions. In only a few years for no reason other than heartbreak and habits. His breakup broke him down to nothing, and I guess there was no choice but to rebuild stronger. I can't understand why or how his will had gotten so strong. Where did the boy I knew go, replaced by this man with no humor and eye-bleeding ambition?

Here I was naked, cooking him breakfast as I had never done for any man anticipating him walking in the door, my body fully exposed and my efforts left for his. I feel like I lost my friend's innocence, laughter, and optimism for this new man I craved with an insatiable sexual hunger with deep wisdom about the world. He had matured so much, and it's as if I never truly knew him.

He was once my best friend, a boy I knew better than I knew myself. A boy I could never see myself serving or giving myself to so willingly. Yet, here I stood, waiting to fulfill his

the taste of his manhood on my tongue so different than anyone else's. I was hungry for his touch, words of wisdom, and attention more than food. I was under the same spell all the other woman fell for so witlessly. Has he truly changed who he is as a man?

Oh my God, have I made the right decision giving myself to this strange man when I fell in love with his former self? I lusted for the new man more than my friend! He was stronger not just in strength but wisdom, focus, and ambition. He rarely laughed, barely spoke, and if he wasn't at work or on tour scheduled far enough in advance to work around, he was home with me working on his projects, and we only started dating!

Have I made a mistake confusing love for lust? Or was he the same person...? I haven't seen the boy I know in over a year from his past relationship. His relationship did truly kill him, and this form was reborn from the ashes like a phoenix. This is what the Almighty God returned to the world, a warrior who fought from the pits of hell for a second chance at life. He was constantly training as if he would have to fight the Devil again. Was this what I signed up for with Chris?

He texted me, saying he was down the block. I began to put the scrambled eggs in a bowl and the pancakes on a plate. The sausage sat in a metal dish to stay warm. I set the table in the kitchen nook table with a gallon of fresh orange juice from

up the stairs. We live on the fifth floor. Why and how did the laughing boy I knew become so willingly intense? Or did I truly know him to begin with because he's been hiding all this time, working for validation and appeasement like every other one of us before deciding to check out and stop?

The door opened, and my heart flew up my throat into a bright smile. I exposed myself, letting him see every inch of me. His new energy and power permeated the room, drenched in sweat with his clothes clinging to his body. His wide smile planted on his face as he panted from near exhaustion. I didn't know this man at all and want to more than anything.

"Wow, baby, you look amazing." he grinned ear to ear with such pride as he entered the room, strolling toward me.

I felt frozen and melted at once. I wanted to be held, kissed but admired from afar like a statue. He smelled putrid from sweat. His grey cotton shirt was see-through, clinging to his skin. His sweatpants cradled his beautiful member in place, squeezing his thickly muscled legs. I loved what I saw before me, even though I couldn't yet have him again. We favored the other from afar, and his joy was palpable. His energy rose not to pin me down but to delight in me. I bite my lips, playing with my hardened nipples as he watched me.

"And look, you cooked in time. Everything looks amazing." he chuckled, kissing me on the cheek.

reactions wanted to fight back and take it as a snide comment, but I knew the truth. I still felt him deep inside me from the morning I felt subdued. I bit my tongue with a stupid smile, more thrilled with how he marveled over my cooking. There was nothing to defend me over and no enemy standing before me. There was nothing but love and commendations.

"I'm glad you like it. Now, go shower real quick." I place my hands on his firm butt as chiseled as his biceps and shoulders squeezed in his tight shirt.

"You are coming with me?" he ran his hands up my curves and squeezed my breast.

I shuddered at the thought, "You know if we both get naked, we'll never leave the bathroom, and breakfast will be cold as ice."

I dipped away from his grip, blushing at his suggestion, my body lit on fire, and my nipples hardened.

"Indeed." He reached for me but stopped himself, "So, why the birthday suit?"

"I want you to watch me with the same unquenchable desire I've been looking at you all this time," I confess, still fondling my breasts.

"I know what you mean. The flesh is willing, but the spirit refuses," he said how I felt perfectly.

you so badly, a pang of hunger and yearning for you. The truth is I enjoyed bonding with you more than sex. I don't know which I'm more excited for, honestly." I sneered.

"I understand. Sex completely undermines what we truly had all these years. It adds a bit of spice to the living situation, I admit." He smirked, squeezing my butt and kissing me deeply with such smug confidence.

"This is what you've been telling me this past year and every day since we moved in together. I finally understand what you mean." I smacked my forehead, letting him go and walking to the stove to get away from his scent.

"I'm gonna go shower, so you stop cringing." he laughs, walking off to the bathroom down the hall.

"I'll be your Eve, and you can be my Ada." I trail after him massaging his muscles as he undresses in the bathroom.

"Eve kind of messes up everything for everybody, then leads Adam to a pathway of hell… let's try Ruth and Boaz, okay?" he rubs my chin.

"I am rubbing you down after breakfast with cocoa butter and oil. Are you ready for that kind of loving?" I lean against the doorway as he looks back.

"My Love," he says as he begins to tear off his clothes then kicks them into the hallway.

I grit my teeth.

"Ha, that was short-lived." he turned around quickly, his manhood swinging as he rushed to grab his clothes and toss them in the hamper down the hall.

"There is nothing at all short about it. God blessed you, My King." I licked my lips, grabbing his jewels and scepter with much respect.

"You are saying that because I have you now?" he asked.

"You always had me." I blush.

"I always had a big cock too," he smirks, that smug confidence again.

"Oh God, go take a shower before I jump on you! Don't start something you can't finish, Choir Boy." I giggle, leaving him to take his shower.

"I'm just saying, I'm blessed to be a blessing. I'm happy to have you too, Mya!" he calls after me as I strut back to the kitchen.

The door doesn't close until I'm down the hallway. He makes me, so it's like he makes me orgasm without even touching me. He's left me exposed to the softest, warmest side of my personality. He nestles so deeply inside my vulnerability, and I can't let you go. I feel it all over my skin. It's like he makes my mind and emotions cum but leaves my flesh untouched.

off!" I shout back up the hallway.

"Why would I ever do that when I have all your personalities?" he calls back from behind the door before the water starts running.

I could hear his hearty laughing, deep from the pit of his stomach. His was a robust gravelly chuckle like a train starting its engine.

I muttered underneath my breath, "Shut up... He's one to talk. He's like a freaking sour patch kid."

I smiled brightly, walking away from his commanding, not contagious laughter. I left him to shower in peace. I was preparing the festivities for his return to me. Waiting to share our presence and explore the new love we had for ourselves and each other.

I never felt so comfortable in my skin than living with him. He made me feel beautiful, and of course, I already know it. His self-control made me feel like a model or painting. Something knows I can do naked yoga in front of a man without him trying to poke me with a hard-on or making a joke of it all. He could sit back and enjoy the show with patience and temperance. He made me feel attractive, not like his fleshlight. Then when I needed space, silence, or not to be gawked at, he respected me instead of calling up someone else to do the same thing he asked of me.

and finishing setting the table before the bathroom door opened. He came into the kitchen area stark naked. His rippling stomach and semi-flaccid cock took my attention. I lacked his internal discipline, nearly dropping everything as he approached.

"I've been waiting to walk around here naked since we moved in." He stretches out with a yawn.

"Me too…" I marveled.

"You always sneak around in your bra and panties. No more of you yelling for me not to come out until you're done making snacks naked. Now, I'm free." he sang.

"I like your newfound liberty." I nuzzled up to him.

"What's up with you?" he asked rhetorically, his eyes sharpened.

"Hahaha…" I chuckle, setting the try down.

"You're real goofy." he was plotting something. His eyes tightened as he sized me up.

"You meant voluptuous and beautiful." I sneer, sticking out my tongue.

"And goofy." he licked his lips.

I put my hand on my bare hips, gripping his chin, "Do you like breathing?"

"As much as I want to be successful." he stared me in my eyes with a deadpan expression.

began pouring the orange juice, bumping him with my hip. Instead of playing along, he got a firm grip of my hip, holding me in place as my butt squirmed. I was gratefully shocked as he began pushing up on my booty. I finished setting napkins on the table, wondering if he had it in him. I giggle, keeping my thoughts to myself and reaching to the other side of the table to fiddle with the fork and knife. I let out a soft moan as he gripped my hip. I looked back at him, watching the look on his face as he began squeezing inside me. I gobbled him up, closing my eyes, biting my lip as our hips smacked against the other.

"Did you seriously just take my yoni?" I cooed

He placed his hand on the small of my back, slowly pulling every inch out of me.

I reached back for him shaking my head, easing my hips back against his until there was no space between us. My tongue hung from my mouth as he pressed on my cervix. He nodded, understanding my true desire better than I did. He pushed back inside me. I drive my hips back so he can reach deeper, leaving none of him outside me. I felt my stomach tighten as he pushed past my cervix. My entire body was tingling, feeling weightless. I was a complete surrender to him. It felt greater than any other man I've had before.

"Kirin, show me how a Warsinger tames his prey." I taunt him pushing my soft butt against his waist.

He begins smashing into me harder, using my own body as a counterbalance. His mushroom cap drowns in my gushing juices as he begins smacking my "act-right-button" near my diaphragm. He reached around to squeeze my breasts as he glides in and out of me with his full-length, grinding against my folds, pushing himself deeper, stirring against every inch, searching for my g-spot.

"Yes, yes, yes, yes!" I beg, wishing he wouldn't stop, stepping a foot on a chair, gripping the table tighter as he finds my spot.

I watched the table filled with the delicious breakfast I cooked, feeling myself cumming all down his length and hips. I came like a waterfall dripping onto the tiled floor beneath me. I could hardly breathe as he down his pace. I slid off his cock and sat down in the same chair, beginning to laugh hysterically. I laid my head in my arms, still laughing hysterically.

He rubbed his neck, completely confused, "Are you alright, Harik?"

"I've waited for you to take me down like that since we met. I never thought you would do it." I couldn't stop laughing from joy.

"Seriously?" he rolls his eyes sitting across from me.

"Yes! This is the best sex I've ever had." I stretched out my arms in ecstasy and joy.

It didn't take a therapist to know I offended him. I let a bit of time pass for us to begin eating before pursuing it. I was hoping it was a bad memory, but I knew it was something I said as he avoided eye contact.

"Babe, what's wrong?" I ask happily.

"It's nothing, Mya. It doesn't make sense to me. I rather keep it to myself. Enjoy your food. I'm good." he gives an uneasy smile, then goes back to picking at his plate.

"You can tell me anything, Kirin." I loved the way his middle name ran off my tongue.

"It's a question that I don't want you to take the wrong way. I'm not angry, mostly confused about your intentions." he looks down, focusing on cutting his pancakes.

"Ask away." I smile ear to ear.

"Were you truly my friend, or were you just waiting for your turn to have your shot at me?" he asked like throwing a dagger at an apple.

He was not going to like my answer. Not even remotely, I already knew. I didn't speak immediately. Looking around the room then stuffing eggs into my face to avoid talking. It was, of course, impolite to speak with your mouth full. It was more impolite to lie.

"Swallow. Why are you acting so suspicious?" he pushes my orange juice toward me.

nervously. My eyes switch between the two a few times more as I tried to get my words together. Once my juice was gulped down, then my words had to come up. The truth had to come out. I can't lie to him! He isn't going to like the truth either. Alright, I'm caught. He's staring dead at me so intensely. I gulp the juice down and let out a refreshed sigh.

"Alright, it's just... I wanted you. I always wanted you to myself. From the very first time I saw you here at the lake, I knew it was you and no one else. I loved you, but I wanted you however I could have you. I was so pissed off every time you dated someone else or a girl hurt you. You never picked me, so I dated other men, but it wasn't the same. It wasn't waiting to be with you! I accepted you probably would never date me or marry me. I was terrified to tell you how I felt. Plus, with all you went through, I wanted to be the one to show you something different, completely different. I didn't expect to wait for YEARS. I gave up hope then accepted we were just friends." I confessed feeling as if it was all one giant breath.

I breathed heavily, trying to suck up all the air in the room.

"Have you ever talked me out of a relationship because you wanted me?" he was borderline furious, remembering all the times I told him there was something better.

Now he knew I meant me.

"Can we just eat? I didn't even want to talk about it, to begin with, Mya." he rolled his eyes, shaking off the feelings.

"No, no! I did it because I know we were meant to be together! I kept having dreams and visions of it. I knew it was you! Rakil, The Almighty God showed me, I swear!" I continued to plead for him to change his perspective.

"We're already past the point where any of that matters, don't you think? I'm tired of talking about the past of anything." he sighs.

"I'm gonna finish my thought." I suck my teeth.

He chimes in, "Breakfast is delicious."

"Don't change the subject. Get used to that gourmet loving and open your ears. So, as I was saying, I seriously loved you since the first day we met. You stood out. Every other guy my freshman year was like wolves waiting to plow me or was like lemmings, all grouped up jumping off a ledge. You were never around ANYONE. You were like a Golden Eagle. You were always to yourself. He was kept as a prize from God. I never made a move because all my friends thought the same. They adored you and spoke of all the things they wanted from you or would do to you. I heard other girls asking me about you, saying the same. No one ever talked about getting to know you. They thought they had you all figured out but never even spoke to you. You're right. Women thought you were too creepy or

that. I felt like I knew a different of you that couldn't be possessed, unafraid to be yourself, and it's not positive, but it's like a jackhammer trying to break through pure stone." I confessed for the first time.

He looked away uncomfortably, letting out a sigh.

"Are you going to pretend I didn't just pour my heart out to you?" I asked, furious.

He shook his head, "That dirty kept secret was your heart? Don't you think you wore that on your sleeve and just lied about it for years? You're ruining your own life with bad relationships instead of just focusing and going after what you wanted? We could have avoided a lot of trauma if you were honest. Then again, we may never have become who we are now." he shook his head.

I scrunched up my face, forgetting who I was talking to and his deep level of thought and questioning. I wanted to be selective in what I told him, but it didn't work with Chris. His mind unfolded and unpacked everything without every effort. It's just how he functioned.

"Okay, I tried my heart, so here's my very soul." I cleared my throat with some juice first.

"If you must continue, then let me give your ranting some guidance. Clarify to me that I didn't lose my best friend because answers I wasn't aware.

"Stop talking like that. You're not losing anything! I- ugh, fine. You want the truth. I wanted everyone to be wrong about you, okay? I wanted to be wrong about you! So, I tried being with other men and different relationships. I saw this guy with God-given purpose and potential, yet you did nothing, absolutely nothing with it! I wanted a finished project. Someone I didn't have to wait for to build, suffer with, or take care of, but you know what? Those men are the worst. They already reached their cap. You were limitless. I honestly didn't love you like this until a couple of years ago. I couldn't stand how you wasted yourself on those bimbos or in depression. Drinking and smoking, it looked like you were throwing your life away. I didn't understand you never did any of that before and were enjoying yourself. You missed classes or skipped assignments. I'm not wrong for gravitating toward men who got things done or seemed like they were doing something with their lives. They weren't, though. They were doing the same thing! They were living the only life they would ever live. There was no joy at parties. It was to recover from their week, not to celebrate life as you and Jared did.

"I honestly wanted to get to know you. Truly and honestly get to know you because no one else knew anything about you. Not sex, or gawk over your looks. Or swoon over all

me off that you never apply. I wanted to know what a real man truly was because you were truly it. The only one left. Not a sheep, a wolf, or a gorilla, or some chump who thinks wearing a suit and kissing up is a success. You won my heart because you're successful completely outside that matrix or paradigm. You created your success. Now, look at you!"

"Whoa…" he scratches his head.

"Yep, you asked for it. I gave you the whole truth and nothing but the truth." I finished off my orange juice to clear my throat.

"Why not date me?" he asked.

"What? Didn't you hear me? All those others chicks always had you! I wasn't about to get cheated on. I didn't know you that well yet. I wanted my own man. I didn't have to kick a chick in the throat over. You didn't date just one girl. You always had a side chick up your sleeve. I was not getting wrapped up in your little game. At least you were honest with them all about it." I rolled my eyes.

"Then why date the others?" he was confused.

"I'll drop some realness on you. When I date, it's like a whole facade until we start getting what we want. It's like walking on your tiptoes to seem taller in pictures. They always tried to seem so much better than they were and were brutally careful not to let the other side of the show. It was never real.

were single or dating. Then, I realized I did the same thing with boyfriends! I wanted us to know the real us, not a facade, not wanting something from the other. I feared I would never get to know you if we possessed each other. I wanted to get to know the real you." I explain.

"You are making me fall deeper in love with you. You were frustrated with my past self, huh?" he chuckles.

I was happy he broke his death stare, "You're right, I was frustrated! You were letting yourself be used by girls who had no business with you. You could have been a King. Instead, you lived in such modesty and mediocrity it was disturbing when I was younger. Outside looking in, I realized that was the reality. I was so used to facades and faking. I realized you were impressed with the facades, and you didn't want the facades or anything other than yourself. That's when you honestly became my best friend. When I learned you were real as the day is long, my whole perspective changed of you about two years ago."

"Yeah, that's how you viewed? Despite my grades being better than all of yours?" he rolled his eyes, "I thought I came to college for an education, not fashion shows and popularity contests."

"Alright, you weren't living mediocre. You were avoiding the traps. You had no one to impress. Your goals were people-oriented. You were living your best life already with so much

wanted to be where you were, outside the lies, faking, and drama but happy, unlike the others."

"Ha, well, welcome to the dream team. Thanks for finally understanding everything I've been trying to teach you. I guess you understood for a couple of years now. Thank you for your initiative in actually getting to know me, Mya." he wipes away a tear with a look of pride.

"Oh baby, I didn't mean to make you sad." I held my heart.

"It's joy, pure joy. Your story was so beautiful. I didn't know I stressed you out so much. That's why you were such a B-

"Hey, watch it!" I stand up, giving him a taste of his death glare.

"Hahaha!" he broke out laughing, falling out of his chair, then laughs even harder.

"Whoa." I giggle, completely disarmed.

I kneel to help my King back into his throne. He pulls me into his lap. I straddle his waist, and he eases his length back inside me. I was shocked at how easily my body received him. I wrapped my arms around his neck, winding my hips, working up his nut slowly. I lifted his chin from suckling my breasts, giving him a passionate kiss, enjoying the taste of organic toothpaste and sheer determination on his breath.

"You were always on my top 3 for women to marry." he gripped my waist.

"Margot used to be number 1 when I first made a list. You were number two. Number three was some songstress I never met before. Now, Margot has knocked off the list, and I don't even listen to Tiana's music anymore. It's just you now." he brushed my braids out of my face driving me insane.

"How are you so hard?" I bit my lip, bouncing on his length, working myself up into excitement.

I felt our juices mix together as I rode him gleefully. The last time I tried this with a guy, he couldn't keep up and could barely reach inside me. I felt my beloved Chris up into my belly. He grounded himself, leaning back to let me enjoy every inch of him. I fell over on top of him. My body shivered from another orgasm. He felt so amazing, so strong and forceful.

"I need to get on the bottom." I moan.

"Wrap your legs around my waist." he smacked my butt before lifting me in his arms walking me into the living room.

My legs squeezed around him, holding every inch inside me, squirming on his length as he laid me out on the carpet. His thrusts were short and fierce. He posted his arms over my head. He bit his lips as he slammed inside me. I closed my eyes, unable to feel my legs anymore, but I knew they were tied around his waist. He began to slow down, moving his hips in circles tickling my g-spot with each swirl.

be picked up by him and put back together.

"Can you walk?" he asked as he helps me to my feet, my legs wobbling underneath me.

I managed to stutter-step into his bedroom. He lay out on the bed, stretching out from exhaustion from his workout earlier on. I got my knees before him, greedily sucking on the bulbous head of his cock. My walls were too exhausted to put him back inside me. He was half-hard by the time he began releasing his nut on my face and breasts. I scoop a taste in my mouth, giggling as he snored lightly on the bed.

I stood up, looking for a towel to wipe myself off.

"You look so happy." I giggle as I wipe off my face.

"That's the best head I've ever had." He swoons.

"Total satisfaction guaranteed. By the way, do you have any weed on you?" I asked, hoping he had a stash on hand.

"You want to smoke? I have work in a few hours, Mya. We can't just nap?" he muttered.

"What? Do you have to go to work? We haven't even finished breakfast, and I wanted to hang out with you all day!" I whined, climbing back on the bed once the globs of semen were cleaned up.

"I have four hours until my shift, babe. We can hang out with smoking. I need some sleep. Let's just ride the vibe. Let's leave you with some bud before I leave, okay?"

"And some money…." I chime in.

"What?" he groans, "Mya, get out my pockets."

"It's for groceries. I need something to do while you're gone! Some money to buy a few things and a bit of bud, come on." I clasp my hands.

"Fine, I got a grip." he sighed, rubbing his neck.

Chris pointed to his wallet on the nightstand on my side. I rolled over to grab it while he slept. I grabbed the soft leather trifold, feeling its weight with surprise. I peeked to see if he was awake, but his eyes were closed. Chris used to never have money out of some strange sense of pride and immaturity. I opened it up to find a Black Card, A Gold Card, and a congress of dead leaders suffocating in the dark leather.

"Chris, where did you get all this money?" If I didn't recognize him before, I was completely at a loss now.

"Don't rob me now." he yawns, giving me the trust and liberty to explore his newfound wealth.

"Can I take the Gold or Black card, pretty please?" I pleaded with uncontrollable excitement.

"For groceries?" he grumbled, not buying it.

"No, I want to flex at the register! I want to pull it out like BLOAH!" I shout, holding it up.

"No," he said curtly without a thought.

"With all that knowledge, I never apply. I read about credit repair, fixed my credit, and built up my score for a few months. I worked it up to a 700. I still have further to go, but I have changed myself around. I fixed Jared's too. He has a freaking 848 now." Chris sits up with more energy.

"You're not going to take a nap?" I ask, hopeful.

"I'm going to compromise and help you out first. I'll roll up a fat blunt for us. You reheat breakfast. I'll smoke you up before my nap, then head downstairs to the office, okay?" he reaches over the edge of the bed to pull out a pillowcase-size bag filled to the brim with weed.

"What the hell are you a drug dealer now? Am I a trap queen!?" I was astounded. My jaw dropped to the floor. "You're not worried I'll smoke your stash?"

"No, I'm not a drug dealer. I used to fight drug dealers as a mask. This is my weed. I bought it off Jared's boy Judah back in Nadia. It's a farm-grown, premium Ecru Life Kush. He gave me a good deal on a pound. I had to smuggle it through customs." he holds the bag out to me, letting me smell the pungent odor.

"I'm horny again..." I confess, having no idea how much he had gotten his life together.

"I'm going to give you an ounce. Do not touch my bag," he says firmly, taking handfuls putting them in my hands.

Friday! I never buy this much." I cried out, wanting to throw it back at him.

"It's for you to keep, baby. So you don't touch my stuff! I'll give you an ounce for you and your girls. I'm going to give you $200 for the next couple of weeks, so you're good after you pay rent." he yawned, motioning for me to take it out of his wallet.

"Are you doing this for sex?" I asked nervously, pulling away a bit.

"I'm not that kind of guy. I don't pay for sex or friendships," he says, offended I even suggested such a thing.

"I'm not that kind of type of woman, so I guess we're perfect for each other." I was warming back up to him.

"You still want the gold card. If you use it, you better fill up the fridge with real food, actual food. And please cook something." he dug in the nightstand on his side, grabbing a plastic bag for me to dump my overflowing hands of weed in, breathing the pungent smell deeply.

"Can I quit my job?" I asked.

"You better not dare!" he cursed.

I laugh, stretching out, "I mean, maybe I can be a housewife for a month or so. I can live off $200 and an ounce of weed. We'll have a fridge of food. Let's playhouse!"

"It's not a game. It's my real life. How do we build more if you're settling for nothing?" he asked with wisdom.

sense of inferiority washed over me. "Why do I have to cook then?"

"It's not even like that. I want things to run smoothly. Don't search for an offense where none is intended."

"Fine." I bounce up and head to the kitchen, feeling an extra bounce and shake in my booty as I walked.

I wondered where he found the time to transform his life while we were living together. I was struggling to balance work and school. He was building an empire with his bare hands. I imagined how much further we could take each other. Thanking God, I was patient for my Boaz instead of turning him into Ahab or Samson. I was very happy with Chris. Beyond so, I wanted to be the primary investor in his new vision. I needed to sit him down tomorrow and figure out what his true vision might be. Once he reached a goal, it was on to the next.

We chilled in his room watching "The Lego Movie" while I enjoyed my bong. He smoked the blunt with me then drifted to sleep, declining my offering. After he fell asleep and the movie finished half an hour later, he was better off staying awake but was dozing off the entire time.

He would be working until close and be on-call until late at night. I wanted to plan a party without losing his trust or my money. He and Opal would come back around the same time. I could at least have a small kickback for the three of us.

feels grounded. He wasn't the excitable type. I never fully knew Chris because he matured. I guess from now on. I just have to keep up with his pace. I needed my pathway to success. I don't want to ride his coattails or live in his shadow. I'll learn from him, but he'll understand my need to have my own life.

www.ingramcontent.com/pod-product-compliance
Lightning Source LLC
Chambersburg PA
CBHW072043190726
48294CB00005B/1386